GREAT NOVELS
OF
EROTIC DOMINATION
AND SUBMISSION

NEW TITLES EVERY MONTH

www.silvermoonbooks.co.uk

TO FIND OUT MORE ABOUT OUR READERS' CLUB WRITE
TO;
SILVER MOON READER SERVICES;
Suite 7, Mayden House,
Long Bennington Business Park,
Newark NG23 5DJ
Tel; 01400 283488

YOU WILL RECEIVE A FREE MAGAZINE OF EXTRACTS
FROM OUR EXTENSIVE RANGE OF EROTIC FICTION
ABSOLUTELY FREE. YOU WILL ALSO HAVE THE CHANCE
TO PURCHASE BOOKS WHICH ARE EXCLUSIVE TO OUR
READERS' CLUB
***
NEW AUTHORS ARE WELCOME
Please send submissions to;
The Editor; Silver Moon books
Suite 7, Long Bennington Business Park
Newark NG23 5DJ

Tel: 01400 283 488

Copyright Sean O'Kane 2001.
This edition published 2011

The right of Sean O'Kane to be identified as the author of this book has been asserted in accordance
with Section 77 and 78 of the Copyright and Patents Act 1988. All rights reserved.

ISBN 978-1-908252-92-0

All characters and events depicted are entirely fictitious; any resemblance to anyone living or dead is entirely coincidental

THIS IS FICTION. IN REAL LIFE ALWAYS PRACTISE SAFE SEX

THE STORY OF EMMA

by

Sean O'Kane

PART ONE: MARTIN.

"Do you want to beat her?" I heard Martin ask as he and his friend Jason settled themselves on the sofa in Martin's flat.

I was pouring out two glasses of whisky for them and a port for me when he spoke and I nearly dropped the bottle in shock.

"It's a gorgeous arse," he went on, "and she loves having it spanked hard."

I spun round in fury and humiliation but he just carried on quite calmly and Jason didn't appear the least bit embarrassed.

"That's a tempting offer," he said. "Will she bend over for it in here?"

"Who the fuck do you think you are!?" I finally found my voice and yelled at Martin.

"I'm the guy who beat you earlier this evening before we went out," he replied. "And Jason here is the guy who's going to beat you now."

I simply gaped at them both. Of course it was quite true, Martin had spanked me before we had gone out to meet Jason for what had turned out to be a very boozy dinner. But this was ridiculous! I thought about hurling a drink at him but then settled for flouncing out and turned on my heel.

"If you leave Emma, don't even think about coming back ever again," Martin said as he read my intention and stood up. That stopped me in my tracks, as he must have known it would. I wasn't in love with him; but I lusted after him like I had never done with any man before. He was completely different to any man I had known before.

For a start he beat me and I enjoyed it.

But bending over for him and just hiking up my skirt and doing the same for a man I had only met that evening were two very different things. And I had a lot fancied the man. A girl who was in my position didn't want to be thought of as an easy lay. Word gets around; especially in the media business.

I was a political journalist in those days. You might well have read my work in the national dailies. After leaving university with a very good degree, I worked for two of them and loved every minute of it. I wasn't above a little flirting with press secretaries and 'advisers' to get my briefings — and yes there were a few 'double entendres' about getting my briefs in return — but none of them did. Too risky; everyone said I was heading for TV.

But I never got there. I would have been good though. A sharp mind in a five foot six body, good enough legs and a thirty four C bra size, trim waist and stomach — even now — and I am conceited enough to admit that I have a pretty face. Wide-set hazel eyes, a chin that someone who later played a large part in my life called 'cute' and the kind of lips that men like to kiss, or be kissed by. Top that with a thick brunette mane worn to shoulder length and I would have been up there making mincemeat of politicians five nights a week, batting my eyelashes, crossing my legs, then hitting them with the question they really didn't want to answer; all the usual tricks of the trade.

Instead I met Martin. No regrets.

It was in one of those West End pubs where hacks of all descriptions hang out. I had just done an interview with a junior minister and was going to write it up the next morning, so I was chatting with a girlfriend who wrote for one of the tabloids when he joined us.

He was tall and dark, but not handsome. He had a pleasant smile though, I do remember that making a big impression on me. I don't want to describe him any more because subsequently he has made it into TV and his face is very well known. But in any case women don't focus on appearances as much as men do to form initial judgements. I just remember an easy way with words, that smile, and a relaxed self-assured manner. A lot of journalists are constantly on edge — always looking for that next idea, that next item — but Martin seemed to know exactly where he was going and was quite certain that he was going to get there.

After some small talk we adjourned to a restaurant a few doors away. All through the meal washed down with a couple more glasses of wine than was good for me, I was aware of that special secret tingle of anticipation and excitement that women get low down in their stomachs when there's sex in the air. And there was. He was a good listener, which is a very sexy quality in a man. After all if a woman is going to end up in bed with a man, she likes to think he at least knows who he is screwing.

His flat was only a short walk away and while he poured out a nightcap I hurried to the bathroom. I was still dressed for work and that meant tights. They had to go! But what about the knickers? They were workaday too, and frankly a bit damp by that time. I wriggled out of them, screwed them up with the tights and crammed them into my handbag. Then a quick comb of the hair and I was ready. The skirt could have been a bit shorter but it would have to do.

There is a very special feeling, any woman reading this will know it, when you decide that the man you are with is going to have you in his bed in a few minutes. There is a wonderful sense of release. That's it, you have burned your boats and all you want now is for him to be as good as you hope he is. It's a hot, moist feeling and the butterflies start in your stomach.

And that night it was unusually strong. As soon as I entered the lounge he kissed me long and hard. He tasted of whisky and smelled of sweat, deodorant and above all; man. His arms held me tight and I pressed into him until I was breathless, then he led me to the couch and sat down beside me — close.

I managed to take a bit of my drink although my hand trembled; the butterflies were running riot and I knew that between my legs I was hot and moist.

"Do you want to tell me you don't usually do this now? Or later?" he asked quietly.

His hand was on my bare thigh.

"Neither. I've taken my knickers off," I told him.

I reached my arms up to pull him onto me, just inched my hips forward and parted my legs for him. I shivered and moaned into his kiss as I felt his fingers slide up my thigh and into the warmth at the top. Expertly he parted the lips and found my clitoris. Just a fingertip at first and then the length of the finger itself as it slid down and into me through the front door.

He was good! He explored every inch of me slowly and carefully, probing up with two fingers, parting them inside, then twisting them and clenching them, sensitising every nerve ending in my vagina until I was getting the first flutterings of orgasm before I was even undressed. And I came properly when at last he went back to the clit and gave it some serious attention. He was rougher with it than anyone had been before, rubbing and rasping his hand up and down, pressing hard. But I responded, it was pleasure so intense that it was almost pain, I broke the kiss and just lay there gasping, pushing up with my hips to grind against his hand harder and harder until I came in full Technicolor.

That was the first of many firsts that night. In bed he went on being patient and slow, but very rough in some ways. I loved every second of it. When he first drove up between my wide open legs, he dug his fingers deep into my bottom, making me arch up under him and cry out as he squeezed handfuls of my flesh between fingers and thumbs, his nails sending sharp little needles of pain to mix with the delight of feeling him deep inside me. I lifted my legs and wrapped them round his hips to get every last bit of him right up there where it counts while I ground my poor clit against the base of his shaft. It wasn't the biggest cock I had ever seen but it could stay the distance all right.

I was almost praying for him to come after two more almighty climaxes had ripped through me, and then he started those big pushes, the ones which seem to go right up to the cervix and beyond. I clawed at his back and he clenched his hands even harder into my bottom. He ducked his head down and started giving the side of my neck a painfully hard love bite. I had always climaxed fairly loudly but I'm sure that when he finally reached his peak inside me and pushed me over the edge yet again I swore and yelled like a madwoman.

It was my first ever experience of the strange alchemy of pain and pleasure mixed. Pretty tame by the standards I have come to expect subsequently but very real nonetheless.

There were other firsts that night. The first time I did oral on a first screw. The first time I ever had a finger in the back door while I had a penis in the front. For me it felt wild and uninhibited. This was new territory and I explored it eagerly. In the warm, after-sex-scented dark under the duvet I licked my way round his scrotum until it tightened into that lovely crinkly sac which means the balls are ready to shoot all over again.

How do men produce the stuff so quickly? Time after time.

I had never been afraid of oral or found it distasteful but this time I went much further, exploring that ridge which runs back from the base of the penis and merges into the anus, then it was back up and open wide for the helmet. It filled my mouth very nicely and tasted richly of his sperm, and acridly of my own juices. I flicked my tongue at that sensitive spot on the underside of the helmet, just where the foreskin gathers and heard him groan. That was enough, I didn't want him coming in my mouth just then. Later maybe but for now I wanted to go for another ride. I heaved myself up and straddled him then lowered myself towards where I held his shaft in both hands. First I guided it to my clit which was fully up again and ready for more punishment, I rubbed the head of his cock against it until I was ready and then sank down onto it. He ran his hands along my thighs, rubbed his thumbs at my clit with brutal hardness which only made me begin to jiggle up and down on him and then he reached behind me. I think I groaned in mock protest but covered his hands with my own when they resumed that grip on my buttocks. When I came that time, I was collapsed forward onto him, being shaken about like a rag doll by his upward lunges into me and beyond all thought.

I know we woke each other in the night and there was more because when I woke in the morning the first thing I became aware of was a stinging, burning feel between my legs, a sure sign that I had had a good seeing-to.

But I wasn't just a well-screwed girl I was also a working one. I glanced at my watch and leapt up, I had an interview to file. Martin sat up and watched me, looking very tempting but there would be other times, for now I was all business.

"You've got a lovely arse Emma," he said. "A man could get off on smacking it good and hard."

"A man could die waiting for the chance to try it," I told him, but waggled it at him playfully.

In a second he was off the bed and onto me. There was a confused minute or two of laughing, giggling struggle. He was naked and fully erect, I could feel it pressing against me as I fought him and could smell the scent of sex. And here was another first; the joy of struggling against a strong man, knowing you're going to lose and he's going to do what he wants anyway. But it feels good to make him exert his strength to overpower you. I thought I was going to get the morning screw but when he picked me up like I weighed nothing at all, he carried me back to the bed, sat on the edge and put me face down across his knees. All I had managed to do was get my knickers on, and these he yanked down.

Suddenly I was furious at being put in such a humiliating position and all the excitement died. I flailed my arms at him and tried to twist but he simply reached down and around with his left arm, trapping my upper body. I squirmed and wriggled but only ground my already sore breasts against the rough hairs on his thigh.

Here was I, a highly paid young career woman put over a man's knee like... like a schoolgirl! No way! But there was nothing I could do.

I heard the first smack before I felt it. It went off like a pistol shot and there was a second's numbness, then a sharp, stinging pain which seemed to catch in my throat and make me gulp for breath. Then he smacked me again, on the other cheek. When I could get my breath I screamed every insult I could think of at him. But he carried on regardless. It was a good hard session too; he put all his strength into it and soon I was ablaze with scalding pain and crying my heart out. I was so hurt and humiliated that I was totally limp when he picked me up again and this time threw me down onto the bed on my back. I yelled as my bottom hit but then Martin was on top of me and I fought again. Nails, teeth, I tried everything but he calmly trapped my wrists and pinned them to the bed over my head while he used his thighs to spread mine and I felt the hardness of his erection rub against my pubes. I went mad then, twisting and bucking, but he waited till I ran out of energy and let his weight pin me. I had lost and all he had to do was hump his back slightly and there he was, nudging at my entrance. My vagina certainly wasn't lubricated, but neither was it totally uncooperative. He was able to get a little way in. I gritted my teeth and tried to concentrate on my fury, anything but think of him easing into the body he had treated so badly only minutes ago. But for a woman to think of anything else while a man is pushing himself up into her is virtually impossible. I stared up into his face, which was regarding me calmly, and spat.

"Next time, I'll beat you harder for that," he said.

That left me utterly speechless. Next time! Beat me again! After what he had done? I was going straight to the police, never mind anything else.

But while I was struggling to absorb this latest outrage, quite suddenly he was fully into me and his whole weight pressed down on me. He let go of my wrists, reached under me and gripped my buttocks again. This time I really yelled, but he stopped my mouth with his own and began to move inside me. Thrust and withdraw, slowly, rhythmically, the oldest rhythm in the world, at the same time he gradually increased his grip on my bottom. My attempted yells faded to groans and then I suddenly realised that my hips were responding to the rhythm and that the pain in my bottom had joined the pleasure in my sex to form one seamless sensation that was neither pleasure nor pain but something quite different.

The previous night's orgasms faded into insignificance. I couldn't tell where his body ended and mine began, I lost all thoughts and very nearly passed out when my climax exploded. I heard him shout something and realised that he had come as well and we bucked, thrashed and twisted as one body while the aftershocks ran through us.

Over the following days I seesawed wildly between hate for Martin, shame and disgust at myself and fond memories of the sex. I felt used and abused but couldn't deny that the climax I had enjoyed after the beating had been the best ever.

Eventually I even stood with my back to my dressing table mirror with my skirt up and my knickers down to see if there were still any marks. There were still scratches and bruises from his fingers, but no red marks from the actual spanking and a treacherous part of me regretted that, so I gave in and rang him.

We met at a bistro in Soho. I was deliberately late but he seemed quite unconcerned and rose to greet me, giving me a quick peck on the cheek as I got to his table. I tried to be all aloof and cool, but it's difficult when you know he got you into the sack so quickly on your first night. And then there had been the spanking and now, here I was again. Back for more? I honestly didn't know, but he had woken something in me, I had to admit that, and whatever I felt about him, it was different to the way I had ever felt about any other man.

While I picked at what was more of a snack than a meal he was gentleman enough to keep the conversation away from the bedroom, but when we were into our third glass of wine I couldn't stand it any more.

"Look Martin," I said. "I've got to know. If I come back to your place tonight, are you going to… you know… do that to me again?"

He was quite unperturbed. "I promised you another spanking, so yes. I fully intend to keep that promise."

The bistro was crowded and I looked round in panic; he had spoken quite loudly and plainly.

"I meant what I said Emma," he went on. "You have a lovely arse. Just a nice size — a good handful in each cheek. And they wobble so beautifully when they're hit."

"Shut up!" I hissed desperately, although I suddenly realised that I had my stockinged thighs clamped together to savour that treacherous tingling at their tops.

"Have you kept your knickers on tonight?" he continued, completely ignoring me.

I had. The briefest thong I owned — and I had on my one pair of stockings — emergencies only. I had wanted it to be secret that I had dressed to look good undressed. But his words felt like they were stripping me in public. He was pushing all the buttons again, totally in control.

Again I gave in.

"Yes," I whispered. "And stockings and suspenders. The whole works. But do you have to do it so hard this time?" That last part came out in a girlish whine.

"Yes, of course. Come on, we're leaving."

I followed him out, weak kneed and fluttering inside.

Back at his flat I got what was coming to me. This time he didn't put me over his knee, he made me strip while he watched. He wasn't giving me anywhere to hide or pretend that I didn't want what was coming.

I had on a simple shift dress so it didn't take long till I was standing with just stockings, suspenders and high heels on. Martin let his eyes wander over me slowly and I felt my breasts start to get that tight feeling as my nipples started standing to attention. Down below I was all heat and butterflies again.

"Come and kneel down here," he told me at last.

I did as I was told, kneeling beside him and facing the sofa, then he had me lay my torso on the cushions so that my bottom stuck out. I tried to bury my face in the cushions to blot out just how exposed and vulnerable I knew I looked. I felt him get up and then heard him undress before he put one knee on the sofa beside me, his left hand on the small of my back and his right on my bottom.

Oh God! This was going to hurt! But I didn't make a move; I wanted to see just how much it would hurt.

"How many am I getting?" I asked.

"As many as I want to give you," he said quietly and then he started.

It was a good beating. Hard strokes delivered steadily so that the heat and sting from one could spread up from my buttocks before the next one landed. I gasped and wriggled, humping and arching my back under his strong left hand as smack after smack rained down. My nipples rubbed hard on the fabric of the cushions as I writhed. And all the while my whole pelvic area glowed and stung and burned in that strange way it had before. It was as though his hands were striking directly into my sex. And although I yelped and whimpered in genuine pain, I was responding as if to a really good screwing.

At last he gave me a rest and I lay panting and twitching, but then he dug his fingers between my thighs and straight into my sex. I gasped at the roughness of the intrusion but opened my legs instead of clenching them shut. It only took a few moments until I could hear as well as feel how my vagina was responding. Shameless squelching noises came from inside me as he worked his fingers. I couldn't tell how many he had in there I was so open and wet.

He chuckled and started in again and I howled and wriggled even more. This time it really hurt and he had to almost lean on my shoulders to keep me down, but even as each resounding smack forced floods of tears from my eyes, I knew I was getting more and more desperate for him to take me. And at last he did. He knelt behind me and had me doggie style. He went in so easily and so fast that it felt like he was going to go right up into my stomach. I was well and truly impaled on him and with his hands on my hips he rode me to three orgasms before he came himself. He never even touched my breasts or my clit, he just rode me like an animal until he allowed himself to come, forcing me to climax under him just as easily as he had made me strip and kneel for him. I was beaten in all senses of the word.

For two months I was the happiest girl in London. I went to his flat when he rang and summoned me, I dropped whatever I was doing and ran to meet him for drinks or dinner whenever he wanted me to. I learned the importance of taking my time, when his summons allowed me to. Showering or bathing, then perfuming every nook and cranny before easing the stockings up my legs and fastening the suspenders, taking hours to choose the right dress or suit, always a suit with a skirt though. And always I wore suspenders and stockings or hold ups underneath.

And for the first time I really got turned on by looking at myself in the mirror and seeing the way the suspenders framed the area of my sex, looking almost like a harness and I began to understand why men love the contrast between the naked and the stockinged thigh — the change from outward appearance to naked intimacy. There's really only one reason why a woman dresses like that.

Once he had me get a taxi to the flat wearing only bra, suspenders and stockings beneath a coat. But always he beat me. And always hard. And every time he did I grew more and more accustomed to the strange regions a woman can be taken to. I bent over every item of furniture in the flat and even learned to bend over in the middle of the floor and hold my ankles.

I really believed I had the strong man I had obviously always wanted. And I probably would have gone on believing it if Martin hadn't taken me to dinner that night with Jason, then let him beat me and offered me for screwing into the bargain.

"No!" I yelled and twisted away, straightening up to face the men, flustered and dishevelled but defiant. "He's bloody well not going to do that, Martin!"

While Jason had been beating me, he had helped himself to another whisky and now he drained it. "So you won't obey me, Emma?" he asked quietly.

"Damn right I won't!" I screamed, too angry to even note the humiliating use of the word 'obey'.

"Sorry Jason. Looks like you'll have to settle for the spanking for now." He seemed strangely unperturbed and Jason just shrugged and made to leave, Martin followed him out and I helped myself to a drink.

"Well Emma," he said on his return, "I promised you something new and now I've got the perfect excuse to do it."

At once I realised what game he had been playing. He had deliberately put me in a position where I had been bound to refuse to do what he wanted. So now I was going to get a real punishment beating, which was something I had never had before. Tingling excitement erupted once again and I decided I would play the game to the end.

"Get stuffed," I told him.

He came close and I could see genuine anger in his face. Suddenly I was scared as well as excited — like you get at the start of a fairground ride. Was he playing or had he really expected me to let Jason fuck me? The risks and dangers of the situation set my pulse racing.

"You let me down in front of an old friend, you bitch," he said and without warning he slapped me. I staggered back and fetched up against the drinks cabinet. "Now I'm going to punish you."

"All right then," I said fingering my blazing cheek and finding I was really enjoying the thrill of the danger. "See if you can make me say sorry."

He slapped me again, on the other cheek sending me reeling sideways into the TV set. I looked up at him, my heart hammering wildly, my bottom still glowing and now my sex fluttering. He stood before me, calm and authoritative; powerful and in control. I melted completely and he saw it.

"Go into the bedroom and take the belt out of my jeans, then bring it to me here for your punishment."

I did as I was told, hardly able to breathe from excitement and fear. I fumbled the belt out from the loops that held it, my nervous fingers feeling the thickness and weight of the leather. Then I took it back to the man who was about to beat me. I watched as he wrapped a couple of turns round his fist, leaving a good long lash to use on me then he had me strip completely and lie on the coffee table.

I went to the long low table, straddled it and lay down on my face, squashing my breasts against the cold wood and feeling my nipples harden into full arousal. I braced my hands, feet and knees on the carpet and waited.

I heard him go to the drinks cabinet and pour another large measure of whisky. He drained it in one go and then came to stand by my right shoulder. I braced myself for this new experience. My first taste of leather. And I nearly jumped out of my skin when the first lash landed.

It cracked deafeningly loudly across my shoulders and I really hadn't expected that. I was so naive! I thought I was just in for a more extreme bottom thrashing, but suddenly I knew he intended to whip my back as well. Images of true slavery leapt to my mind even as the second lash cracked home. This one was across the buttocks and started a strange, burning, itchy sort of stinging; quite unlike a hand spanking. Then he moved his target to my middle back, then the shoulders again. He was plainly intent on keeping me guessing as to where he was going to strike next. The physical sensations were far from pleasant at this stage of the whipping but mentally I was incredibly turned on by my own submission and vulnerability, and now by Martin's coldly calculating way of tormenting me further.

More lashes fell; the noise of leather smacking down onto my own flesh had me squirming with excitement even as the stinging they caused began to escalate into a fire of breathtaking intensity.

When he had me giving little breathless gasps at each lash, he stopped.

"Don't move," he said, still cold and distant.

Again I heard him go to the drinks cabinet. I should have told him then how excited I was and that I was quite happy for him to carry on; to take me further into the strange landscape of pleasure and pain that was opening up before me, but all I could do was hang my head down and try to get my breath back. I realised that I had shifted my hands and now they gripped the table legs with white knuckles. Then Martin was back and the belt swung in again. The second batch was far more intense. The lashes built on the earlier ones and I moaned and kicked and writhed as my whole body seemed engulfed by white-hot flames.

I had no idea how many I had taken when he finally stopped, but I just lay, panting and gasping as the fires raged. Deep inside me though there was a certain pride and peace. I had taken my punishment and in so doing had come to know myself fully. I had been whipped — how that word went round and round in my head — and when Martin took me as he surely would do, he would find me open and ready for him. He did indeed take me, right there and then, still face down on the table. He tore off his clothes and rammed himself towards the crease of my vulva where it was plainly on view between my now well-whipped buttocks. He used his hand only to guide his shaft, there was no preliminary fingering but he slid into me with no problem and I cried out at the depth and speed of the penetration. He laughed at how easily he went in and, careless of my discomfort pushed his whole weight down onto me. I could smell the whisky on his breath as he lay on me and pumped in and out hard and fast. I came very quickly that time and the orgasm blended and blurred all the borders between the vaginal stimulation, the white heat in my back and buttocks and the way Martin's body was crushing mine down onto the hard wood. It was simply mind-blowing and I just lay like a wrung out rag while he rammed himself to his own climax and finished with me.

However much pleasure I had taken in being punished with the belt, Martin had taken more in delivering that punishment. He was insatiable that night and drove me to the point of begging for mercy after God knows how many orgasms. He took great delight in digging his fingers hard into my back and bottom as he thrust into me when he took me to bed and it had never felt so good. Especially when he whispered that the next day he was going to buy a cane. By the time I sank into an exhausted sleep I was quite certain that I had found the man I wanted, and that I had also found myself.

I couldn't have been more wrong.

PART TWO: BEN.

I struggled up into wakefulness, stinging and aching all over, to find Martin sitting on the edge of the bed, his back to me and his head in his hands. When he heard me stir he turned and I could see how haggard he looked.

"I'm so sorry Emma," he croaked in a morning-after-whisky voice. "Can you forgive me? I lost it… I really lost control. I'm so sorry."

It took a few seconds for the depth of his betrayal to penetrate my sleep fuddled brain but only a few minutes later I was stumbling home, my eyes filled with tears of humiliation and rage.

I thought I had submitted to the anger, and the hand, of a strong man. A man strong enough to overpower me with his will; to make me quite literally bend before him. But after that terrible beating, as it now appeared to me, he had revealed that he had had to have a drink to get up the courage and had then had too many so he had been more than half drunk while he thrashed me.

If only he had said nothing and carried on I would never have known, but now he had actually apologised and begged my forgiveness, all my illusions were shattered and my self- disgust at the pleasure I had found in being so abused knew no bounds.

That summer was the worst of my life.

I was so depressed, confused and lonely.

I couldn't bear to talk to Martin after I had walked out on him that morning, so there was no-one I could talk to about my confusion. At first I tried to simply put it all behind me and throw myself back into my work, but re-runs in my mind of the whipping at Martin's hands just wouldn't leave me alone. And it was hardly the sort of thing I could discuss with a girlfriend over lunch.

I had been brought up to believe that straight sex was the only sort, and I was naive enough that I never really believed other people could enjoy alternative sex. I was convinced that I was totally alone in taking pleasure in pain and submission and on top of this there was the question of sex itself. I had tasted it at an intensity which left everything else standing. It had become a major part of my life and I missed it terribly. I tried going out with a few men but it was no good, the sex was bland without that added spice of secret illicit pleasure. Once I tried asking for a spanking and the guy tried but he just couldn't do it hard enough to be of any use to me, and anyway he too apologised afterwards. So I resigned myself to celibacy and masturbation; something I had never done before. I found I could do a good job on my clitoris, better than most men anyway, but when it came to penetrative... well fingers just didn't do it. I plucked up every ounce of courage I had and went into a sex shop to buy a vibrator. And while I was in there I saw that they sold whips, restraints and paddles. So there really were other people out there doing it! I resolved to try asking the next man I fancied. I would give it one more try and then if that failed and he reacted in horror, well maybe an advert in the personal columns somewhere...

For two weeks not one eligible male came within range and mentally I had begun composing an advert, but then I met Ben again.

I had known him for some years really but had not met him since well before Martin. He was an MP and in his mid-fifties. I liked him; he had never made any secret of the fact that he fancied me a lot. Okay so he was a lot older than me but he was tall, grey haired and hadn't run too badly to fat. He often gave me interesting titbits of news and gossip, one of those unnamed sources that political journalists use so much. I knew he was only trying to get inside my knickers but he was so honest about it that it had become a bit of a game with us. It was the more slimy ones that made my skin crawl.

No, Ben was all right.

I was attending a reception at 'The House' in honour of some visiting dignitary and was engaged in the usual business of pumping all and sundry for signs of splits or policy changes when I felt an arm go round my waist.

"Let me take you away from all this, my lovely Emma," a voice breathed in my ear.

"Ben. You know I'd love you to, but I have work to do," I said without looking round.

"I've got some really spicy stuff for you, and I'll spill the beans over dinner — if you see what I mean."

I laughed, and it seemed like the first time in months. What the heck, I told myself. Take a night off and enjoy the company.

"Okay," I said, and laughed again at the look of surprise on his face. But when it came to adding everything up the next morning, Ben had won hands down on surprises.

We went to a small Italian place off the Strand where neither of us was likely to be recognised.

"Now then Emma, what's up?" It was at the end of what had been a very good meal with some very good wine and now Ben steepled his hands and looked at me seriously. He had given me some useful stuff; he never let me down.

"Nothing," I lied.

"Emma, you know I have lusted after you for years and as ever I was watching you tonight and I can tell you're not happy. There's something on your mind, you're just not as professional and focused as usual. With a beautiful woman that usually means man trouble."

He should have been the journalist! A heady mixture of good wine, compliments and well aimed probes to winkle out the truth.

I looked at him closely. He wasn't at all bad looking; distinguished I think you'd call him, and anyway it wasn't as if I was going to leap into bed with him, I told myself — I just needed to talk to someone. He knew I had always respected his confidences and never quoted him.

"Strictest confidence? Between friends?" I asked.

"Of course." And despite everything that happened subsequently he was as good as his word.

I told him everything, propelled over the rough bits by some more wine. He listened calmly and silently until I had finished.

"Well I must say Emma you're the most surprising and certainly the best looking submissive I've ever come across," he said at last.

It took a second for the full import to hit me.

"You've come across others? How? Where?" I spluttered.

"Like you said, you're not the only one. I've been lucky enough to dominate quite a few over the years. Would you like me to take you on?"

I was to come to learn that he had a habit of coming straight to the point in these matters. But I had to think, he was a lot older than me but then again he wasn't unattractive. He was a high risk to my career just as a lover; let alone as a lover of the sort I needed. But I trusted him. All these thoughts whirled round my brain while I used the usual female ploy of retiring to the ladies' room to repair makeup and gather my thoughts.

In the end one thing decided me; he had experience of submissive women and I wanted that.

"Okay," I said as soon as I sat back down. "Where do we go from here?"

"My place. And Emma," he reached over and gripped my upper arm in an unexpectedly strong hand, "understand this. Everything starts from now!"

And it did.

The change that came over him was extraordinary. The mischievous, smiling Ben was gone. In his place was a tall and commanding man of experience who was close to the corridors of power and who knew how to wield it. In the silent taxi I felt that tingle in the pit of my stomach and had to shift in my seat a couple of times as my knickers became uncomfortable. When he paid off the taxi he took me to the doorstep of his Kensington house.

"I suspect that as you did not know you would be coming to me tonight, you are somewhat over dressed under that delightful gown. See to it and then ring the bell." And he was gone, leaving me staring at my reflection in the highly polished front door. I was so totally shocked that I never even thought of hailing another cab and going home.

I looked down at my dress. It was a much loved friend, black velvet with a tight and very low-cut bodice, underwired so no need for a bra — thank God! It was under the full skirt that the problem lay. I was going to have to get my knickers off before he would allow me in, and it was entirely up to me how I managed it standing at the top of his front steps in a London street. I turned and faced away from the door. It was quite late but there were still people around, couples returning from pubs — two gay men, arm in arm, even a Kensington nanny taking a wakeful baby out in its pram. In the end it was the very full cut of the skirt which came to my rescue. I backed up to the door and fumbled the back up over my bottom, grabbed the hip straps of my knickers and wrenched them down to my knees. Once they were there it just took a couple of wiggles and a stamp of each foot to coax them the rest of the way. I looked around me and no-one had noticed, so a quick lift of each foot, being careful not to tangle my heels, and they were off. I stuffed them in my bag and rang the bell. My heart was hammering away and I just wanted to get in off the street.

"Yes?" Ben's voice was tinny on the intercom.

"It's me, Emma. Can I come in now?"

"Have you taken off what I required you to?" Infuriatingly calm.

"Yes, yes!"

"Tights as well?"

"No! I've got stockings on. Please Ben!"

The buzzer went and I piled into the hall in just the shaken and flustered state he had wanted. He was standing a few feet away and smiling.

"Stockings! How very sensible for a modern girl, well done!"

He turned and went into the lounge; I followed.

"Kneel down here in front of my chair, Emma." He had settled himself in a big leather armchair, a glass of wine at his side and a cigar burning in the ashtray. I squared my shoulders and did as I was told. I knew I was being tested but was determined to measure up to whatever was required. This was what I had wanted after all, no-one had forced me here.

I made sure that the skirt spread out round me prettily and that he could get a good view of my cleavage, and even with the underwiring built into the cups and the velvet itself I could feel my nipples pushing out tightly. I glanced down proudly, yes he couldn't fail to notice the little peaks.

"Now then. Here are my rules. Whenever you come here, from the moment you enter the door you will be at my command. You will call me 'Sir' at all times. You will not speak unless spoken to or unless you ask my permission. Under your clothes you will be properly undressed. I have no time for fumbling with feminine fripperies. Clear?"

"Yes B... yes, sir."

"Good girl." Even that most patronising of compliments made my heart swell with pride. I was going to be good for him.

"Whether I require you to be naked or to retain stockings and/or shoes, or restraints you will accept my instructions without demur and at all times keep your eyes modestly cast down. You will leave your name behind you when you enter. I will refer to you simply as 'K'..."

I was so startled I looked up quickly from his expensive, hand made brogues at which I had been gazing while trying to absorb these outrageous 'rules'.

He met my eyes and smiled again. "That will be added to your first punishment."

My stomach lurched and melted all at the same time. I looked down again quickly.

"My first slave was 'A', so from that you may deduce the experience of the master into whose hands you have placed yourself. You will notice that I have a glass of wine, I will not indulge in anything stronger during a session with you, you have my word on that, K. You however, will not be allowed any alcohol at all; it is not fitting that a slave should have her senses dulled in any way. She must be fully aware of what is required of her and experience fully whatever her master wishes her to. Especially when she is beaten."

I had been kneeling back on my heels with my legs together and had become increasingly aware of the moist heat building down there. But at the word 'beaten' something seemed to turn it up another notch and I drew in my breath at the sheer strength of the surge.

Ben must have known because he leaned forward and cupped a breast in one large hand. I moaned in pleasure at the pressure against the nipple.

"Now K, stand up and let's see what you have to offer your master."

Proudly I stood up, unzipped the dress and stepped out of it. He allowed me to retain stockings suspenders and shoes. For a man who had, at his own admission been dreaming of having me, Ben had done a hell of a job in keeping cool and in command. Okay, I thought, let's see how he does when the goods are on display.

It was no contest.

If I had been expecting him to crumble before my blatant nudity, take me in his arms and have me there and then. I was sadly disappointed.

He walked round me slowly while I fixed my eyes on a patch of carpet and tried to control my heartbeat and wildly fluttering vagina. In his suit he seemed to tower over me and made me feel deliciously vulnerable. At last he stopped in front of me and took both breasts in his hands. He stroked them, cupped them, weighed them, rubbed at the nipples till I closed my eyes and nearly lost my balance, at which point he held the nipples hard and twisted them. The sharp pain brought me back to my senses, and then I gasped in shock as he gently slapped the breasts themselves, left and then right; again and again, making them swing across my chest and judder under the blows. It was not an unpleasant feeling, and as I watched those intimate parts of my femininity being so casually treated for a man's pleasure I felt they made an intensely erotic display and that helped me keep my hands by my sides and let him play with me. Again I moaned as a fresh flood seemed to break loose inside me. Ben laughed.

"Good, very sensitive. And you are a sensual creature aren't you? This is what you've always wanted isn't it?"

"Yes sir," I breathed.

"Over to the sofa. Lie down, raise and spread your legs, hold your knees."

I went over to the leather ottoman he indicated and did as I was told. The leather was so cold under my back! But I tried to ignore it and instead concentrate on the display I was being asked to make. With my legs doubled up and my hands clasped behind my knees, I knew that from where Ben now sat, just beyond my backside, he could examine my sex and even my anus. All nicely framed by the straps of the suspenders and the dark stockings. And he did, just as a doctor might. I stared at the ceiling and bit my lip when I felt him pull my labia apart so he could see my inner lips, my entrance, my clitoris…

"Good plump lips. I like that on a girl, and good sized inner ones too, and all very wet."

I jerked as I felt a finger go deep inside me and then I cried out when it withdrew to wipe itself on the straining little button of my clitoris. And then something thicker invaded me, I craned my head to look down between my legs and saw his thumb sink in right up to the second knuckle but then I bucked and twisted, nearly letting go of my legs when I felt a finger stab at my anus.

"Lie still!"

I tried to and bit my lip harder as I felt it press, and my sphincter tighten, but he pressed again and was in. It was only the second time I had felt that weird urge to move my bowels, and tightened still further, but it was no good. He clenched finger and thumb inside me and I nearly bucked right off the sofa as I felt my rear vaginal wall gripped and squeezed. Then suddenly he withdrew again leaving me gasping and quaking. And I yelped in surprise as he then smacked both buttocks twice, hard.

"Good," he said, standing up and smiling down at me. Too late I realised I was looking into his eyes again and he laughed.

"You're going to be a delight to punish, K. An excellent body to take it and an excellently adjusted mind to accept it. Now stand up and walk to the far wall."

Shakily I got to my feet and again obeyed, turning when I got to the beautiful antique writing desk which stood there. He watched coolly as I approached him, acutely aware of how my breasts moved and swung as I walked. I went close to him and then stopped. He reached out and grasped my pubic hair to pull me closer and I whimpered a little as he yanked at it. I felt the cloth of his suit brush my aching nipples.

"Now down onto all fours, on your dress." This time I could hear his voice was throaty. At last I was going to be taken!

He knelt behind me and I heard him unzip himself, then his hand ran down my bottom crease and into the folds of my sex, prising it open again. And then at last I felt him plunge into me. It wasn't an exploratory shove, he was aiming for my very core and he got there. His size took me aback; I arched and yelled in abandon as he slid up and up until I felt his pelvis grind against my buttocks. And then he simply battered me into complete surrender, my arms collapsed under me as my orgasm finally exploded and I knelt with my bottom in the air as he drove me mercilessly up to the heights again. I shouted and gabbled mindlessly as the colours blinded me and my whole body whirled out of time. I never even felt him come.

When I revived I found I was sprawled out on my dress and already Ben's semen was leaking out onto it. Exactly what he intended of course. Roughly he grabbed my tousled hair and yanked me up to my knees. This time I had no choice but to look him in the eye.

"Thursday night at eight o'clock you will report here."

I nodded as best I could.

"I will cane you then. For now you may go."

Dazed and utterly humiliated I dressed. I had been prodded and poked, tested and screwed brutally, even my best dress had been soiled and now I was being thrown out. But I had passed the test! And even the humiliation of being so carelessly dismissed was made sweet by that realisation. He rang a cab while I tried to compose myself and find a way of holding my dress to hide the semen on it, and when he led me to the front door, he pointed to the coat stand in the hall. In the bottom of it stood three riding crops.

"They're one implement of our craft which can be openly displayed K. But it will be the cane for you on Thursday, after that we'll see. Then he opened the door, took my hand, kissed it, and was gone.

And so I became simply 'K'. And I liked it, yes it made me excitingly depersonalised — just a female body with no name — but it still sounded like a name nonetheless. The experience of existing for Ben as just a nameless body for his use and pleasure I found intensely arousing. Even at work or wherever I was I became very aware of my body. I was proud of it, really proud of it for the first time. I stood up straighter, I started wearing smart, tight fitting clothes even when I was just working on my laptop at home. And I even began walking more self-consciously... but I'm getting ahead of myself.

After that night there were two endless days of combined terror and excitement before the big night came! I put on cream holdup stockings. Why? I just did. I knew he liked suspenders so was I deliberately inviting trouble by not wearing them or was it just that I thought they suited me? There was no question of knickers so I showered as close to the time I had to leave as possible, and gave my bush a quick trim as well as a good squirt of scent, hissing through my teeth at the ferocious stinging that always set up, then a crisp white blouse and my cream linen suit on top. The skirt was just long enough to cover the stocking tops — but only just. Still I wasn't going to be wearing it for long. I did a twirl in front of the mirror and thought I looked pretty good.

We women really are creatures of vanity. I was going to get a real caning, and I wanted to look my best for it.

Again I was flustered and unsure of myself when I rang his bell. There was a pause, then my heart skipped a beat.

"Yes?"

"It's me, Emma... I mean K!... Sir!" Damn! Off to a good start. The door buzzed and I went in. Ben was waiting for me, dressed in a blue silk dressing gown which he wore like an old fashioned smoking jacket, since under it he had his trousers on, but he was barefooted I noticed as I carefully fixed my eyes downwards. Without a word he turned and went into the lounge. I supposed I was meant to follow and did so. I found him in his chair again. He pointed to the middle of the floor and told me to strip. I could feel his eyes boring into me as I fumbled with jacket, blouse, bra and finally skirt.

"Hands on top of your head, legs apart ... further. That's right. It's Position One, K. Learn it."

"Yes sir."

He walked round me and then stood close behind me. "Look at the sofa."

Oh God! There it was. The cane! Lying on the leather cushions, long, smooth and terrifying. I think I moaned when I saw it just lying there waiting for me to bend over. I didn't think I could last much longer, I just wanted to get it over and done with but Ben wanted to torment me some more. He asked me if I had had a 'safe word' with Martin, I told him I didn't know what one was. He explained the idea and then to my dismay, dismissed it in my case.

"Firstly I am very experienced, and secondly, I don't think you want one. I think you want me to take complete charge of you, you want to trust me. You may answer."

My mouth was dry and my legs trembled. I didn't want this! I didn't want decisions but he was waiting.

"I want whatever you want, sir," I managed. *'Oh just get it over with,'* I was begging him mentally.

"I want you to commit yourself entirely to my control."

"Yes sir," I whispered.

"Good girl. Go and stand behind the sofa then bend over it." At last!

Again I shivered at the chill of the leather as it met my stomach but my attention was riveted on the cane lying just below my face. To the left and right of it were lengths of white nylon rope; one end of each was tied through steel loops which were sewn into thick leather straps with buckles. Ben duly buckled these tightly onto my wrists and then looped the other ends of the ropes around the front legs of the sofa until I was bent over and grunting under the twin strains of trying to keep my toes on the floor and the pain of the sofa digging hard into my stomach. Only then did he tie them off. It was my very first experience of restraint and I liked it. It was terrifying and exciting and the feel of the leather tightly gripping my wrists was very sexy indeed.

My hair hung down round my face but I could just see his hand reach down and pick up the cane.

"Oh God!" I couldn't help myself when I saw him adjust his grip and heft it to get the feel of it. He chuckled as he moved round behind me and used his foot to nudge my feet wider apart. He was getting a grandstand view of everything I had to offer. I twisted my hands so I could grip the ropes and hang on for dear life.

"By the way, holdups are okay every now and then, but darker ones in future."

"Yes sir. Please sir?"

"What?"

"Please... please start! I can't stand it any more!"

"Oh you can stand a lot more K, believe me. But you learn fast, I was going to make you beg me to take the cane to you in any case. There's just the matter of how many strokes now. Six for pleasure I think and another six for the various offences you have committed."

I gaped in horror. Twelve! No-one could take that, could they? I was about to beg for mercy when I felt his hand softly stroke down along my sex and his fingers split the lips then rub at the clitoris which sent a jolt of such intense excitement through me it went way beyond pleasure.

And then at last he started. His fingers left me, there was a sudden whooshing in the air behind me and a fleshy smack as the cane bit. A second's numbness and then all hell let loose. A wave of fire swept through me. Tears sprang to my eyes, my head went back and my throat tightened so I couldn't breathe or scream or anything. Then the second landed and I was pulling at my ropes with all my strength, bouncing up and down still gulping for breath. The third, and I started screaming.

I couldn't stand this! He had to have mercy on me! I had no idea that anything could hurt so much; I took it all back, I didn't want this!

I sobbed and begged my way through three more strokes, and then he stopped. I gasped and gulped and sniffed until I could fully appreciate the fire now raging in my bottom. It seemed to throb in waves which engulfed me and swept me away. But now that the cane was no longer landing, strange things were happening to me. I knew my whole sex was blatantly on display between my agonised buttocks and spread legs. And just like when Martin had strapped me and spanked me the white heat of the cane seemed to have gone deep into my very core and I knew I was moist down there. I sniffed up some more snot which had trailed from my nose and realised that Ben was standing in front of me. His dressing gown had come open enough for me to see the bulge in his trousers. He had enjoyed that, and he was going to enjoy me even more when he finished.

"All right K?"

I managed a nod. He poured himself a glass of wine and took a drink while I gradually calmed. Now the feelings were merely overwhelming rather than agonising, and there was a definite excitement growing in me. I had done it! If I could weather six; I could take twelve.

"Ready to go again?" he asked, standing behind me once more.

I nodded. I was ready this time but I still howled like a banshee as the next six carved themselves into me. But this time I was conscious of the erotic sound of the cane striking my stretched bottom and the fires grew and grew, each stroke adding to the last, but also adding to the excitement of giving myself so totally to this man offering my pain for his enjoyment, and so turning it into something that wasn't mere pain.

And the pride when he untied me at last!

It was some time before I could straighten up and I realised that all my writhing had tugged my stockings down. I pulled them up, straightened them and walked over to Ben as best I could. I was desperate to rub my cheeks but I was so proud of having taken twelve good whacks that I was determined to show him that it was no big deal to a tough cookie like me.

I remember that I spent an hour or so in Position One, with my back to him while he occasionally stroked my backside and ran his fingers along the still scalding lines carved onto my buttocks. And he questioned me further. Had I enjoyed it when Martin slapped me? Had he ever whipped my breasts? I jumped at that. Surely a woman couldn't be whipped there!

"Oh my dear girl, there is virtually nowhere the female can't be whipped, provided one knows what one is doing," Ben told me when I dared question it.

I took some time to absorb that and felt very vulnerable between my open legs all of a sudden.

I learned more positions that night; Two was down on hands and knees, back arched, head up. Three was knees and forearms, head down and bottom up. Ben explained that this was useful for swift and minor punishment as well as buggery. Four was standing with hands behind head, elbows well back, good for breast display. Five was the waiting position, hands behind back, legs apart and facing the wall.

Over the next few weeks K spent a lot of time in Five as her master was keen on waiting as part of her training. He would announce which implements were going to be used on her, or how he was going to take her and then put her in Five to let her think about it for an hour or so. It was very effective and he always got a moist and excited girl when he finally began.

But I finished that first night tied to his bed. Ben explained that it was the only way I would share it with him, otherwise I would be sent to one of the spare rooms when he had finished with me or else I would be tied to the foot of the bed. I was very impressed with the neatness of the wrist restraints and their clips when he fed my wrists through the bars of the bed head and clipped them together. He then put more restraints on my ankles and fastened them wide apart to each of the posts at the foot of the bed.

My bottom still burned and stung deliciously under me and the evening's activities plus my wide open bondage were doing devastating things between my legs and when Ben finally mounted me I took him for a wild ride. He was heavier than Martin but so far as I could I bucked and pushed under him as he thrust into me, deliberately I squirmed my hips about to stoke up the fires in my bottom and propelled myself as loudly as ever into orgasm twice before he came.

And how I loved his final pushes as he climaxed! I felt so totally used; beaten, bound and screwed by someone who really knew how to dominate a girl. Before he fell asleep beside me Ben told me I was the loudest girl he had ever had — either under punishment or during sex. He would beat that out of me, he said.

I smiled happily in the darkness and tugged at my bonds a couple of times to enjoy the feeling of helplessness to the full and finally fell asleep myself despite being unable to stop Ben's semen oozing coldly down my bottom crease.

Dressed in my smart linen suit the next morning I left Ben's house to resume being Emma. But I was a different Emma now; knickerless and with a stiff bum, an Emma who felt a complete woman at last. A woman who was prepared to give everything to her man and who had braved the cane to provide him with pleasure and found her own overwhelming joy in the tortured regions of submission. Ben had been so clever, he had known that it was the cane which held the most fearful fascination for me as it was what I had been looking forward to with Martin, and he had broken me in by making me face it straightaway. Now I was over that hurdle, I could face anything.

In the following days I threw myself back into work with a vengeance. Going for stories like a terrier, worrying at people and hounding them till I got what I wanted and then writing with a vigour and energy I had never had before. And the part of me that was now K was insanely proud of my wounds and every evening I would strip in front of my mirror and examine the marks left on it by Ben, my master.

I was fascinated by the narrow tramlines which striped each buttock and how the flesh had bruised darkly around them, especially where the inner, softer flesh had been struck. I was also very impressed by how close together they had been laid on me. Ben had a very good eye and all twelve strokes had been laid neatly on the main buttock flesh without straying down onto the thighs. I learned that he had been going easy on me for my first time.

It took a week for the bruises to run their course through purple and red to yellow and brown and finally begin to fade. Meanwhile I awaited my next summons impatiently. It came in the middle of an editorial meeting. My mobile rang and Ben simply gave me a day and a time, told me he was going to whip me with a crop and then hung up. I melted inside at the sound of his voice and my thighs clenched together under the table. I hardly heard anything from then on. I was K again.

On my second visit I duly got the crop. I wore my blue dress, a nicely tailored waist and twirly pleated skirt; over dark stockings it looked very prim and proper.

As soon as I was inside Ben had me take the longest of the crops out of the coat stand. I could feel the weight of the thing, the cord on the shaft and how whippy that shaft was. It made my skin crawl and once more I experienced pure terror. I thought I would be so much braver after the cane… but no way.

When I was naked — even stockings and suspenders this time, only my black court shoes left — he had a good feel of me and that calmed me down. It was just as if I was a horse he owned. He stroked down my sides and my hips, and ran his hands across my buttocks again and again and then played with my breasts for ages. He only slapped them after he had felt them very slowly and thoroughly and then pulled at the nipples till my eyes were watering.

"You've got good tits, K," he said. "Nice wide sweeps of upper breastflesh and pleasantly convex too. And good curves below the nipples as well. When you're ready for clamps and pegs you'll find there's plenty I can work with there."

I felt so grateful that he was getting to like them so much that I almost thanked him without permission. But I didn't, I was learning.

Then he went for the jackpot and my knees nearly buckled when he touched me there. One finger up first, and he had no trouble getting in believe me, then two and after a quick rub at the clit with his thumb — good and hard — he got three in and started stirring things up. I couldn't help groaning and moaning; it was wonderful. I think he was trying to make me break my position and he damn nearly succeeded. I had my fingers clenched in my hair and my legs were locked so rigid they ached by the time he finished. Then he reached under me and ran his wet fingers down between my buttocks and over my anus. He stopped there for a bit, just tickling it and pressing a little, while I clenched my teeth and waited for him to go in, but he didn't.

"Later K," he said. "When you've been cropped you'll have earned it."

I didn't know what to make of that but at least he put me in Five and went to have a bath. I stood and stared at the wall beside the writing desk where he had positioned me and tried to recover. The way he had felt me and played with me had got all tangled up in my mind with the forthcoming beating and I couldn't decide which one I was getting myself all wet thinking about. In the end I just decided to enjoy feeling so horny and to relax and leave everything to Ben.

When he came back he was wearing just the blue dressing gown, I saw him from the corner of my eye and heard him pick up the crop. He ordered me to follow him, naked and trembling down the hall and into the dining room. There was a superb walnut dining table with eight beautiful chairs around it, and portraits on the walls. I just about took that in as he guided me across the room and had me stand under, and in between two wrought iron wall lights. In the ironwork of each I wasn't surprised to see a ring hanging down. Ben buckled on my wrist restraints and clipped them to these rings so that I was held face first against the wall, boobs slightly squashed and arms raised and spread.

Then he took up the crop and began to stroke it over my back and bottom, letting me get the feel of the shaft and the keeper at the end.

Then he asked, "Now K, what do you have to say?"

I knew how this bit went and although I was scared and thrilled I managed to keep my voice steady. "Please use the crop on me sir. I'm ready."

"I wonder about that," he replied. "Anyway turn your head to the side so I can see your face. Whenever possible it is desirable to be able to see a slave's face as she is whipped. They look very pretty when they wince and gasp and scream."

I had been standing with my forehead pressed to the wall and now I turned towards him. And I think as I did so he saw just what an effect his words had had on me. I was definitely ready to go. The open way he had talked had me feeling like molten lava inside. The casual brutality of whipping a girl to enjoy how pretty she looked while undergoing it! I loved the idea, and best of all he had used the word 'slave' for the first time. He even brushed my hair forward off my shoulders so that nothing would get in the way of the crop and I swear I nearly came to orgasm at that bit of cruelty.

Anyway, this time I could see what was coming, Ben had stripped off and I saw his lovely erection swaying as he moved his arm back

How can I describe that sound? It was a sort of swooshing, like with the cane, but there was a much louder report when it hit me. I suppose it was a kind of Whhhhack! Or Shhhwack! Words just can't do the job! But it was more than just the sound, very sexy though it was, it was the instant burn on the skin of my back, the impact which jerked me against the wall, my nakedness and helplessness and most of all opening my eyes after each lash to see Ben staring intently at my back, aiming the next stroke while the heat of the last sank into my whole body.

And being tied like a real slavegirl for the first time made it the most incredibly erotic experience! I blinked and gasped after each of the early lashes, then clenched my teeth against the screams as the beating went on and the agony mounted. But I was mesmerised by watching the shaft swing in towards me and strangled shrieks at last burst out of me as the blows built the fires across my back and bottom into white hot lances of flame which went far deeper than pain.

In the end I think I came. It felt as if I did. Something was fluttering and clenching inside me as the lashes kept on coming. It was far better than the cane. Every nerve in my back was registering overload and by the time Ben started in on my bottom, I swear I was grinding my pelvis against the wall, trying to drag my clit up to rub it.

Soon after that he stopped and when he released me I just slid down the wall and stayed there gasping like a landed fish. But unlike a normal orgasm I didn't feel content and satisfied afterwards, what had happened to me under the whip had left me desperate to have Ben inside me, somewhere... anywhere.

As my head cleared I wiped away the snot and tears from my face and heard Ben's voice.

"Crawl to me K. Thank me with your mouth for that whipping. You looked exceptionally pretty while you were suffering."

Oh yes I had suffered all right, but I had loved every second of it and I crawled over to where he was leaning against the side of the table. His erection was sticking up hard and inviting, just waiting for me to explore and taste every inch of its soft sheath of skin. I knelt up when I reached him and very gently began to lick him, thanking him for the fires still raging over my body, thanking him for having put me to the whip. Payment for that scarlet mist of agonised delight I had just experienced.

I slowly licked every inch of that lovely shaft, a master's sex; the very essence of mastery. I explored every vein and every fold of foreskin, holding the base with one hand and running the fingernails of the other up and down his inner thighs. I ducked my head and tasted the tight scrotum, rolling the balls on my tongue, moving along and licking as far up towards his anus as I could, smelling the sweat between his thighs. Then I moved back and began to make my way up towards the helm, running my hands up to his chest so he could hold them there and force me to work with only my mouth. And slowly, ever so slowly I slid my lips around that wonderful smooth, polished helm, already exuding its first rich tasting drops of liquid. His size made me open so wide I thought I was going to dislocate my jaw. I was so full of him I could hardly suck and just slid down and down, until he was pushing right into my throat. That was the most I had ever got in, I think the aftermath of the whipping which was still dominating my body let me relax much more than usual and suddenly I realised my nose was almost brushing his pubic hair and my face was stuffed to bursting with penis.

It was time. I had to go for it before the gagging reflexes set in. And the thought of having him spurt directly into my throat was so exciting I just had to do it. I started that nodding motion which always milks them but I did it far better than ever before, moving right up till I felt my teeth on the edge of his helm and then all the way back down to almost nuzzle his bush. I was in some kind of frenzy I think, I was pure sex, whipped and desperate to please but getting a bigger hit out of oral than I had ever had in my life. The crisis came with that lovely swelling and stiffening and then the pumping began, I could feel the pulses run along the whole length I had in my mouth and throat. And God could he pump! There was gallons of the stuff and I locked onto him tensing everything except my throat, just letting it jet straight down me, but when I felt the spasms begin to fade I lifted back so I could taste the last few drops on my tongue.

And the best of it was that he obviously thought I did really well. He tied me to the bed like the first time, but woke me twice to kneel over my face so I could lick him all over again, but he wouldn't untie me so I could do it properly, all I could do was crane my head up and kiss it as best I could, but at least I could have a really good go at that bit behind the balls. What an obedient little slavegirl.

And the next morning when he said goodbye, I got the kiss of the hand and then he told me that next time he was going to bugger me… and I couldn't wait.

He was as good as his word. I bet every girl who has been taken like that can remember her first time. It's much more traumatic than losing your virginity, at least in my opinion. But even now, when that back passage is so well used it can take virtually anything up it — and pretty well has — I have never taken as much pleasure in being given a good shafting there as in the other two entrances. I do enjoy it, but it's more mental than physical pleasure, I love the degradation more than the act itself.

Ben summoned me over a week later. I had been keeping a careful eye on my marks, especially the ones left by the keeper — the leather flap at the end of the crop — rectangular bruises with pinpoint dark red spots inside them, where it had snapped at me a split second after the shaft had raised its long, livid weal. But they were well on their way to disappearing, I could move without any stiffness and I was up for more.

I wore a tight fitting jumper and pencil skirt that time, and was looking forward to another night of mind-blowing forays into the darker regions of my personality so I stripped almost before he gave the order. I was allowed to keep stockings, suspenders and heels on, he said it would make me look much more attractive when he took me, and I had to agree with him. He made me adopt my positions to make sure I remembered them, then had me walk for him. He said he was going to teach me to display myself much better by making me place one foot directly in front of the other as I walked and getting me to sway my hips more. He flicked at me with the cane as I practised and

I learned quickly. He cut at me across the fronts and backs of the thighs which I found out instantly was much more painful than getting it on the bottom.

After about an hour of this he put on my restraints and had me kneel on the sofa, facing the back, with my knees just on it so I could bend right forward and get my head down, jammed up against the back. Then he made me spread my thighs and put my arms back between them and tied my wrists to my ankles so I was trussed up neatly with my backside jutting up and out for him. He caned it then. Just six but I was so tightly stretched it hurt like the devil and I knew he would be able to see my labia peeling open as the pain and pleasure built. A very special humiliation that is. I couldn't see very much with my head jammed down, but peering back through my open legs I could see just enough to watch some of the strokes coming and I am sure I made a very pretty picture, jumping and making "Aaah!" sounds each time the rod cracked across my suspender-and-stockings-framed buttocks.

Once he decided that six had warmed me up well enough I saw him unzip his trousers and free his sex. I moaned at the sight, reminded of just how thick it was. He reached for something I couldn't see and then I jumped again as cold and sticky stuff was spread round my anus and the finger doing it slid up inside me, quite easily. Then it withdrew and he spread some of the stuff on his helm before stepping closer to me. He didn't say a word but I started to beg him not to do it as I watched his hand grip the base of his shaft and bend it down towards its target. Quite properly he ignored me and in fact punished me for speaking out of turn on my next visit. But my protests faded into gurgles and groans as I felt the blunt helm nudge at my sphincter and begin to push the muscles apart. They seemed to stretch impossibly wide and I screamed in panic, quite sure that something would have to give; and it was going to be me, but Ben just carried on regardless. The stinging got worse and even eclipsed the heat from the caning but still he wasn't in. I was in such pain by then that I longed for him to get in, anything to stop that awful stretching. And at last it happened, quite suddenly, with a smooth suctioning feel the helm slid into me and my poor abused anus clamped tight around the shaft. I yelled all over again as he began to push farther in and provoked that instinctive urge to push downwards from my bowels.

"Relax K. Just relax and take it in."

Easier said than done, but I tried. Despite the lubricant my rectum was so narrow that I could feel the tissues inside being pulled as the shaft worked its way up. It seemed as if I had yards of Ben's body impaling me before he was finally in completely, and then it was time for the thrust and withdraw. I tried desperately to relax but he was so intent on coming that he yanked my innards backwards and forwards with him while I whimpered and moaned under him. At last though, I felt him slam up against my bottom again and again in short, sharp thrusts and felt the sperm spurt into my tortured passage. That was the only pleasure I took in the whole experience.

He was obviously displeased with me because he could have stayed inside me till he began to soften and shrink but instead he wrenched himself out while still fully erect and that made me scream again as the helm brutally gave my sphincter one last stretching to remember it by. And to judge by the weird feeling at the base of the rectal passage, some of me must have stuck to him and for a second some of the lining actually came out before freeing itself and snapping back. I gave one last strangled yelp of fright and disgust and then it was done. Ben left me while he went to wash and when he came back simply told me to get dressed and go.

He had released me and I stood clutching my buttocks and hopping in discomfort at the stinging from my anus. I burst into tears when I realised I was being dismissed, but he was adamant, just pushing me towards my clothes and repeating his command. To my utter dismay I understood that I was to return home with his sperm seeping out of my bottom hole.

I was too miserable to protest any more and squirmed on the taxi's seat all the way home as the cold, sticky fluid smeared itself over my agonised anus and all over my caned bottom to remind me of my first failure as a slave.

I rang his home number every day for a week, blubbering tearful apologies to his answering machine and promising to do better next time. Either he was playing with me or he decided to relent and two weeks after that night I went back into training.

He used an inflatable butt plug to stretch me and I even took it home and inserted it myself whenever I had an hour or so, pumping it to the point of real pain and then leaving it there. He made me ring him whenever I did that so that I could tell him how much I hurt, and so at least I got some pleasure out of knowing that he knew I was waddling about naked and in tears. We settled into some kind of routine but it was difficult. Both our jobs demanded odd working hours and there were times when I really couldn't respond to his summons. I was allowed to cry off twice in a month without incurring punishment. Equally there were times when he was required for late night sittings in the House, and on one occasion he was paged to get to the Division Lobby while we were in full session.

By the time that occurred I had graduated to a room at the back of the first floor of the house where Ben kept all the equipment he had collected over the years. There were all kinds of trestles, benches, chains and some things which I simply had no name for back then. But I was immensely proud that I was regularly disciplined there, it meant that I really had been accepted as Ben's slave. On that evening he had me lying face down on a wide wooden bench, ankles restrained and shackled, head hanging down off the end and my arms pulled painfully back and up, my wrists shackled to a chain from the ceiling. I was about to get a prolonged session under a whip wielded across back, buttocks and thighs — no short skirts for a week or so — when his pager went off. He simply laid the whip down across my back and left me.

I can't begin to describe the torments I went through for the next three hours. The pain was one thing but it was the fear, the desertion, the vulnerability that really got to me. By the time he returned I was sobbing and groaning uncontrollably, my tears had formed a puddle on the bare wood floor under my face. I heard him enter and approach but all I could see was his beautifully polished shoes, spattered with raindrops.

"All right K?" he asked.

"No sir! I was so scared!" I sobbed. "And my arms…"

"Are pure agony," he finished for me. "But don't worry, I'm back now and you won't notice your arms in a minute or two."

I was so relieved that he was back his words immediately triggered the fires between my legs, and I welcomed the thrashing once it began at long last. It was my first experience with a proper whip and it was a real eye opener in all senses of the word. The skin-burn was more diffuse than with the cane or crop and took longer to penetrate and blend with the excitement in my belly. So I got longer to appreciate the slave experience of pain and helplessness before I got the pay-off and began to lose myself in that mist of pleasure/ pain which had me drumming my pelvis up and down on the bench while my bottom and thighs were laced with red-hot wires.

And he was right, I forgot about my arms until he released me and then I really felt them. Subsequently of course, I came to learn that release from bondage can be even more painful than undergoing it. And very shortly I was to learn that the release of nipple and labial clamps holds a very special torment for a submissive.

That night I spent in the spare bedroom which was next to his. I used it quite frequently by then and kept a small wardrobe for emergencies, that night was a case in point, as I had to have a knee length skirt for work the next morning to cover the whip marks on my thighs. Before he chained me for the night he took me from behind again and by then I was doing much better. I could let him in with minimal discomfort and control the bowel urges — even enjoy them — and then clench hard around him to give him a nice tight tunnel to pleasure himself in. And it was made better by my having a flaming red back for him to dig his fingers into as he rode me. And so I eventually came to terms with having three entrances open for business.

For a moment I have to leave K and return to Emma. She was living a pretty intense existence herself at that time. A general election was looming and the government of the day was staggering from crisis to crisis while the opposition went from strength to strength. My paper's editorial stance was pro-government and my editor was in despair as scandal after scandal rocked it. But at last we got a breakthrough. One of my sources, not Ben this time, tipped me off to just a whiff of scandal surrounding an up and coming opposition back-bencher, hotly tipped for a ministerial position after the election. I shall call him simply Guy.

Anyone who has worked with me will know that in my professional life I am in no way submissive at all. And after I left that meeting armed with just a couple of phone numbers and names, I was a tigress. I spent hours on the phone using assumed names, I doorstepped shamelessly, browbeat ruthlessly and downright threatened people until I got what I was after — an exclusive!

Two weeks later I broke a story which was a humdinger. It had a hint of local government corruption, selection procedure anomalies and a sprinkling of photogenic women. The man concerned hadn't quite done anything illegal, but the lapses in proper procedures were enough. Hard on our heels the rest of the pack closed in and I was there when he left his house to face the press. He saw me right at the front of the crowd and his look left me in no doubt about what he would like to do to me if he ever got me on his own.

As the weeks went by both Ben's and my life became even more hectic. The election came ever closer and Ben found it hard to make time for K. As a result our sessions became more intense. I missed a lot of them and ran up some impressive beatings.

I was broken into wearing a collar and lead. It was a two-inch high collar in thick leather, with studs and rings round the outside. Ben said it suited my small chin very well, and I fully agreed. It was kept discreetly in the bottom of the coat and umbrella stand in the hall and it was the first thing I put on and the last thing I took off on my visits. Walking the way Ben had taught me to, hips swaying, naked apart from stockings and heels, and pulled along on a collar and lead, I felt I presented a pretty inviting image of available womanhood. And Ben took full advantage. When he wasn't caning or whipping me tied to the wall or over a trestle, he was making full use of all three passages open to him. His stamina was awe inspiring and he was capable of starting with my mouth, just letting me get the helm inside and savour the taste and feel on my tongue, then moving to the vagina and giving that a really good reaming, and while I lay gasping and twitching in the aftermath, he would turn me over and finish himself off in my rectum. Quite often this was done on the flogging bench upstairs, but sometimes he did it in the kitchen, with me bending over the table, and sometimes in the lounge. It would only take him half an hour or so and a glass of wine and he was off again. I would either assume Position Two and offer my back as a footstool, or Position Five and stand patiently facing the wall until I was required again. The humiliation was so thrilling, my submission to him so complete and so comforting that I didn't even protest when he began taking me vaginally first, then anally and only after that, finishing his pleasure in my mouth.

Once the election was called, I knew that Ben would have to leave town and go and fight for his political life back in his Home Counties constituency, but I just blanked it out of my mind until one night I turned up in answer to a summons from him and found that he had gone.

He gave me no warning at all. That was my first experience of the fact that a master does not owe his slave any explanations. Her business is to just accept whatever he does.

When I pressed the intercom that night, there was no answer to my statement that it was K, just the buzz of the door unlocking. I stepped into the hall and found myself face to face with Ben's wife.

I had known he was married. He had been quite open about it and even showed me her photograph once, it had been a mainly financial transaction between two old 'county' families but Ben and Clair had discovered that they shared an interest in dominating girls like K, and so it had suited them well enough and they rubbed along quite nicely. But never in my wildest dreams had I thought that he would turn me over to her care.

She was in her late forties I guessed, wearing a high buttoning jacket and knee length pleated skirt in matching light grey; smart and businesslike, and she took her time examining me while I stuttered, blushed and then made to turn tail.

"Come here you silly girl," she barked — just like a headmistress. "He wants you to read this."

She handed me a note with just the letter K on the envelope. Inside was the note which I have kept to this day.

'Dear K,
You of all people will know why I can't be in town just now. But I put you in the capable hands of my wife to continue your training. Don't worry, she has my permission to do anything she wants to you, so you won't feel neglected.

Of course you can refuse to hand yourself over to her, and if you do I will accept your decision and make no further contact with you. If you go ahead, she will report your progress to me.

Ben.'

The threat was crystal clear. It was all or nothing; I either did what he wanted or I would lose him. But I knew it would involve me being naked in front of another woman, and who knew what else as well? And there was another aspect which Ben must have known about. Up until then I had told myself that I had allowed myself to be whipped and abused out of devotion to the man who was strong enough to do it to me. If I went ahead with Clair, then I was admitting that it was the submission itself which turned me on. I didn't know her; she didn't know me, it was going to be domination and submission purely for their own sake. But even as I hated Ben for forcing me to make the decision, I realised I had opened my bag and dropped the note in. I guess my body decided for me, any domination is better than none when you are a submissive.

Resignedly I followed Clair into the lounge, just like I did with Ben, and there was another woman there — a girl really, about twenty — she was plump and pretty with a cheerful face and a mass of thick black hair.

"This is Janet," Clair told me. "She's my own slave. She calls me Madam at all times and so will you. Understand?"

I nodded. I knew what was coming next and I was going to have to do it front of two women, and not just one!

"Don't just stand there, K. Strip! Let's have a look at what I've got to work with."

I nearly cried with shame but I did it. Even the stockings went and I just stood there while Madam stalked round me as if I was a cow at auction. She pinched my bum hard several times and then came round and had a look at my boobs. I had to close my eyes and pretend it was a man's hands squeezing them and pulling at the nipples. I got a good hard slap round the face for that.

"Don't look away from me! It's not your master's hands, it's mine. Your mistress's."

I blinked back the tears and tried to stare ahead. But then her hand went down my stomach and started to play with my pubes. I was in Position One, legs spread; and when she slid her hand down and then along my lips I had to close my eyes again. I couldn't stand being touched by another woman. Another slap, even harder and then before I knew it her fingers were inside me. I knew they had slipped in easily and could feel them stirring up the juices.

Madam laughed. "Ben told me you liked getting slapped a bit. Okay, you'll do."

She pulled her fingers out and stood back. "Not bad tits but not on the scale of Janet's milkers. Show her Janet."

Madam used really coarse language to compensate for not being a man, and to make a female submissive as conscious of her body as she would be if a man were there. She said 'cunt' the whole time, and always referred to 'tits' 'teats' and 'udders'. In its own way it was quite effective.

Janet stood up and stripped in front of me. She was the complete opposite of me, all curves and chubbiness where I was slender. Madam said that, but added that my 'arse' was pretty good nonetheless. Janet really had got the boobs — sorry — tits that I had always dreamed of having. Not that mine are small, but hers were really big and yet still high and firm. God! The men I could have had if I had had a pair like that! And their crowning glory was their teats, the nipples were incredibly long and pronounced. Madam made sure I noticed them and told me that they were 'slavegirl teats' and mine should be like that, in fact she would make it her business to work on them over the coming weeks.

Upstairs, I was sent to kneel against one wall, while Janet was spread out against the opposite one and her restraints clipped to some of the rings. She was spread out like a letter X with her back against the wall. And while Madam put a ball gag on her and then opened a cupboard which Ben had never used she talked to me.

"If I know Ben, he'll have beaten you soundly enough by now. Right K?"

"Yes Madam."

"What's he used?"

I told her and she grunted approval while she laid out a range of steel clips, chains and clothes pegs on the whipping bench. Janet gave a muffled moan as the items appeared but Madam ignored her.

"He's a good man with a whip but he neglects the more feminine areas. I think frequent and prolonged tit torture does a girl the world of good. And it's high time you had some, so watch. It'll be your turn next."

I watched all right. I couldn't take my eyes off what I was seeing. Evil little spring loaded clips with serrated jaws were clamped straight onto Janet's nipples, making her heave and twist at her bonds. But then Madam slowly added clothes pegs. One by one. She gathered big pinches of breastflesh between finger and thumb before letting the jaws of the pegs close slowly onto them, while Janet sweated and moaned into her gag. At last Madam stood back and surveyed her handiwork on the left breast. An entire ring of pegs surrounded the areola, making the breast itself look like some bizarre sort of sunflower. There must have been about twenty of them, and she still hadn't started on the right breast.

"Want to leave, K?" Madam asked. I wasn't tied, I could walk out quite easily. And part of me wanted to walk as far and as fast as my shaking knees would carry me. But the K part of me was full of that reckless abandon which I got when I knew Ben was going to whip me. And I wasn't going to back down in front of a woman. No way. Ben knew what he had sentenced me to and that was good enough. I told her I was staying and I watched the whole process slowly repeated until two tortured sunflowers adorned Janet's chest.

"If I really want her to suffer, I whip them off," Madam told me. "But it's late and I've still got you to see to."

She took the pegs off and Janet's writhings became even more frantic as the blood flowed back into the squeezed flesh, but at last her tits were naked again, with livid red lines radiating out from her areolae, where the pegs had been. She gave Janet a slap on the rump and sent her off to get a cold flannel to cool her tits off and then beckoned to me. I could hardly stand and must have tottered over on my high heels, and by the time I was fastened as Janet had been I was openly crying in terror. Madam said nothing but once she had me chained she stripped off her suit and revealed a black leather basque and stockings underneath — no knickers, just a thick bush of dark hair at her pubis. Her body was in good shape, spare and muscular, and she looked so dominant and threatening that I very nearly wet myself.

"No gag for you, K," she said. "I want to see how you perform. I like to hear a good bit of moaning and crying, but I get very angry if it's loud enough to distract me, understand?"

I nodded and got another two hard slaps. They were a godsend, pulling me out of my terror and steeling my resolve as well as stoking up the dormant fires between my open legs.

"Yes Madam, I understand," I managed to whisper.

And I reckon I did pretty well. I didn't scream when the clamps bit into my 'teats' after Madam had played with them enough to harden them up. And I bit my lips and stifled the screams as peg after peg went on. I couldn't help looking down in fascination as my tits sprouted brightly coloured plastic petals, but the pain was something else! Nothing like the whip, no violent, sexually charged imposition of dominance; just a slow build of throbbing aching pain, coupled with a slow burning fuse of excitement as the abuse grew worse and worse. At last I couldn't stand any more and began to let out cry after cry, shaking my head, looking up at the ceiling and wrenching at my wrist shackles. But then it was over and the agony reached a plateau. I realised my crotch was sodden and aching in its own way. I blinked away the tears and saw Janet on her knees with her head between her mistress's legs. Madam had fistfuls of her hair and was forcing her pelvis against the girl's face, her eyes were closed and her face had an expression of fierce concentration on it and I realised that for the first time I was watching another woman approach orgasm. I almost forgot the pain in my tits, the ache in my vulva was so strong as I watched her climax. I needed to come as well.

That was another step forward. I didn't need Ben, or the whip in particular, just someone, anyone to tie me up and cause me pain and I did the rest myself! Submission for its own sake.

Janet chained me to the spare bed after I had experienced the entirely separate torment of having pegs taken off my tits. She gave me a chaste little kiss and told me she would be back soon. I heard her go into the master bedroom and then listened and counted twenty meaty smacks, it sounded like the riding crop and I visualised her broad expanse of buttock flesh rippling under the strokes. It made me more desperate than ever and I was squirming with urgency by the time Janet returned. I didn't care about doing it with another girl by then, and when she knelt between my legs and put her fingers up me, my hips lifted and I went straight into overdrive. But when she really got down to it and used her tongue, she left every man I had ever known standing. Her tongue knew every crevice of the female anatomy and exactly how to excite it. I went off in blinding firework displays of ecstasy time and again. And then I got my first taste of woman. When Janet kissed me I got second-hand Clair mingled with second-hand me, but later, when Janet unchained me and lay down in her turn. Well I can't pretend I hesitated. And I was fascinated by exploring another vagina

Mind you I was glad of the dark. Giving another girl oral with the lights on was still a bit advanced for me. But once I got used to the taste, it wasn't so bad. Pungent and acrid but very animal and very sexy. Making her come was fun, a different challenge to making a man come but satisfying and afterwards I kissed her bottom all over to cool it down.

And so for a hectic few weeks I became Madam Clair's slave. Sessions were hard to arrange as the election came closer and closer, but there were landmarks on the road I was now travelling down even so.

Clair had obviously decided to cram as much training into those few weeks as possible, after all none of us had any idea whether Ben would be back at all.

I got my first 'tit trembler' as Clair called it. I was tied backwards over the trestle, and very uncomfortable it was, although Janet did put a pillow under the small of my back to cushion me against chafing on the wooden crosspiece. I was left there for half an hour or so, staring, upside down at the multi-lashed whip which was going to be used on me, hanging from its hook on the wall. And by the time the actual flogging got underway, K was in her usual state of moist excitement and fear. A state which Madam confirmed by putting her fingers inside me before beating me. She worked them in me until I was squelching at one end and moaning with pain, lust and frustration at the other. But the really devilish thing was that she kept her hand there while she flogged my boobs. Even upside down and stretched because my arms were tied behind me, wrists to ankles, my tits still trembled all right. I could crane my head up and watch the leather lashes coming down but I couldn't watch the actual strike; that was too much. But I could feel the weight of the lashes smacking into the soft flesh and how it shuddered and swayed even through the blazes of pain. And all the time she kept her fingers working inside me until I howled my way to a shattering orgasm.

Then there was the night she took us to a club.

Janet and I were only dressed in 'uniform', collars, wrist restraints, a scarlet basque for Janet and just suspenders and stockings for me. It wasn't until the following week that I was sent off to get my first basque. We both wore long coats with the collars up and the lapels held across to cover the slave collars. Madam and Janet exchanged smiles in the back of the taxi as I blushed and squirmed in embarrassment at my nakedness under the coat. But once we were in the club all my discomfort and shame vanished. Janet and I were led around by Madam, she held leashes attached to our collars, and I just gawped at everything around me. Although all I wore were high heels, stockings and suspenders, plus of course a generous rash of weals from my last beating, I was by no means alone.

There were leather-clad male and female dominants in weird and wonderful costumes, leading their own slaves around; some of whom wore less than I did. The music was thunderous and the light show made it hard to take in everything in detail as figures in extravagant concoctions of feathers, latex, leather and strange masks seemed to flicker about the place. Janet and Madam seemed quite at home though, but I pressed myself close to Janet as we trailed around behind her. I was truly glad of the collar and lead, just like when I was tied for beating, it allowed me to hide behind the dominance of someone else; I had no choice so it was okay for me to enjoy whatever was going to happen.

My eyes were particularly drawn to slavegirls who had piercings and from whose nipple rings weights and chains dangled and swung. But most of all I stared at the slaveboys. I had been so bound up in the exploration of my own submissiveness that I swear it had never crossed my mind that men too could enjoy the strange world of slavery. It shocked me to my naive little heart.

I was devoted to Ben and I instinctively felt that these slaves humbly following their mistresses and with horrible piercings in their genitals were an insult to him somehow, and to all the men I had ever known. But even as the carnival unfolded around my fearful and horrified gaze I felt an insidious response between my legs to this open display of the delights of domination and submission.

There was a voyeurs' room and we paused to watch the pumping male buttocks between the soft skin of spread female thighs, the wide open mouths of girls on their knees with their masters' penises deep in their throats and the smooth curves of female bodies intertwining. Then Clair dragged us on and we moved to an area where there was a whipping frame occupied by a slavegirl who had fresh traces of a beating on her back and buttocks. Her legs were well spread and her master was busy fisting her cunt. I had never seen that done before and frankly just couldn't believe that a vagina could take a clenched fist and about four inches of forearm to boot. But there it was, the man's arm was twisting, withdrawing; the fist pulled back to the point where it caused maximum distension of the vagina before pushing back up into her body while the girl herself looked down and watched with that expression of frowning concentration which I now recognised as the onset of female orgasm.

"I suppose Ben never did that to you?" Clair asked me.

"No Madam," I replied without taking my eyes off the girl who was now beginning to rock and circle her hips as her stuffed vagina and her whipped back propelled her to those heights I was becoming so familiar with. Her groaning and writhing nakedness were having a real effect on me and I felt myself becoming increasingly warm and moist in sympathy.

"Hmm… we'll have to see about that," Clair said and before I could make any response she yanked my lead hard and I stumbled after her to where another scenario was being played out. A male slave was tied face down over a trestle and his mistress was whipping his buttocks with a suede flogger. She must have been at it for some time as his skin was an impressive shade of red by then.

Over the music I couldn't hear the lashes land but I could see him jerk at each stroke. If it had been a girl I would have loved watching but instead it revolted me, seeing his tightly crinkled scrotum behind a stiff erection jutting forward under the crossbar he was tied over. His mistress had long, flaming red hair which clashed magnificently with her scarlet leather catsuit, and boots with stiletto heels. When she had finished whipping him she reached under him and using one gloved hand began to milk his erection like a dairymaid would milk a cow. I saw her hand clench his shaft and work up and down it until the slave's body tensed, his head came up and I got a glimpse of fluid spurting down onto the floor.

I felt sick and would have turned away but Clair jerked me forward again and she approached the pair just as the man was standing up and I could just about hear him thank his mistress for wanking him. His humility revolted me. That wasn't what a man should be — but the rest of him definitely was. He was powerfully built and even though his mistress was a tall woman he looked as though he could crush her with one hand, and yet he calmly let her turn his buttocks into a reddened mass of weals... just like I let Clair and Ben do to me, I thought to myself ruefully. His cock was softening now but still remained pretty impressive and what really fascinated me was the glint of steel at the helm — right in the slit. I couldn't take my eyes off it and remained staring at it while Clair and the redhead chatted away like old friends, which they were as it turned out. Eventually I realised that beside me Janet was doing exactly the same as me, but far more obviously and was actually flirting with the man who stood in the classic eyes downcast slave position, seemingly ignoring Janet's attempts to flaunt her boobs at him. For some reason she irritated me and I turned my attention to what the two dominants were discussing.

"If he's as well trained as that," Clair was saying, "bring him along." Here she jerked my lead. "A dose of slave spunk will do this one good. Ben hasn't really got her under control yet; she's still a bit prissy."

It was all I could do to suppress my outrage but when Clair turned to me and I saw her smile I knew she had been taunting me deliberately to test my obedience. I bit back the words I wanted to say and the other dominatrix came towards me. She reached out and caught my cheeks between a strong finger and thumb. It was the hand she had used to bring her slave off and I caught the strong aroma of sperm off it. I tried to twist my head away but she was too strong and forced me to meet her eyes.

"Hmm. She's good material, spirited but submissive. And you're right, I reckon she needs taking further; well my Danny's the one for that alright." She grinned maliciously and I had to gaze into her cold green eyes for a moment before she let me go and then ignored me completely.

For another hour or so we were led around, accompanied by the woman whose name it appeared was Mistress Scarlet and her slaveboy Danny. Janet contrived to get next to him and rub her thigh against his but he continued to ignore her. For my part I was still gazing around at the bizarre costumes which flickered before my eyes as people moved through the strobe lighting as the music pounded. Occasionally hands would grope our bottoms or boobs, mainly they were gloved ones, sometimes in smooth leather but sometimes in leather which was cruelly studded or spiked. I jumped and squeaked each time but Madam just turned and grinned at whoever had done it and passed the time of day with them. Sometimes Janet or I were lined up with another slavegirl and our figures compared while the dominants discussed our capabilities under the whip or tit torture.

I had never seen so many body piercings. It seemed as though Janet and I were the only girls without nipple rings at the very least. And there were plenty who had tongue studs, septum rings and labial rings; while the amount of steel some of the men carried on their genitals made my skin crawl at the thought of having a shaft of combined flesh and steel rammed into my tender vagina or rectum. But as ever there was a tingle of excitement at the same time.

It wasn't until we reclaimed our coats that it fully dawned on me that Scarlet and Danny were coming with us. We all shared a cab and I found myself wedged next to Danny who was encased in a long leather coat. I was horribly aware of Clair's words earlier concerning 'slave spunk' and even my revulsion at Danny's submissiveness and the crudity of the words couldn't repress the tingles of arousal which ignited in my nipples as they rubbed against my coat. Janet just sat opposite and made cow eyes at the man while he himself continued to maintain a stoical disregard for everyone except his mistress, at whom he occasionally glanced. The two dominants chatted about acquaintances they had in common and seemed to ignore us. But once we were all back in Ben's hall and we three slaves were virtually naked again, Madam rounded on Janet.

"You horny little slut!" she yelled and landed a stinging slap on her face. "Did you think I didn't notice the disgraceful exhibition you made of yourself?!"

Janet rubbed at her cheek and stared, terrified at the bristling Madam.

"Hands on your head!" she snapped and once Janet had obeyed she landed a series of roundhouse slaps to her breasts. Left and then right. Left and then right again, drawing her arms right back and hitting the huge melons full on. They swung so hard they almost pulled Janet off her feet. And Madam didn't stop until Janet was fidgeting from foot to foot, her eyes welling with tears and she was making little "Oow!" yelps at each thunderous impact. After that she was sent to stand facing the wall in the lounge in Position Five.

Meanwhile Danny and I were ordered into Position Two and served as footstools while our mistresses enjoyed a drink before starting work on us. They had us arranged so that Danny was behind me and his face was only inches away from my bottom. I could feel his breath between my buttocks, and the hot air tickled my anus and vulva. The dominatrixes made comments about us looking like a dog and a bitch on heat, the humiliation of which only served to make me behave like one. Madam chuckled when she removed her feet from my back and then bent over to put a couple of fingers into my sex and rummage about. Of course I was wide open and moist and I blushed with delicious shame as she made me squelch down there and then had me turn around to watch Danny lick her fingers clean.

"That'll give him the scent," Mistress Scarlet said. "Now let's go and whip them up a bit."

Upstairs Danny and I were mounted in the rectangular whipping frame, wrists raised and spread, ankles wide apart. We were tied face to face, our bodies pressed hard against each other's for their entire length. Because of his height my face was pressed against the hairs of his chest and I could feel his flaccid penis against my midriff. It didn't stay that way for long. As soon as I had been positioned against him and it became clear that we were to be whipped in that position, I felt it begin to tumesce and had to draw in my stomach to allow it to jerk into its fully upright position. In the meantime I saw Madam selecting a heavy, flat bladed flogger and my nipples attained full erection against Danny's muscle-ridged torso. Mistress Scarlet disappeared for a moment and came back with the longest and whippiest of the crops.

What followed was the slowest beating I had ever taken, and the most exquisite. They took it in turns, circling around us, so that I got the thumping impact of the multi-lashed whip followed some time later by the searing bite of the crop. They took their time too, comparing the marks the different implements left on the male and female body, and the way the lashes wrapped around my slenderer back to thud into the side of my breasts, while Danny's back took it full on. It was obvious that these discussions were for our benefit, making us wait for the next lash while we savoured the full effect of the previous one. The result was that I felt each stroke of the whips as a steady build, the third lash re-igniting the pleasure and pain of one and two, the fourth building on the previous three and so on. But it was so slow! Cool fingers traced the weals on my back and buttocks and comments were made on how much more easily my flesh marked than Danny's. I became aware that I was moaning in frustration and burying my face against his chest as I waited for the next lash, then it would come, scalding my shoulders and jerking me against Danny who was, in turn, pushed against me by the force of the lashes across his back. I felt his cock press harder against me and began to rub myself against it, rocking and circling my hips, licking at his chest. Laughter came from behind me, but I didn't care. I really was in heat by then; I needed the whip and I needed that cock deep inside me. The whipping began to pick up pace at last and the slow burn from the lashes really took hold between my open legs. I rubbed everything I could against the hard male body I was tied to but the only response I got was the jerk of his hips at each lash. He made no sound at all while I shamelessly moaned and yelped as the heat built up. I had no idea of how many lashes I had taken when I felt fingers run down my buttock crease, along my sex lips and then push up into my vagina.

"A few more yet my little bitch and then we'll let Danny loose on you," Madam said.

Both dominants then let fly for a few minutes, a full-blooded flogging, no more teasing. The whip hammered down on my back and I slammed against Danny, time after time, with an ache in my sex and my lips fluttering in desperation to get his cock into me. I was nearing a climax of pain and agonised pleasure from the whip and from my blatant frustration when they stopped and took us down. I was practically sobbing as they did so and couldn't take my eyes off Danny's throbbing erection with its steel piercings. They no longer made my skin crawl, I was just desperate to find out what it felt like to have them deep inside me.

I had never had sex in front of an audience before but even that prospect didn't bother me. My whole body throbbed with whip heat and desire — pure lust. Fortunately the two dominants were turned on as well by then and wasted no more time. Madam hauled me over to the whipping trestle and made me brace my arms on the crossbar while sticking my rump out and spreading my legs. I hardly had time to settle myself before I felt Danny's helm begin to push my swollen lips apart and slide smoothly up until he had full penetration. I gasped in appreciation and dimly noted the feel of the barbell at the base of his shaft as it came to rest against my lips. Inside I got a definite feel of more than usual friction on my front vaginal wall from the piercing through the helm. As soon as he was in I started moving on him, swivelling and rotating my hips.

Madam pulled my head up and began kissing and nuzzling me.

"You're in for the fuck of a lifetime," she whispered. "He's trained not to come until she tells him to. And we're going to make you beg for mercy before he shoots his load."

Naive little fool that I was I nodded eagerly at that prospect. Being fucked was a new experience for me. I mean just having a man in me for the pleasure of the physical sensations without any kind of relationship at all. Martin and Ben had had me plenty of times obviously, and lots before them. But always there had been some kind of relationship. However rough Ben was with me after a whipping, I loved being taken by him precisely because it was him doing it to me. But that night all I knew was that I had a complete stranger's penis right up me and I was loving it. It could have been a dildo for all that I cared.

"Shove it to her, Dannyboy," Mistress Scarlet called out, and I heard the crop land on his buttocks. "And if you dare come before I tell you to, you worthless lump of shit, I'll make a pincushion out of your balls and keep you in your kennel for a month. Now fuck her!"

He immediately grabbed my hips and began to batter at me, his pelvis slapping against my bottom while his shaft rammed in and out, the steel balls at his helm and his urethra rubbing my inner tissues. Madam laid a couple of lashes across my shoulders and I began bucking and pushing against him in earnest.

"Fuck him, you bitch!" she yelled and lashed me again. To their shouts of encouragement and for their pleasure we two slaves performed a frantic coupling. I came very quickly with all my usual yelling and crying, while whips slashed and Madam and Scarlet shouted obscenities. It was a shattering orgasm but even while the lights were fading in my brain, I felt Danny grab my hair to brace himself better and just keep on going. In, out, in, out. Rubbing constantly at my vagina and already starting me on the way up again.

Madam grinned down at me as she saw realisation begin to dawn on me.

I've been taken by many slaveboys subsequently. My present Master in particular has enjoyed watching me servicing them while I am forbidden an orgasm myself. But I've never liked them; they just feel wrong to me. Danny was something else though. Later on I found out that his mistress made a small fortune hiring him out to bored trophy wives and rich older women. I wasn't surprised, he was just an endless fuck on legs. How she had trained him I never did find out, but the result was that he could quite simply go all night without coming.

My arms buckled under the assault of my second orgasm and I finished it slumped over the crossbar. But Danny hauled me up again by my hair and just continued pistoning in and out, slowly, relentlessly. My sex began to sting but it was so juicy I could feel as well as hear how it was overflowing around his cock as it withdrew and then rammed in again.

"No, please Madam!" I begged. "Please, rest…"

She laughed into my now seriously frightened face. "Did you know, you whip-hungry little slut, that to a slavegirl like you Danny's tool can be more terrifying than any whip? How many orgasms can you take, do you think? Well, we're going to find out."

They did but I lost count long before I was allowed to stop.

In that first session I can remember counting four climaxes and then the orgasms came so fast they overlapped, like waves pounding onto a beach.

At last Mistress Scarlet must have told him to stop because suddenly he withdrew completely and I almost screamed in shock as my muscles suddenly clenched round nothing and my lips fluttered in spasms. My knees buckled under me and I collapsed onto the floor cupping my sex with both hands. It burned and stung like never before and I writhed for a moment or two until I realised that I wasn't the only groaning female in the room. Slowly I raised my head and saw that Janet had been fetched from her position of disgrace downstairs. She was now backed against one of the walls with the two dominants on either side of her, tweaking and pulling at her nipples while she masturbated with a monstrous dildo. Her legs were spread wide apart and I could see how the huge shaft spread her labia as she rammed it into herself so violently that her breastflesh quivered at each thrust. She was nearing her peak and was gazing at Danny's still rampant sex with shameless lust. Her cries mounted until she froze at her climax, both hands holding the dildo at full penetration and the two dominants pulled and squeezed her nipples spitefully hard. She gave one last shuddering cry and subsided.

I was grateful for the rest but it had been all too short. Madam saw me sitting up and strode over to haul me up and lead me over to the broad topped whipping bench. She pushed me down on my back and immediately I began begging for mercy. I had a horrible feeling that Danny was nowhere near finished with me and I didn't think my sex could take much more pounding. For the first time ever, I became seriously frightened. I was scared of what damage that glistening pole which jutted out from Danny's black pubes might to do to my insides. Madam made no response to my pleas and I could only struggle weakly. In a few moments she had rolled me half over, clipped my wrist restraints together behind my back, rolled me back again, raised and spread my legs and clipped my ankles to a spreader bar hanging from the ceiling.

"Okay, fuckboy," Mistress Scarlet said, "she's ready to go again."

"Noooo!" I managed a scream but it was choked off by a grunt of pure agony as he speared me again. I was tight but still sodden with juices so he had little problem getting in, but from my side it was terrible. It felt like he was splitting me wide open. I craned my head up to beg him for mercy but he was expressionless as he placed his big hands round my upper thighs and began rocking his hips back and forward in that murderous rhythm I was now so scared of. But there was absolutely nothing I could do and pretty soon the inevitable happened. The orgasm was so intense I nearly passed out and they let him stop for a moment until my heart stopped hammering, but then they made him start again. I was terrified of the next orgasm and screamed as it hurtled over me, blinding me, throwing my body helplessly against its bonds, paralysing me with an ecstasy which overloaded every sense and every nerve. It wasn't pleasure and it wasn't pain; it was simply the outer limits of both. And I've come to believe that it is a region that only slavegirls attain. And having watched other girls forced there by their masters, I can see why they enjoy pushing us to those limits, we make a spectacular show as we arch and twist and scream in sexually induced dementia. Maybe there is some envy there; it's one place we go to where they can't follow. Maybe, but I've never had the courage to ask a master about that.

"Now that was a true slave's orgasm, K." From a long way away I heard Madam's voice. Slowly I opened my eyes and looked blearily up at her. Danny was still inside me but he was waiting for the command before he began shafting me again. I saw no end to my torment in her expression, and worse, she was running the lashes of a strange little whip through her fingers. I couldn't speak, just shake my head desperately. The lashes of the whip were thin and only about a foot long, they looked almost like thick shoelaces and I could see that Madam's gaze was fixed on my heaving chest as I fought to control my breathing.

Whack!

With no warning she swished the whip down and I arched in agony as a stinging like a hundred bee stings burst over my left boob.

Whack!

Again those thin laces bit down, into the soft flesh of my right boob, the very slenderness of them allowing them to bite more spitefully than anything I had yet experienced. She paused to let me gasp and whimper for a bit while I contemplated what she had in store for me next. She waited until I was about to beg again, then she nodded at Danny and simultaneously brought the whip down.

How I twisted and bucked and howled as Danny mercilessly shafted my burning sex and Madam flicked that awful little whip again and again over breasts and hardened nipples. But once more I was helplessly drumming my bottom on the table as my body prepared to throw itself into the abyss again, and again I hurtled into the darkness of tormented orgasm. And this time I couldn't stop. Danny battered at me between my legs and Madam slashed at me with that horrible little whip and time and again I dissolved into helpless overload until at one final peak, which I thought would surely kill me, I fainted into merciful oblivion.

I was still on my back on the table when I came round, but my wrists and ankles were free. I was immediately aware of the agonising pain in my crotch and moaned as I rolled into a foetal position to cup it with both hands.

"Ah, she's back with us," Mistress Scarlet said. "Come on, Danny hasn't finished with you yet." She hauled me up to a sitting position and I just leaned against her, too exhausted even to beg, too dazed from the orgasms and too badly beaten by Danny's prick and the whip to do anything more than accept whatever was coming. But I would gladly have gone under the whip again if it meant avoiding another session on that wretched cock.

Scarlet yanked me off the table and I crumpled into a heap on the floor, my legs just wouldn't work. Madam bent down and showed me the bootlace whip, I groaned and made an attempt to get knees and elbows under me but it still took several cuts across the buttocks before I could even kneel up. And when I did I found myself staring at a still-rigid, steel pierced weapon which even after all that, jutted in proud erection from Danny's thick pubic hair. It gleamed with my juices.

"Suck him. And do it well or I'll have him fuck you again," Madam ordered.

I nodded and shuffled over on my knees. I couldn't speak; I needed all of my remaining strength to avoid being fucked unconscious again.

When I got to Danny I had to reach behind him and hold his buttocks to support myself, and for a while all I could do was lick the scrotum and tease at the two gold rings which pierced it there with my tongue. I can't say whether they excited or repelled me by then. All I was concerned about was doing a good enough job to escape having him screw me again. Some female readers might find it hard to imagine a woman being so desperate to avoid having a good sized cock inside her, but all I can say is that being driven helplessly to repeated orgasms without end until your body is quite beyond any control is far more frightening than a whipping.

After a few minutes, and in response to a growl from Madam that I should 'get on with it' I began licking up the shaft, investigating the barbell and then moving up again until I could lick around the strange piercing at the slit of the helm which emerged from the underside of the urethra itself — a Prince Albert as I subsequently found out — and finally I stretched my mouth open to its fullest extent and let my lips close softly over the whole of the polished roundness of the helm itself while my tongue flicked at the slit and tasted the metal of the piercing. I got the softest of groans from Danny as I did so and began to relax — I was doing okay. Even though he obviously had permission to come in my mouth, he held out for quite some time, but at last he grabbed two fistfuls of my hair and began bucking his hips at me and ramming my face down onto him simultaneously. I dug my hands hard into his buttocks and tried to ready myself for his ejaculation even as I felt him begin to slide right into my throat at each thrust. I tried to relax but then suddenly I felt that tell tale swelling of the urethra and he erupted. That's the only word I can find for it. It was as if he was manufacturing sperm at the same rate at which he was discharging it. At first I took my usual pleasure in having stimulated a man to orgasm in my mouth but as fast as I swallowed he pumped more into me. Once again he reduced me to panic; I began to make muffled squeals of fear as he held my face down onto him and my throat worked overtime but the panic tightened it and slowed the swallows down. His shaft filled my mouth and I had no choice but to choke through my nostrils so that the salty emission splattered out onto him as I snorted and coughed while spurt after spurt splashed out into the tight little cave of my mouth.

I must have made a pretty picture of defeated femininity when he finally let me go. I was laced with crop marks and had bright red patches from the flogger all over my back, my breasts were striped with thin, livid welts, my vulva was reamed raw and sperm dripped from my chin and face. I just lay in a heap while Janet was summoned to lick up what I had spilt and then Danny picked me up — still without a word having passed between us — and took me to bed in the spare room. And still Madam hadn't finished with us.

Janet was chained down first, spread out on her back then I was laid down on top of her face down and chained in exactly the same way. Then the two dominants left us and took Danny with them — it was the only blessing we were granted. I was totally exhausted and in desperate need of sleep, but Janet was just plain desperate. She had only been permitted one climax all night and had had to watch me being fucked unconscious. She heaved and squirmed and moaned under me, squashing our boobs together and trying to grind her pubic mound against mine. All I could do was let her lick my face to get the last of Danny's 'slave spunk' off and then I fell into a light sleep despite Janet. My last thought was that surely, surely this time I had plumbed the depths of sex slavery. It comforted me enough to allow me to sleep, but of course I was wrong.

By noon of the following day I was back at home, had had a long wallow in a hot, foam filled bath and was feeling a little better — even a touch proud of myself. After all it is not every girl who gets to be screwed into oblivion by a stallion like Danny, even if it is terrifying at the time, and the various floggings had been satisfactorily painful. I could admire now the mesh of thin stripes across my breasts and feel proud of having endured it. Ben would be proud of me.

I was only wrapped in a short silk dressing gown and was slumped in a chair reading the papers, beside me I had a bowl of tepid water with a flannel in it, and every now and then would pause to stand, spread my legs and press the flannel against my throbbing sex. At least by then I felt no permanent damage had been done, but I hoped no-one would want to use it for a few days. I groaned when the front doorbell went.

Once I saw it was Janet though, I opened the door for her quite eagerly and then gasped in surprise as she entered. She was dressed in a simple cardigan, which strained across her breasts, and tight jeans. Not only was I astonished to see her at all but to see her, a slavegirl, dressed in jeans really took me aback. Ben didn't mind me wearing them if I wasn't with him, although I very rarely did, but I knew that Madam chose what Janet wore every single day and didn't approve of anything other than skirts. She laughed at my expression and walked in with a stiff legged gait.

"Madam's off playing with Scarlet somewhere so she said I could come round," she explained. "She said she thought you'd be sore so she sent me to 'lick the slut's cunt better and teach her more about being a slave'."

I blinked at the obscenities being so calmly uttered in my cosy sunlit lounge.

"Look Janet," I began. "You're a great girl but I'm not in slave mode just now. I'm tired and..."

"Sore. Yes I know, but girls like you and me are always in slave mode, K. We are slaves. It's not what we do, it's what we are. Look here..."

She was right, and it hit me like a ton of bricks. Just because I was at home didn't mean I wasn't a slave, it just meant that no-one was currently flogging me or using me. If Ben or Madam had walked in, ordered me to bend over and caned, whipped or paddled me, I wouldn't have made a murmur of protest. I had given them every right to do so. They simply hadn't done it up till now. While these thoughts raced through my mind, Janet had unbuttoned and discarded her cardigan.

"Bloody hell!" was all I could say. Her wonderfully full and hugely areoled breasts looked as if she had slept face down on a basket weave bed. They were covered in a criss-crossing mesh of narrow, livid stripes. They were just like the ones I was sporting but Janet had taken far, far more than I had.

She looked down proudly, hefting and cupping her boobs with her hands. "Pretty good eh? Bet you thought I was being a right little tart last night, rubbing myself up against Danny and giving him the eye."

I had the grace to blush while I stared at her lacerated boobs and ribs.

"Listen K," she sent on seriously. "There's nothing Madam likes better than to see me getting a seeing-to from a slaveboy. So by flaunting myself at him I knew she couldn't allow it. No master or mistress can let a slave set the agenda, but that doesn't mean we can't pull a few strings here and there. It was worth missing out on the action you got and getting all frustrated, so as to get a really good punishment this morning. And that was what I really wanted. Madam knows perfectly well what I was up to, but she'll never admit it of course and that made the punishment all the harder — so everyone's happy.

"Now what you've got to do is stop being such a mousy little goody two shoes. Make the buggers work for it. Be disobedient every now and then. They love you for it; it keeps them on their toes — gives them a break from having to invent ways of making you fail, and a real punishment stops either of you getting bored. Understand?"

I did. In the space of a few minutes I had understood that I was a slave wherever I was and that K (how very unlike Emma!) was too meek by half; but mostly I had understood that submissiveness itself could be used to exert some control over dominants and provide a slave with some pleasure on her own terms as well as ensuring her master's attention was fully focused on her for quite some time.

But while I absorbed all that I was still staring at Janet's breasts.

"How many lashes?" I asked.

"I lost count after fifty and two orgasms." She giggled. "So it was worth the wait."

I laughed with her; it felt like we were two schoolgirls who had got one over on a feared teacher.

"Now take my jeans off, K. She always makes me wear them after... well just do it."

They were very tight and after I had undone the stud, she had to breathe in sharply so I could slide the zip down. I had to kneel down to pull while she wriggled her hips but when at last they slid down her thighs I gasped at what stared me in the face.

Madam had been at work with that bootlace whip again. And this time she had worked it across Janet's inner and outer thighs, hips, stomach and her sex itself. Bright red lines crossed the pubic thatch and the plump labia themselves. I helped her get the jeans off her feet, one at a time, while I imagined the harsh denim material and especially the seam pulling tightly up into the crease between those tenderised sex lips.

"Madam's always furious with herself when she's had a good time with a man — and they don't come any better than Danny." She grinned at her own pun. "So she had plenty to take out on me. 'Tits for punishment, cunt for pleasure' she said. But what she meant was 'tits for my bad behaviour, cunt for hers'."

I really could understand why she sounded so happy with her appalling treatment. For a slave, offering herself up for a punishment which she has in no way deserved, but which the master or mistress will enjoy inflicting, is taking submission to its extreme and is better than getting a deserved punishment. And those weals really did suit her generous, curvaceous form very well.

I felt an overwhelming affection and admiration for Janet who understood and accepted so much more than I did. I leaned forward and gently kissed the tops of her thighs as she spread her legs apart and then let my tongue begin to lick and soothe the hot labia, then delve between them to explore the complex folds of her fleshy inner lips.

She groaned in pleasure and then whispered that she wanted me to take her to bed. And I did for four, slow, soothing but passionate hours. I flung off the duvet and made love to her in broad daylight, no longer caring that I was caressing another girl orally. We made each other rise to orgasm very gently — the complete opposite to how our dominants did it, and a welcome change. We dozed in each other's arms for a while after a series of sixty nines had brought gasps and cries of sheer delight from both of us. But when we woke we knew it was not enough, pleasure on its own might be enough for some, but slaves need more. We rubbed our boobs against each other's and then Janet kissed me hard.

"Hurt them for me, K," she whispered hoarsely. "Make my tits burn all over again."

"Yes." There wasn't a second's hesitation in my response.

I found a thin leather belt in my wardrobe and Janet held onto the bedhead while I whipped her. My heart thundered in pure joy as I looked down on the rippling, shuddering flesh I was lashing. I finally understood the ecstasy of whipping such vulnerability, extending the pleasure of caressing to the point where pain had to be inflicted in order to satisfy the fierce passions such vulnerability aroused.

And even as I whipped the groaning twisting girl beneath me, my other hand was between my legs and I couldn't wait for my turn to have my breasts lashed.

When Janet left I didn't bother with even a short wrap. I was so proud of my welts and loved the feel of the air on them. We kissed deeply before I let her out.

"Don't forget, K," Janet said as her parting shot. "Don't be too bloody obedient. Make yourself a little bit of a challenge every now and then, you'll get the best out of them that way."

I assured her I would and we parted, but I was sure I would see her again sometime.

But then it was polling day and despite the government's defeat Ben came back victorious. Madam and Janet vanished as suddenly as they had appeared. I did indeed see Janet again; she still belongs to Clair and always will. I envy her, though I think she hates me now.

With the sitting of a new parliament, work was overwhelming for a while and K just had to twiddle her thumbs while Emma got on with business. But she no longer had it all her own way. K's desires were becoming ever more strident and when Ben and I finally managed a dinner date, I was determined to move things along quickly. K was impatient to be back under the sway of her master.

Ben had made a rule that although dinner dates were outside 'sessions' and I would be Emma, I would always dress either smart business or smart casual, that meant skirts of course, but nothing too obviously tarty. The stockings and suspenders, and now my basques, would be discreetly hidden until we got back to his house. Ben always had to be careful. But that night I tore up the rulebook.

We had agreed to meet at a restaurant in a quiet North London suburb — an Indian one which had a reputation which attracted quite a lot of rock stars, but not many journalists. We like to hit our expense accounts a bit more heavily! They are too rich to care. But it was perfect for what I had in mind.

I booked a taxi for a time which would get me there about half an hour late. And when I finally arrived, Ben, seated in a dimly lit alcove as I had known he would be, was plainly furious. By the time I had sauntered over to the table, he was coldly enraged. For a minute I felt a knot of real fear in my stomach; I had never seen him so angry. But it was too late to go back now; I had to play it all the way.

I had deliberately worn the biggest, gaudiest, jaw bashing earrings I could find; my makeup was well over the top, dark eye shadow and bright red lipstick with a layer of lip-gloss. I wore a blouse knotted up under my breasts so that my stomach was bare and I had stuck one of those temporary tattoos just below my navel so that the dragon it depicted disappeared down under my black leather miniskirt. I was bare legged — and showing a lot too — with strappy high-heeled sandals on my feet. In short I looked outrageously tarty. But I didn't stop there.

I really was so glad to see Ben again that the next part wasn't too difficult. As soon as I reached the table I bent down and kissed him full on the lips — a real tongue plunging, minute-long smacker. Everything was designed to be the exact opposite of what Emma would want to do or what K would be permitted to do.

And when I slipped into my seat I could see that if we had been on our own I would have been slapped from here to kingdom come before anything else. That settled me, that was what I wanted and so I just cocked an eyebrow at him flirtatiously and asked if he was pleased to see me, while underneath the table I shamelessly ran one foot up and down his leg.

He made no response until he had ordered me a gin and tonic and it had been served.

"You know Emma," he said at last, "when I left London I had a very docile slave by the name of K."

Docile!? Janet had been right, it was high time I made him work a bit harder. "What do you mean by 'slave'?" I asked innocently.

"A girl who lives to be beaten and abused by her Master. A girl who will literally do anything to please the man who dominates her, but who most of all obeys him in all things."

Good, he was playing along.

"Do such girls exist Ben?"

"Oh yes. And after the meal I'll tell you what I would do with her if she were here now."

We locked gazes and smiled at each other. Game on.

The food was good but I'm afraid we didn't do it justice. We both wanted to get it out of the way and get on with the main business. Ben ordered two cognacs and we got down to it.

"This K, does she really do anything you ask? Or are you just having wet dreams?" I asked him.

That got him. I saw his pupils contract in fury for an instant. Crotch whipping I thought; no way I was going to get away with less than that. Oh well.

"I assure you Emma that if K was here and I told her to expose a lot more cleavage than you are doing; she would obey me."

"What a tart!" I feigned deep outrage. "But would it turn you on if I did that?"

He made a so-so gesture and then grinned as I reached down and undid two buttons of my blouse. That didn't leave many left and really only the extremities of my boobs were covered, the upper and side curves were on full view with only Ben between me and the rest of the room. That thought made my nipples swell into almost instantaneous erection and further heightened the effect of my decolletage. Ben sat back and considered the view.

"Your tits are as nice as hers," he decided. "But if I told her to take them both out and press an ice cube against each nipple — she wouldn't hesitate."

"Anything that slut can do..." I carefully didn't look to see if anyone was watching I just watched Ben. I pulled the blouse apart, completely baring my areolae and nipples, reached into the water jug, took out two ice cubes and applied them in my cupped hands. It was impossible to hold back a gasp as they made contact with the hot, engorged flesh. I closed my eyes and drank in the feeling; absorbing the shock, as I would a cane strike, 'freezing fire' was all I could think. Meanwhile down below, having my boobs out in a restaurant was having an effect which was just plain hot. I held the ice pressed tightly against me until I could open my eyes and look squarely at Ben again.

"Not bad," I said at last, taking my hands away but leaving my boobs on full display, I dumped the ice on my side plate and then calmly reached into my bag for a tissue, dried my nipples and then shrugged the blouse back just enough to cover them. "But I expect this K, or whatever her name is, would chicken out after that."

"Certainly not. It would only serve to encourage her to put her hand up her skirt and masturbate to a climax under the table when I told her to." He waved a waiter over and ordered more cognac, for which I was grateful. I hadn't expected that order; I was thinking more of dropping another cube down my skirt and into my knickers.

Ben read my mind.

"After that of course, you have an advantage over poor K. She is forbidden to wear knickers, so at least you will be able to cool yourself down by putting an ice cube in yours. That is if you have the same courage as K does."

I was too busy working out how I was going to cover the noise I always made when I orgasmed to argue too much. Eventually I grabbed my napkin in my left hand and held it over my mouth while I jiggled about in my seat until I could reach up under the tablecloth, under my skirt and get the gusset of my knickers out of the way and start rubbing at my already erect clit. I could only get one finger up inside myself with some difficulty at that angle but I let Ben know whenever I did by making little grunts of pleasure. I had to stage a real coughing fit to cover the orgasm which overcame me pretty fast. I was flooding down there and thanking Janet over and over again. I was getting the best out of Ben all right and we still had the whole night ahead of us.

Once I had finished and was amazed to find that I hadn't attracted any attention, I patted my hair back into place, composed myself and reached for the iced water again. But Ben grabbed my wrist and held it in that strong grasp I had missed so much.

"I think you're very hot down there so if it were K, I'd tell her to take her time, rub it up and down the crease of her cunt and savour the cooling effect."

That put paid to dropping it down and making a quick run to the Ladies. He was working well.

"And this K tart would thank you for that would she?" I tried to rally.

"Oh, yes." He smiled his most irritating smile. "But then of course she's just a scrubber and wouldn't think twice about it, whereas you're..."

"Whereas I can do what any cheap tart can do!" I was getting into this. Not only enjoying the exhibitionism but also letting the Emma and K sides of me slug it out.

It was not easy getting my hand down the front of my skirt. I had to shift my bottom forward in my seat so the tablecloth would cover my hand going down there then lean back and breathe in sharply to make room for it. I gasped again as the ice made contact with my hot, tender flesh. I had trouble breathing for a moment, just as if I had dived into cold water. It was delicious torment and Ben beckoned a waiter over at that precise moment.

I was leaning back and slightly to one side to get my hand down to my crotch, the tablecloth barely covering the action, and I was gasping and wincing at the shock of the cold. Ben ordered another cognac for himself and the waiter looked at me.

"Is Madam all right?" he enquired.

I tried to get my hand out but couldn't and clung to the tablecloth to cover my predicament. Ben frowned and leaned over.

"Are you okay dear?" he asked, oozing concern.

"Y… yes… fine!" I managed to stutter.

"I expect it's just a touch of indigestion," he said to the waiter. I nodded furiously and he left, while Ben looked at me, suddenly hard and authoritative again. "Move it up and down, and make sure you rub it on your clitoris… hard!"

I gritted my teeth and went for it, doing exactly what he had told me to while he smiled at the grimaces I was making. He wouldn't let me stop until my whole vulva was numb with cold and soaking wet. Icy water was trickling down the cleft of my sex and puddling under my bottom. Thank God the skirt was black leather and lined, I thought, it should help to mask the damp patch.

At long last I got a terse nod from Ben and was able to extract my hand and sit up again.

"If this bloody cow K was here, would she be allowed to go to the Ladies now?" I asked bitterly as I dropped the depleted ice onto a plate.

"I might allow it... but only if..."

"All right, please can I go to the Ladies?" I ground out — fierce with desperation.

Ben gave me his most infuriating grin yet and helped me slide past him. But at the last minute he grabbed me by the arm.

"Of course K would always say, 'Please sir,'" he whispered.

"Fuck K," I spat back. The cold water was now running down my thighs and I had had enough.

"That comes later!" he retorted instantly. "After I've flogged her raw for breaking every rule in her book!"

He let me go and I tottered off, weak with shame and excitement. I suspect that only a woman can fully appreciate just how exquisite the humiliation was. My hair was a mess, my tits were almost hanging out — and despite my efforts with the tissue, I had damp patches over my jutting nipples which made it look as if I was lactating. Trails of moisture were glistening on my thighs and only I knew that it was water. From the corner of my eye I caught some startled glances and practically broke into a run.

Once safely in a cubicle I tore my knickers off and wiped myself dry with toilet tissue, and maybe I did rub at myself a bit harder than necessary while I contemplated the total success of my strategy. I regained my composure and revelled in Ben's threat. Once back at his place I was in for a real session, I was going to suffer for this night's work, and in the upside down world of SM, my punishment would be my reward. But not one groan or scream would be faked although I was looking forward to the pain.

I ran a brush through my hair did a quick bit of repair work, disposed of the knickers and returned with a little more dignity although the back of the skirt was horribly cold and damp. I decided to risk winding Ben up just one more notch when I got back to our table, and instead of sitting opposite him, with my back to the wall, I slid into the chair on his left. My bare legs immediately felt the rasp of his trousers against them and sent a tingle spiralling down into my naked sex. I desperately wanted him to reach out under the table, slide his hand up between my thighs and touch me there, take possession of me again. But somehow I kept my mind on my aim of provoking him one last time.

"You know, I bet even your shameless little whore has never done what I'm going to do next," I told him, and before he could say anything I gave a mock squeal of dismay and dropped my clutch bag on the floor. I pushed my chair back hurriedly and dived down right under the table, tucking my legs under me as best I could. Ben's hand shot out to grab me and haul me up but I avoided it and reached out to hold the bulge of his erection. I had him then and I knew I was being very unfair; because of who he was I knew he wouldn't dare draw any more attention to us that evening. So I began to stroke his rod between my thumb and forefinger, moving them up and down slowly. I longed to open his flies and take him into my mouth but that was going too far — for that night anyway.

Instead I spread my thighs, grabbed one of his legs, pulled it forward and began to rub my crotch up and down against it. There really wasn't much Ben could do to stop me and I grinned at the thought of what he was going to do to me once he got me home, but then to my horror I saw the waiter's shoes approaching.

"Your bill, sir," I heard him say.

I froze while I listened to Ben take out his credit card, but the waiter didn't leave. He must have seen my feet and ankles poking out from under the table.

"Er...?" he began.

"She's lost a contact lens," Ben explained smoothly.

I smothered a giggle as I saw him walk away and re-surfaced, wiping at my eye with my napkin and snorting with suppressed laughter. Even Ben's look of pure, tight-lipped fury couldn't entirely quench the giggles. But in the cab back to his house I did my best to resume the serious, obedient demeanour I knew was expected of me. I only really achieved it though when Ben took the wind right out of my sails.

"I've more than half a mind to take you straight back to your flat and leave you there for good," he said quietly. "I could send any clothes back to you tomorrow."

I stared at him in horror. This wasn't supposed to happen. This wasn't what I wanted at all!

I slid off my seat in a complete panic and knelt in front of him on the filthy floor, pulled his strong hands to my face and smothered them in kisses.

"No, please sir," I begged. "I'm sorry! I just wanted to show you..."

"Show me what? That Clair and I have been wasting our time? That you consider this a girlish game? That you're a spoilt little brat who's always got to get her own way?"

"No! No!" I sobbed openly. "I want to serve you! I really do, I just wanted you to have an excuse to really... to really punish me, sir. I've missed my master so badly, I wanted him to have every excuse to... beat me... do anything he wants with me." I looked up at him, blinking back the tears. "I want my master to know that I belong utterly to him and I welcome the pain of the punishment he is about to inflict on me."

I shocked myself. These were thoughts that had previously only been in my head, never had I expressed them so openly, but I knew that I meant every word with all my heart. If Ben dumped me I wouldn't want to go on living, I knew that now.

For what seemed like an eternity he stared down at me impassively and I cried in terror.

"I can play games as well, K," he said at last with a tight smile. I sagged with relief and realised that after all, my little rebellion which had nearly gone too far, had left me where I wanted to be. He had put me firmly back in my place.

I don't think any master could have wanted more from his slave than Ben got that night. The terror and relief made me more obedient and responsive than ever.

Once I was naked and collared he clipped my hands behind me and hobbled my ankles with a two-foot length of chain clipped to ankle restraints, then, still in the lounge he began to exact his revenge. He gave me a really good slapping to start with and that was why he started in the lounge. I had plenty of soft things to fall into and over. I held my face up to him like a normal woman would if she were expecting a kiss or a caress, but welcomed the jarring of the slap and the burst of lights behind my eyes as I staggered back in my chains. Inevitably after only a couple of slaps I lost my balance and sprawled onto the sofa. It took me some time to get back on my feet and face up to the next which sent me crashing to the floor. I knew Ben would be enjoying the sight of me, naked and chained, crawling and struggling at his feet. It took me quite some time to get my legs under me and kneel up, but with my hands held behind me I had to use the coffee table to support my torso while I straightened my legs. It must have been an erotic display of humiliation, particularly as I was struggling to get up purely so I could be knocked down and do it all again. I managed to weather a left hand slap to the face followed by a right across my breasts and then a left again to the face which spun me helplessly across the arms of his chair. That was a bruising impact and he let me take a break after I had doggedly shaken my head to clear it, got my legs under me and levered myself up. I wasn't going to fail him again.

But that was enough he decided, however much he could see I was loving it. His hand reached between my legs and I felt his fingers slide up into me, I shuddered and moaned immediately but he gave me a tap across my breasts and shook his head, then removed his fingers grabbed my right nipple, and twisting it hard led me stumbling and crying out, up the stairs.

He tied me face down across the whipping trestle and whipped my bottom to start with. It was a hard whipping, much harder than I had grown used to with Madam, and much harder I suspected than he himself had ever delivered before. I counted twenty lashes out loud and thanked him for each one and then he began on the needles. I had seen them in the cupboard while Madam had been there and had trembled at the sight of the long thin steel spikes. But I had never had them used on me, nor seen them used. Now Ben put some disinfectant on a cotton wool pad and spread it over my throbbing buttocks, then, making sure I could see, he took one needle at a time off the crossbar beside me and stuck them into me. It wasn't so much the pain, which really wasn't so bad in comparison to the aftermath of the whipping, it was just the thought of all those spikes going in that had me moaning and pulling at my chains. The last few went into the soft flesh of my inner thighs which were chained wide apart and I yelled at those, in fright as much as anything else. Ben left me for a while and when he returned he was naked. He also carried a mirror. He dragged my head up by my hair and made me look at my reflection. Behind and above my tear-stained and reddened face I could see the mounds of my buttocks and sticking up from them were the needles. It was an intensely erotic sight and I did hope that maybe Ben would stick the gorgeous erection he was sporting just next to my face straight into either of the entrances I was displaying between my decorated cheeks.

But instead he hot waxed them next. He lit a large white candle and a red one in front of me and held them for a while to get the wax running and then moved behind me. I leapt and yelped as each blob dropped onto me. Ben had propped up the mirror so that I could see the candles and watch the wax melt and gather then, as Ben tipped them, watch it run slowly down and drop. It was a horrible extension of the Chinese water torture, irregular intervals between sharp scalds on already abused flesh. Every now and then he would let a dollop fall between my cheeks, right onto my anus and sex. The gyrations of my hips were not purely from pain by then, I was trying to tempt Ben into sampling the excitement he was causing. But he was coldly and cruelly back in charge now and I had still got a lot to pay for.

Even when he put the candles down he didn't let me up. He clamped and weighted both labia and nipples and then left me again after taking a crop to my shoulders and back. Just a quick ten, enough to make me scream, jerk and set the weights swinging at each stroke to increase the pull they were exerting.

But when at last he did come back he took the needles out and removed the clamps before letting me up. I could feel the wax cracking as I stood up and stretched, then waited for whatever was coming next. I could tell by his look that there was still more, and I wasn't disappointed. He pulled the spreader bar which hung from the ceiling right down to the floor and ordered me to sit.

It felt very odd with the wax cracking as I bent and stretched. Ben replaced my ankle restraints with wider, softer ones and clipped them to the spreader bar. My heart raced as I watched him work. I was going to get an ankle suspension. I had seen Janet get one and had thought it was the most exciting thing I had ever seen. The experience of undergoing one though, completely eclipsed just seeing one. Despite the wider restraints the tension on my ankles and legs was incredible — both scary and exciting — and as Ben hauled me up until my arms swung clear of the floor and my wide splayed crotch came level with his face, I became more acutely aware of having my legs open than I would ever have believed possible. The urge to close them, one so deeply ingrained in women was almost an ache. I could feel the muscles in my vagina and my anus clench in a vain attempt to shield themselves. I even tried to bend up so that I could get my arms there, but Ben pulled them back down and clipped them to the ring at the back of my collar so they couldn't interfere with his plans. I hung there, just like a slab of meat on a butcher's hook, just a female body for her master to amuse himself with, the sinews in my inner thighs still twitched every now and then as the urge to close my legs grew worse by the second and the distress and the pain of the suspension itself set floods of hot juice oozing out into my sex. Ben picked something up and then approached me until I could nuzzle and lick at his scrotum and the base of his shaft. Having my face upside down and helplessly pressed against him like that made me whimper with desire for something to fill my own sex. All I could do was rub my cheeks against the soft skin that coated his shaft, flicking my tongue and then taking long lascivious licks. I urged him on hoarsely when I at last felt his fingers part my labia.

"Yes, sir. Please!" And then I screamed and thrashed in my bonds, my stomach clenched as I frantically tied to curl up around the burst of agony which had consumed my crotch. Ben stood back and watched me twist, curl and stretch, screaming and begging for mercy at the same time.

He tutted and then squatted down so I could stare upside down into his face.

"It's just a clit peg, K. A good bolt of pain like that will open a slave like you up nicely."

I had no choice but to bear it, and he was quite right.

He fisted me and I took it quite easily. I really was getting to be a pain freak. He worked three fingers inside me, giving me a running commentary on how wet I was as he worked on me, then four fingers, then he flicked at the clit peg a bit to make me scream again and then he went for it; his whole hand. I held my breath as I felt my lips spreading wider and wider and then wider still and finally he was in and making a fist inside me. I could feel my insides being stretched and rubbed as he twisted and thrust down into me then withdrew. I could feel everything so much more forcibly than with normal penetration, I was sure that if I could only crane my head up I would be able to see a bulge in my stomach where his fist was. He made one violent plunge down and I was catapulted into an orgasm so suddenly that I hardly felt the onset. I just went into spasm after spasm while he fucked me with his fist and I twisted and spun. I screamed and gurgled and sobbed and he played with me, ramming down into me to make me scream, pulling out to make me choke as my labia stretched but I tried to hold him in, then sobbing as he twisted his fist right at my entrance. Then he did it all again. And again. Until I was nearly unconscious. He didn't wait for me to come round properly, time was running short, I had been suspended for quite a time by then. So even while I twitched and whimpered in the aftermath of the orgasms which were still running through me, he flogged me. Walking round and round my body he swung in blows to every part of me with a multi-lashed whip. I just swung and moaned at the swish and crack of the strokes, my whole body racked with pain. I didn't care where he whipped me or for how long, I was bathing in my pain and the fact that I hung upside down in front of my master, available and helpless.

But my lethargy was rudely shattered when he began crotch whipping me. I didn't think anything could hurt like that. I didn't think the universe contained that much pain. I couldn't even shriek for the first few blows, just stretch and arch as if I had been electrocuted. He struck so that the lashes bit down along the whole of my vulva, hammered across my anus and then splayed out to further inflame the already flogged, scalded and pierced buttock flesh. What engulfed me was a tidal wave of purest agony and only shock, I think, prevented me from orgasming more intensely than even with Danny. I was still crying and gasping when he took me down and carried me to his bed.

He didn't chain me that night and I slept happily curled in his arms after he had taken me. Once I fully realised all I had endured that night, I was ecstatic and when Ben had kissed me and congratulated me for my stamina, in a whisper I begged him to fuck me, fuck me hard, make me hurt all over again. I relished the carnal brutality of the word itself as well as the knowledge that I had spoken out of turn and would have to be punished. And he did it. Making me his own again as he sank deep inside me, re-awakening the pains in my tenderised sex flesh and driving me to wild orgasms until I reached utter joy when I felt him attain his release inside me. I was his property to hurt and abuse as much as he liked and I fell asleep still murmuring how much I loved him. And I meant it too. I really did that night.

I was punished and happy again in the weeks that followed. And even politically there was the honeymoon period while the new government settled in, but there were lots of briefings to attend, interviews with new cabinet ministers, 'portrait' pieces to write about new figures on the political landscape. So I was kept busy.

Ben now had much less pressure on him and he devoted more time to me. Once or twice he came round to my flat and we had sessions there. I think he understood my dual personality very well and judged it important that Emma should have nowhere to herself. K should be everywhere. But as I lived in a modern apartment we had to be a bit careful about noise. I had a wrought iron bed though, which made tying me to it very straightforward. The most bizarre thing was that when he rang to say he was coming round, I went into a cleaning and tidying frenzy. How typically feminine!

Ben wouldn't have batted an eyelid at the piles of knickers on the bedroom floor, the rumpled bedclothes or the chaos of my dressing table, but I was determined that whatever Ben did to me, he would have a tidy flat in which to do it.

It was really weird seeing him wandering round there, inspecting my pictures, my furniture; it was as if he had found another piece of me which he hadn't dominated up till then. But even after he left I could still feel him there. It wasn't just the chains on the bed posts, the selection of dildos in my underwear drawer or the whip coiled up in the bottom of the wardrobe, it was that he had been there and I couldn't ever pretend when I was on my own that I was not a devoted sex slave. Janet was quite right, it doesn't matter where you are or what you are doing; once a slave, always a slave.

I remember the first time very clearly. I opened the door to him dressed as he had instructed, basque, stockings, high-heels. I was proud of that basque, it was black satin with good boning and half cups with scarlet bows on them. I had worn it around the flat a couple of times to get used to the constriction and was now highly appreciative of what it did for my figure, particularly the way it made my hips and bottom and boobs swell out so invitingly. I had spent hours on my makeup and knew I was looking good, the only marks I was carrying were from the bootlace whip which Ben had used on me the week before and I had made no attempt to cover the faint stripes which fanned out across my upper thighs, dived between my legs and then fanned out again on my buttocks.

I was delighted with his response when I let him in. He smiled and gave a low whistle before making me do a twirl for him, then sending me off with a resounding smack on my bottom to make coffee for him. I knelt beside him while he drank it and asked me about various trinkets and pictures I had collected, idly stroking my hair, running his hands across my breasts and my shoulders while he did so.

He had brought a suitcase with him and had me open it when it was time to get down to business. Inside were a cane, a crop, a whip, restraints and a selection of dildos and chains.

"This is just an experimental session, K," he explained, as he laid everything out for me. The implements looked so strange, lying on my lounge carpet, bathed in summer sunshine, but even so I got the familiar tingling from nipples to crotch as I looked at them. We started with me bending over the coffee table and bracing my arms on it while he caned me. Almost immediately it became clear that that wouldn't do. The Sshwack! of each stroke in that small room was going to attract attention even if we turned on the TV or my little hi-fi. We tried the crop with the same result and even after only four or five strokes I was beginning to give breathless little screams — the usual prelude to my full-blooded ones.

We went into the bedroom and, as I had known he would be, he was delighted with the bed and showed me the chains he had brought. They were ingenious. Each link in them had a spring-loaded catch so the lengths could be altered with the minimum of effort simply by adding or removing links. I stretched out face down and he attached my restraints and then sorted out the correct length of chain for each limb. And with that done he whipped me. One of the great things about a basque is the way it leaves most of your back naked, so you can take the whip without having to bother with undressing. We found that the slap of the twenty lashes landing was much more diffuse than the sharp crack of the cane and crop and Ben decided that I would keep that whip so that it was always to hand when he chose to come round. He was nothing if not thorough, and it took thirty lashes before he was quite certain that he had made the right choice.

He took a bath after that and I waited on him, soaping him carefully all over and making sure that his penis was properly clean. I made very sure of that, my back was hot and throbbing and as ever that had started the fires down below. When I had dried him we went back to the bedroom, taking with us the dildos, and while he lay on the bed, letting me watch his erect sex which twitched every now and then, he had me masturbate with each one. They ranged from a pretty standard five inch one to an eight inch one with a really thick shaft. That filled me very pleasantly and Ben allowed me to work it in myself until I came to a shuddering climax which left me barely able to stand. But there were vibrators too in the same size range, battery powered of course but one had a remote control and wasn't a vibrator at all. It was a wicked little phallus which was designed to deliver a shock whenever the switch was thrown on the control unit. Ben demonstrated this while he had me make more coffee. We established that its range coped quite easily with my small flat, and from the bedroom he could make me spasm and stagger helplessly time after time. It wasn't an unpleasant feeling, it was just like when a doctor does that knee thing to test your reflexes, it just set my vagina twitching and clenching as it would do in the middle of really good sex. Most of the arousal it set off in me was due to the fact that my insides could be controlled by someone who wasn't even in the same room.

Each dildo was assigned a number and my vagina was given the letter A, while my anal passage was assigned the letter B. This, as Ben explained gleefully was so that he could ring me and give me just a number and a letter. I would then have to wear whatever he told me to until he told me to remove it. He also had me note that some of the dildos had wide flanges at their bases so that they could be safely used anally. Strangely I didn't find that very comforting. He had also bought two long lengths of jeweller's chain, one of which would wrap round my waist, while the other clipped onto it then ran down between my legs, back up between my buttocks and then attached back to the waist chain. It would make sure that whatever I was plugged with would stay where it was.

Once all that was explained and demonstrated he buggered me. It was quite deliberate I'm sure. The first time he took me in my own bed he used me in the basest way of all. And I knew that I would never sleep in that bed again without remembering him forcing into my upturned backside while I groaned into my pillow. While he had been away, that passage had scarcely been used and had tightened up. He had quite a struggle to get in and caused me considerable pain which only made me reach down between my legs and rub at my clitoris fiercely once he was able to thrust and withdraw. He came at almost the same time I did and when he had finished with me he wrenched himself free, hurting me again and went to clean himself up. I lay where I was for a few moments savouring the depths of my humiliation. I was propped up on my elbows, my face buried in my pillow and my bottom raised. In my own bed I had been whipped and buggered, and I had loved every second of the pain which both had brought with them. Ben was whistling happily as he cleaned himself up in the bathroom so I had to wait until he had finished before I could clean myself. And I noticed with grim foreboding that he took the remote control unit for the shock dildo with him.

There was nowhere for Emma to hide now.

All my worst fears were confirmed the following week. I had a function to attend at the embassy of an eastern European country and two hours before it Ben rang to give me the number of that wretched little dildo and the letter A. I pleaded and begged but he was implacable. And so I duly turned up in a brand new evening dress which had cost a small fortune. It was my usual style, low cut neck, slashed skirt as far as was acceptable, all guaranteed to loosen the tongue of whichever male politician I was targeting. But underneath I wore Ben's chain and moving inside me with every step and churning my stomach with fear and excitement was his wretched dildo.

He tormented me mercilessly.

I would catch sight of him from time to time and beg him with my eyes but he would just smile and sometimes put his hand in his pocket. If I was lucky I made it to a table to put my wine down before the bolt hit me. Mostly I didn't though and spilt a lot of wine that night. Some people asked in concerned tones why I kept giving those odd little half skip, half jumps and I concocted a story about suffering from sciatica which caught me every now and then. It was a nightmare; I was trying to be a professional journalist but was being totally controlled by my vaginal responses, which in turn were controlled by someone else. Ben couldn't have made me more acutely aware of my femininity and my sexuality if he had hung me up and flogged me there and then, right in front of the whole gathering.

To make matters worse, I was so hot and moist by the time I got home that I had to use the thing by hand to bring myself off before I could get any sleep. I rang Ben the next day, something I rarely did, and swore long and foully at him. I knew it was totally against all the rules, and completely overlooked the fact that he hadn't forced me to wear it, just told me to. It was my own submissiveness which I was furious about.

He listened in silence and then quietly asked if I wanted him to stop doing everything he did to me.

I sighed and thought of how sluttishly aroused I had been the previous night and how I had kept the lights on in the bedroom while I stood in front of the mirror and watched myself working the dildo up and down until I came.

"No," I said at last.

"Good. Have you got any holiday owing?"

"Yes, lots. Why?"

"Take a fortnight from next Friday. I'm taking you away."

"Would I be right in thinking that this won't involve palm-fringed beaches and cocktails by the pool?"

"You're a clever girl. Beautiful, clever and…"

"And a treat to beat. Yes I know."

He laughed and hung up.

He picked me up from my flat. I had been told to bring no luggage, just the clothes I stood up in. I had asked if there was anything special I should wear but was told that it didn't matter. From that I concluded that I was either going to be spending a lot of time naked or that clothes would be provided, as it turned out I was right on both counts.

I found it genuinely hard to decide what I should wear, I was so used by then to being told what was acceptable and what wasn't. In the end I settled on a classic sun dress as the weather was glorious that day. It sorted out my major problems very neatly, it had no shoulder straps, the neckline was low and the bodice was very tight and made a bra unnecessary, while the skirt was full and knee length. All I took apart from that was a white bag to match the dress. Ben seemed well enough pleased when I stepped into the car; in fact he even leaned across and kissed me. Like any good master he rationed kisses very carefully. He understood how important to a woman they are.

So when he broke the kiss, which left me breathless and excited, nipples already forcing little peaks in the dress, I dared to enquire why I had been so honoured.

"Because you look excited and fearful and that always makes your eyes sparkle," he told me, stroking my left breast quite openly.

"Can I ask where we are going now?" I pushed my luck.

"No. But when you come back I think you will be even more of a slave than you already are."

He never spoke a truer word, but even he had no idea of just how much I would be transformed by the two weeks which followed.

I settled back, well pleased with how the day had begun, but after only a few minutes Ben reached into the glove compartment and produced a pair of sunglasses which he told me to put on. After that kiss I was not in a mood to be anything other than obedient so I did as I was told but couldn't help pulling them off again straightaway. They weren't sunglasses at all. The lenses were of solid black plastic; even the wraparound parts at the sides were thick and completely opaque. It was a blindfold.

"Of course it is," Ben agreed cheerfully when I pointed this out. "None of the girls where we are going have the faintest idea where they are. It's not only safer that way, it's good obedience training. Now be a good girl and wear them until I tell you to take them off."

Locked away in my own personal darkness I had no choice but to concentrate on the sounds of the traffic and the motion of the car. It was strangely restful and reassuring somehow, the warm leather of the upholstery cosseted me and I was safe in the hands of my master, who would take me to the brink but never let me fall.

"Play with yourself." Ben's voice broke into my soporific darkness.

With no hesitation I hiked up the dress to my hips and did as he said. I had no way of knowing whether anyone could see me and I didn't care. I couldn't see them so they didn't matter. I knew how Ben liked me to masturbate but it was a bit of a struggle in a car seat. He liked to watch me get my fingers well up inside myself, not just rubbing at the clit, and in order to get the right angle I had to shuffle my hips forward and eventually get my knees up against the dashboard before I could perform properly. I was bare legged that day, completely naked under the dress and he was pleased with me and kept stroking my right thigh every now and then. I came three times before I was allowed to stop and then dozed in the warmth of the afterglow and the sun on my bare skin. I woke when the motion of the car and the engine note changed. We seemed to be going more slowly and stopping every now and then, there also seemed to be virtually no other traffic. Country lanes I guessed, and was proved right when we stopped and Ben allowed me to take the glasses off. We were at the edge of a lane which ran through ancient beech woods and there were banks by the side of the lane which made me think of Devon. Ben got out and came round the car to my side, ordered me out and then had me bend over and place my hands on the passenger seat. I didn't know if I was going to get a beating or just a quick screw but I panicked about being seen and protested, but Ben just pressed me down with a hand in the small of my back and lifted my dress till it was bunched up on top of my buttocks. My protests faded into incoherent moans as his fingers delved into the hot wetness of my crotch. He confirmed that I was good and ready for anything and then thrust himself straight into me. My earlier performance had obviously excited him because he just rammed into me without any subtlety, intent on finding his release as quickly as possible. I felt him come long before I was ready to and within seconds I was back in the car, blindfolded again and feeling his sperm trickling out of me. All of which left me desperate for my own release, but that was forbidden.

"You'll have noticed that I haven't beaten you for over a week," Ben explained. "It's a tradition where we're going that girls arrive unmarked. But it is better if they arrive frustrated, it helps them settle in more quickly."

And with that I had to be satisfied. But when, after about half an hour, we finally did arrive I was definitely in the state he wanted me.

I found that we had parked outside a long low, Georgian building which could have come straight out of a Jane Austen dramatisation. It was truly beautiful and it stood in large wooded grounds which I was later to explore. I have been back there on several occasions but I still have no idea where it is, or even what its name is. I have always been blindfolded, but some girls arrive in the boots of their masters' cars, so I haven't done too badly. From the look of the rolling countryside around the house, I tend to think it is somewhere in the West Country.

But that first afternoon, all I could think about was the crusted sperm on the back of my dress as I followed Ben into the hall. It was cool and dark, luxuriously carpeted and at the back stood a reception desk. I realised that this wasn't a private house, it was some kind of very discreet hotel. The woman behind the desk, in her early fifties I guessed, with iron-grey hair and a strong, handsome face, greeted Ben warmly and he signed us in while I gazed round at the mounted stag and fox heads on the walls.

That done, Ben smiled at me quickly and left me, disappearing through one of the panelled doors which led off the hall and closing it behind him. I didn't even have time to call after him before the woman caught me by the arm and led me firmly into a small office behind reception. She guided me to a chair and then sat herself behind a cluttered desk.

"Read this and sign," she said curtly, handing me a sheet on a clipboard. My eyes flicked across phrases like; "…accept all and any punishments," "…agree to be at the complete disposal of all guests," "…will obey all orders unquestioningly,"

"I don't understand… what's going on?" I hated the quaver that came into my voice.

The woman glared at me. "He hasn't told you?"

I shook my head and she sighed, then explained.

The house was owned and run by herself and her husband Mr Hepworth with their partners Mr and Mrs Dixon, with some outside help. Both she and Mrs Dixon were slaves themselves and well used to 'patching up girls' as she put it after an evening in the dungeon. There were fourteen girls resident at the moment and they were all there to be used by any of the guests in any manner they chose. By day we would serve as chambermaids, cleaners and assistant cooks, but once the dinner was prepared and ready for cooking later, we were free to enjoy the facilities until tea time, which was when the guests returned from wherever they went during the day. From then on we were to take turns helping in the kitchens or waitressing until after dinner everyone retired to the dungeon and the real business of the day began. In a bit of a daze, and reflecting that this holiday was not going to be rest and recuperation, I signed the document in front of me which gave my consent to everything that either management or guests wanted to do to me. And I have to confess that the thought of fourteen men all having complete freedom with my body, both in and out of a dungeon, sent that familiar tingle coursing through my belly. Ben was going to share me around! He was going to watch other men enjoying me. This was an exciting extension to my slavery, I really was just a slut to be lent out for whipping or whatever and my opinions, my feelings, were totally irrelevant. In short I was being given permission to be a completely submissive whore.

The girls were housed in the stables and the minimum of conversion had been done. The stalls had been widened slightly to allow for two simple pallet beds in each with a small bedside table between them. Chains looped down neatly from rings in the wall and draped onto quilts and pillows. It was our first duty of the day, I learned, that after we were unchained we were to make the beds and tidy the chains. Opposite the stalls was a long dressing table, just a wide shelf really with a mirror running its full length. At intervals there were tidy groups of hairbrushes, lipsticks, blushers, foundation and all the familiar feminine accoutrements. The old stable doors had been bricked up and central heating radiators had been installed under the dressing table I noted with relief. At the far end of the room was a row of toilets, with no doors, and a shower area with four showerheads. About half way along the stalls we came to one bed which had clothes laid out on it. We stopped there and I was told to strip, which didn't take long, and then I was given my uniform.

First came a basque in deep purple satin which didn't cover the breasts at all. It constricted the waist even more harshly than my own ones and then supported the breasts and pushed them together and out in the most inviting swells of soft female flesh. I caught a glimpse of myself in the mirror and gasped at the erotic display I made with my hips flaring out from my impossibly narrow waist and my boobs just begging to be felt and stroked. I didn't need the mirror to tell me that my nipples were already betraying my reactions. Mrs Hepworth chuckled as she saw them swell and harden. Next came black stockings and then a skirt which matched the basque. It was no normal skirt though. The ruched and gathered satin in thick pleats with a frilly white underskirt tacked onto it was sewn onto a wide belt which buckled round my waist, and once I had fastened it I realised that the skirt stopped about in line with the fronts of my hip bones. That meant I was completely exposed from there forward, while behind me I trailed a frothy concoction of floor length satin and white petticoat. When I had slipped on black, four inch high heels with silver buckles and delicate silver chains on their fronts, I was staggered at how blatantly sexy I looked. Although parts of me were clothed, my breasts, sex and thighs were utterly naked. Mrs Hepworth had me parade up and down and satisfied herself that I looked good enough for her and then added the finishing touches. These were the familiar leather restraints at wrists and ankles and a black leather collar from which dangled a plain metal disc with just the letter 'K' on it. Then I was shown my section of the communal dressing table and instructed in how to sweep the skirt behind me before sitting so that I would always sit on my naked bottom. The only lipstick available to me was a brighter shade of red than I would have chosen, but with the costume it made my mouth and nipples a blatant invitation. As if to underline the implications of my dress, I was handed a spare lipstick and a large plastic hairgrip which I was to keep in the pocket which I found in the skirt. The lipstick was to be used after I had served any of the guests orally and the hairgrip was to put my hair up with when I stripped in the dungeon. It was these last two additions which had my heart thudding as I followed Mrs Hepworth back into the main house and was put to work.

I was taken to the kitchen where Mrs Dixon was in charge. She was a younger woman, and rather skinny, her face as sharp as her temper, I discovered. Like Mrs Hepworth she was conventionally dressed, but round her, making tea and coffee, assembling trays of snacks and carrying them out were my sister slaves; all dressed like me in purple, black or dark red uniforms depending on complexion and hair colouring. There was no ceremony, I was simply handed a tray, told to load it from the main table and take it into the lounge.

"Don't worry," the girl I found myself next to said. "Just follow me, and watch what I do. I'm your stall mate. My name's Anna."

"Stop gossiping over there!" Mrs Dixon's called across. "Or I'll have the crop taken to you first thing tomorrow!"

I discovered that quite apart from the beatings we took in the dungeon, we could also be sentenced to morning punishments in the stables for any reason Mrs Dixon or Mrs Hepworth cared to dream up. Mrs Dixon was responsible for most of them.

I followed Anna's rather voluptuous figure along a corridor and into the lounge where the men sat laughing and talking. I saw Ben but he completely ignored me, chatting animatedly with two friends. For the next hour I got a taste of what I was in for. Every time I bent to serve anyone at the low tables between the leather armchairs, hands would stroke and weigh my boobs, pull and twist at my nipples or simply dive straight up between my legs. I had never been so publicly fondled or treated so casually but I knew that whatever Emma might be shrieking in my mind as a stranger's fingers explored the extent of my vaginal lubrication — without the man even interrupting whatever he was saying to his companion — K was lapping it up. I kept my eyes firmly focused on what I was trying to do and concentrated on stopping my knees from buckling under the continual stimulation. At last Anna managed to whisper to me that if I knelt while serving, it was easier to cope with, and from then on I managed much better and was able to pull my shoulders back to show off and offer my breasts to the careless male hands.

I was clearing up and making my way back to the kitchen with a piled high tray when a man with thick black hair and a distinct Yorkshire accent hailed me. He was standing by one of the elegant sash windows in the corridor outside the lounge and as I approached him he reached out and took my locket.

"Ah, K! So you're Ben's new one."

"Yes sir," I replied automatically, even as I tried to adjust to the fact that Ben's earlier slaves had passed this way. Why not? But I couldn't repress a sudden stab of jealousy.

"Put the tray down and bend over that chair," he ordered. After such a strange day it was comforting to be under orders again, anyone's orders. I did as I was told, bending over and bracing my hands on the seat of one of the mock Jacobean chairs which lined the corridor. I felt the man lift my skirt and throw it forward so that it fell right over my head. I could imagine what a sight I presented to him from behind, pale thighs and buttocks framed by stockings and white petticoat, and a sex which was fully open and which felt like it was in full flood. It obviously was because he didn't even have to finger me, just thrust himself home in one easy push. I made a little "Oof!" noise as he filled me and pushed my head against the back of the chair. Then he just held himself there until with a moan I gave in and started rotating my hips slowly and then a little faster as my need grew more urgent. I could hear people passing back and forth behind me but all I could really concentrate on was the rod of flesh which filled me and owned me for that moment. Suddenly I heard a voice over my left shoulder which momentarily jerked me out of my sluttish reverie. It was Ben.

"How're you finding her, Phil?" he asked.

"Not bad. A comfortable fit." He slapped my bottom. "Tighten up a bit girl."

I obediently clenched my inner muscles around him as hard as I could and was rewarded by a pleased grunt from the man who was taking me.

"Quite strong, that's good," he said.

"Her arse is still good and tight, and her mouth is a real treat," Ben replied casually.

Somewhere deep, deep inside, Emma screamed in protest but K was in full cry now and I felt fresh hot surges of pleasure inside me as I was so crudely assessed.

"Under the whip?" the man enquired.

Ben laughed. "Howls like a banshee, comes like a stoat."

He took his leave without even a pat on the shoulder for me and the man got down to business. It was a crude rutting... a fuck, pure and simple. He reached under me and grasped my breasts while he pistoned in and out at a speed which obviously pleased him and this time I was able to achieve a climax myself just after he started pumping himself into me. Then he pulled out and left me as abruptly as Ben had earlier. I straightened up and tried to repair my appearance as best I could. A couple of the girls came by and winked and laughed companionably. I noticed that one of them had telltale glistening streaks of sperm on her thighs and seemed to be making no attempt to clean herself. So I took my lead from her, gathered up my tray and went to the kitchen.

After tea every day we were sent to serve our own particular masters and help them bathe and dress for dinner. This was a clever routine as no form of punishment, beyond what a master could deliver with his hand, was permitted in the bedrooms. As a result there was a lot of flirtation, but no fulfilment. I used to soap Ben all over and wash him off, sometimes being allowed to suck him, my face almost under water. Sometimes he would take me on the bed after his bath and I would have to clean him all over again afterwards. But apart from the occasional slap or spank, there was nothing that could make it properly satisfying for me. The rest of the girls all said the same and this left us eager to serve the dinner, have our own frugal meal in the kitchen and then get down to the dungeon.

But there was one more ritual involved in that process. Each night in the kitchen we drew lots by pulling cards from a deck, the lowest card was the winner; in the event of a tie the winners cut again until one girl won and she was presented to the guests as the entertainment during dinner. As it was my first night I was automatically selected.

Flogging was considered too energetic and noisy for the quiet ambience of the dining room, so usually the selected girl was tied in strict bondage — Mr Hepworth being an expert — and then nipple clamped, labia clamped or both. Sometimes she was weighted as well, sometimes she was suspended. Moans and cries were considered pleasant without being too distracting, but if you got too noisy you were gagged and then cropped the following morning. On that first night I was put to a devilish contraption. It was a chest high steel frame with a crossbar with two pulleys set at right angles at the ends. But from the centre of the crossbar another steel bar protruded forwards. I was placed so that this bar nestled against the centre of my chest. My wrists were clipped behind me and my ankles were chained to the machine's base. Everyone, apart from Mr Hepworth who was working on me, ignored me so totally that I hardly felt any shame or even excitement at being exhibited for others' entertainment. Instead I watched the preparations with a curious detachment, as if this wasn't my body at all. And of course it wasn't. I inhabited it but Ben owned it and decreed what would be done to it. Mr Hepworth screwed C shaped nipple clamps tightly onto me, forcing a hissing intake of breath from me as the plates squeezed down onto the tender, engorged flesh. Then he fed the chains which were attached to them through the pulleys and hung pear shaped lead weights onto the ends of the chains. I gasped as he let the weights go and looked down in shock as my nipples were pulled out so far that my breasts lost all roundness and stretched into odd pointy shapes. The weights were far heavier than anything I had experienced before and the pain was immediate, coupled with the pounding of my blood as it tried to force through the constricted flesh.

The meal lasted for an eternity. Through tear blurred eyes I watched as course after course was served and leisurely conversations were carried on at the tables. I could see Ben but he never even glanced at me, being more interested in fondling the blonde who was waiting on his table. I gave way to groans and cries at last, was duly gagged and cropped the next morning, but at least I earned a hard beating from Ben later, although I didn't like the displeasure I saw in his eyes as he beat me and resolved to do better next time. I didn't. Some days later I was wrist suspended with labial weights and the same thing happened.

I was, and always will be a hopeless case when it comes to suffering in silence.

That first night in the dungeon was one long blur of wonderful pain and pleasure. I can only remember odd moments from it, mainly because of events which followed shortly after and which submerged it. But I can clearly remember a man tying me against a wall and attaching suction caps to my nipples before taking me, my legs wrapped hungrily around his waist. I know Ben at long last paid me enough attention to put me in a whipping frame and breast whip me. After two bouts of nipple torture, the whip just shredded me and orgasm after orgasm exploded through me. I know several men took me from behind while I was tied over a trestle and I know I took someone in my mouth, but who it was I had no idea. Mainly what I can remember are the other girls. It was the first time I had seen slaves being used en masse and the whole dungeon seemed to be filled with quivering female buttocks and bouncing, joggling breasts. Some bottoms were ample and ideally suited to the extended floggings they were getting, some were almost too thin to my way of thinking but they still got the treatment. Big breasts, small breasts, up-tilted ones, droopy ones, firm ones; they were all on display and all looked beautiful.

During that fortnight I really came to understand and be proud of the beauty of we slaves. Night after night my eyes drank in the sight of those soft bodies, flinching, jerking, twisting under the lashes, performing whip-driven ballets. The sweat gleaming on the curves of breasts which jumped and rippled under lashes and crops. The strange shapes the masters sculpted those breasts into with tight ropes and straps. But most of all what I fell in love with was the sound of the gasps and screams of tormented, orgiastic female delight which echoed off the stone walls. The way a girl's head throws back at her climax while the whip still burns and stings her back. The bitten-back grunts and moans which accompany the grimaces of determination when a girl watches the whip descend towards her breasts or sees how far her flesh will stretch under the weights and clamps. And always, always the slap, smack and thud of whips, canes and floggers.

And the men, the masters. Their harder bodies also sweat-shiny in the soft dungeon light, the smell and taste of their sweat as I was allowed to savour it in the aftermath of a session with one or other of them. I still belonged to Ben, but he would have to claim me back from belonging to the dungeon I realised after only a couple of days.

When at last they had finished with us, one by one or in small groups, naked but carrying our uniforms we would be led to the stables by one of the owners, allowed to shower and then we were chained by our wrists to the wall at our bed head and allowed to sleep. Usually we were so exhausted that there was virtually no chatter. A sure sign that a roomful of women has been well and truly used by their menfolk. But the mornings were different. I had never been to a boarding school but I reckon it must have been like one, but with all the brakes off. Either Mr Dixon or Mr Hepworth would come in and thwack his crop against the wooden walls of the stalls to wake us, then work his way down the line unlocking padlocks while we slowly sat up and groaned, stretching and yelping as cuts, bruises and welts were rediscovered. On only my first morning I was called out for punishment, together with a brunette called Marie who had been slow to make herself available for a guest the previous day — or so Mrs Dixon said. We were made, while the others stood to attention by their beds, to bend over onto the dressing table, crossing our forearms and resting our heads on them.

It never seemed to matter how badly marked we already were. Punishment was ten of the crop, duly counted out loud by the victim who also thanked the executioner for administering them. If the punishment came on top of heavy marking a girl was sometimes excused flogging for the following night and wore a red disc on her collar.

That was quite rare though, which made my three day wearing of the red disc the following week all the more of an event.

Once that ritual was over there would be a sudden upsurge in noise as fourteen of us scrummed good naturedly for the showers while war wounds were compared and admired, punishment victims were sympathised with and those girls who had been requested in bedrooms overnight were returned. I think I averaged about one every other night. In the dark we would be roused and pulled from our beds by one of the night porters — there were four of them who came in to help — who clipped leads to our collars and led us naked up to whichever room had requested us. It was always for pure sex, the guests knew that anything else would get them expelled. Of course during the days and in the dungeon we were all taken time and again, but often a reviving liqueur in the bar after the dungeon was emptied would give a man an extra lease of life and he would require his bed warming. Ben only ever sent for me once.

Showered and hungry we dressed and trooped over to the kitchen for a breakfast of croissants and coffee before we served the masters. After that we cleaned, unless anyone required us for sex. We made beds and cleaned bathrooms, swept and polished — often being interrupted for a quick screw or grope. We all found the fact that our masters had given our bodies to other men so openly, wonderfully liberating. We had been freed to admit that we loved the idea of being 'anybody's', something most straight women would die rather than admit. We loved every cock which demanded entrance to our vaginas, our backsides or our mouths. And we were truly grateful to them every time they pulled carelessly out of us and left us seeping sperm, licking the last traces from our lips or wiping it from our breasts. They were demonstrating to us just how deeply enslaved we were. There is something deliciously degrading about having to fall to your knees in full daylight, undo flies and accept an erect cock into your mouth which takes arrogant advantage of your obedience to spurt its pungent, salty load of sperm down your throat.

The hardest job was the dungeon itself, but we loved it. You had to mop the floor clean of wax, sperm and sometimes traces of blood, disinfect it, sterilise all the needles (sometimes ones you had had used on you) wipe down all the frames, benches and trestles and finally oil the whips and make sure they were all neatly in their racks ready for the evening. Every time you went in you got the wonderful smell of sex, leather and sweat; the smell of slavery.

Once our chores were done we were free. The men drifted off gradually to golf, fish or do whatever men do and we could wander in the grounds. This awakened yet another part of me which I had never suspected existed. The exhibitionist. It was lovely weather and in our half naked state it was intensely exciting to walk outdoors with our skirts swishing in the grass while the cool morning air hardened our nipples into erection and stroked beguilingly between our thighs. If one of the men didn't find us there, and most of them did from time to time, we would frequently stop to kiss each other's breasts and fumble between each other's legs. In the grounds this was punishable. I earned two more punishments that way, both with Anna, my stall mate. She was thirty-eight and had been with one master for twenty years. She was running to fat a little — the tops of her thighs were beginning to dimple with cellulite — but the rest of her was still firm and lush — that's the only word I can use, there was so much of her. Her breasts were magnificent, forty inch D, and as we rapidly became good friends I couldn't keep my hands off them, especially as they were permanently marked by the traces of whip, rope and needle; the masters sharing my love of them.

On both the occasions we were discovered the men concerned pushed us against trees and plunged straight into us, not caring that our naked and already sore backs were being rubbed by the bark. It was that animal rutting that a slavegirl most enjoys in the privacy of her mind. A short sharp fuck which takes no account of her feelings whatever, and thereby guarantees that she will love it. The pleasure of these rough screwings was further heightened by the men whispering to us, even as they plugged us to the hilt, that it would mean the crop for us the next morning. One of the men, after he had reminded me about the crop, even kissed me full on the lips while he came inside me and it had been so long since anyone had done that, that the accompanying orgasm was shattering. I took a very long time licking him clean afterwards on my knees, grateful and respectful.

But if sex between us girls was forbidden in the grounds it was tolerated in the leisure complex where we spent the majority of our time. It was lavishly equipped with a pool, spa bath, sauna, steam room and gym. Fourteen wet, naked females disported themselves shamelessly there and I came to delight in the exploration of all the little differences between one vulva and another. The plumpness of the lips and the shape, the contours and convolutions of the inner lips and the slight differences in the placing of the vaginal opening and the angle of the channel. Then there were the tastes, some more acrid than others, some almost perfumed-tasting — but all of them intensely arousing. In between swims and long sessions in the spa bath with our legs open to let the bubbles massage our sexes, we formed ever-changing groups of writhing bodies, tongues and fingers endlessly exploring. I frequently found myself enthusiastically licking even anal openings, tracing the little ridges and whorls of the tight entrances and sometimes even forcing my tongue inside. Even with my eyes closed I could tell Anna though. Her master was very keen on anal sex and she was so open there that my tongue just slid in without any effort. Sometimes I would feel a girl's tongue pressing at my own back door while I was tracing the weals of a crotch whipping across another girl's sex with my own tongue and I would reach round behind me and pull my buttocks apart to help her.

By the time the masters returned we were a seething mass of sexually aroused femininity, ready for anything and everything — quite certain that that was what we were going to get.

Over a week passed like that, and whenever I was alone with Ben before dinner I kissed his feet and thanked him for bringing me there where I was truly amongst my sisters. I really think it was the happiest time of my life, it was the company of so many women who were like me and who understood me which came as such a welcome surprise.

But early on in our second week, everything changed, and changed forever.

As these things do it came out of a clear blue sky. I had picked up my first tray of the afternoon and taken it into the lounge when I saw that a new guest had arrived. I stopped in horror and was about to try and run for it when he saw me.

It was Guy... the man whose political ambitions I had wrecked as part of my job. As part of Emma's job.

He looked at me in amazement at first and then a slow malevolent smile spread across his face. How he must have revelled in the look of utter confusion and horror on my face. I must have half turned in a futile attempt at escape, but where was there to run to? And my pathetic attempt merely confirmed for him that he had me at his mercy — and that I knew it.

If you are a woman reading this, you will probably understand the full humiliation and terror of my predicament. It had taken months of training with Ben just to get me to feel at ease with my body being naked and available to others, but they had been 'safe' others. A woman's instincts are to cover her vulnerability at all times. Quite unconsciously, at work, at home, wherever, we keep our legs pressed together, we cross our arms over our breasts, we feel daring if we expose even a bit of thigh or cleavage.

But there I was, my breasts naked and whip marked, my sex exposed and my pubes matted with recently spilled semen. There was nowhere to hide from him or from myself. He was looking at Emma, the go-getting journalist but here and now I was K — the slavegirl. As that thought came to me it suddenly felt as if my schizophrenic personality had suddenly been put under a spotlight. Previously Ben had been the only one who knew, but now the one man in the world I really didn't want to find out, had done so. Emma and K were as exposed as the body they both inhabited. My knees shook and I tried to put my tray down but he clicked his fingers and beckoned me. I had no choice but to obey. As I approached I could see his eyes sliding over my body, taking in every detail which he had probably lusted after in secret but never thought to see in the flesh. His blatant leering somehow reduced the threat he posed to me and I was able to summon up some defiance. Alright, the cat was out of the bag, but I wasn't ashamed of K, and nor was I ashamed of my body — weals and all. K was a tough girl in the dungeon; I had heard several men comment on that. So I was damned if I was going to be afraid of him.

Emma had got me into this mess, but it was K who was going to get me out. Both parts of me came together then and have never separated since. Emma's grit and determination joined with K's submissiveness and made me what I had been waiting to become, a proud and completely dedicated slave.

"Well, well," he gloated. "Who would have believed it? Emma 'the spitting cat' Stewart, as we all called you, and really you're just a little kitten aren't you? And a submissive one at that. Well Emma, I'm going to enjoy myself more than I would have thought I ever could."

"My name's K, sir." I said quietly.

He shrugged. "Do you scream much when you're whipped, K?"

"I am told that I am very loud, sir," I replied as steadily as I could. Then added recklessly, "But I can take quite a thrashing."

I broke all the rules and met his eyes squarely, challenging him. He didn't miss a beat and just returned my stare.

"I'll have to declare an interest in you to the management or I'll be risking expulsion if I lay a finger on you and someone finds out — and we wouldn't want that would we? Who is your master by the way?"

I told him and he burst out laughing.

"The sly old fox!" he said. And just then Ben entered the room. For a split second he faltered when he saw

Guy and I could see his lips thin as he walked over to greet him very stiffly. Mercifully he waved me away and I had to try and get through the rest of the afternoon with my hands trembling so hard I could hardly hold anything. I could feel Guy's eyes boring into me all the time and I knew that the men were discussing my fate; deciding between them what should be done to, and with me. It was simply none of my business. At any other time, with any other man, I would have accepted that. But this was personal.

"He has the right once he has declared 'an interest' in you, to request the use of you in extreme session, under supervision," Ben told me when at last we were up in his room. "It's a safety rule to prevent any outside resentments threatening any of the girls here. If he had failed to declare it and had whipped you or touched you in any way, he would have risked instant expulsion. Mr Dixon is a doctor and will keep a check on you during the session."

He looked very serious and concerned as he added, "I'm sorry K. I had no idea that he would be here, but now that he has abided by the rules there is nothing I can do… except check out this minute."

How could I tell him? Since I had felt the two halves of my character come together I was looking forward to the evening with a mixture of fear, excitement and determination. A heady cocktail. Whatever Guy wanted to do to me; I wanted to see how I handled it. I wasn't going to beg for mercy or run scared. What I really wanted to say was that just at that moment I felt that it was nothing to do with Ben. This was between me and Guy.

"I'm sure I'll be quite safe," I said carefully. "And anyway I'm sure you'll want to watch and make sure I behave myself."

He smiled at me, pulled me onto the bed and took me.

In the dining room, Guy's slave, as the new arrival, provided the entertainment over dinner. She was a raven-haired Spanish girl, very pretty and ringed at nipples and labia. She was slung up by her wrists and ankles, her legs wide apart and her dusky lipped sex on full view to the room. Her nipples were chained and stretched up to the hooks which held her wrists, while her labia were chained and weighted. Her head fell back and her long hair trailed on the floor while she writhed and groaned all through the meal, loud enough to earn a cropping the next morning.

The other girls all seemed more concerned about what was to happen to me than I was. I felt curiously at peace and even smiled at Anna when she tried to commiserate with me hurriedly outside the kitchen.

I was actually quite impatient to get all the clearing up finished and to get on with it, so it was a relief to finally strip off with all the other girls, hang up my uniform, put my hair up and face Guy and Mr Dixon in the middle of the dungeon.

Although the masters tended not to go in for fetish wear, Guy certainly did that night. He had on tight leather trousers and heavy boots. His surprisingly well-muscled torso was naked apart from wide studded leather bands on his forearms and his head was encased in a leather hood through which I could see his eyes glittering coldly as he surveyed my nakedness. He looked excitingly dangerous, like a medieval torturer.

Mr Dixon, tall and thin, stood between us like a referee at a boxing match and explained to everyone what Ben had already told me and then added, "If K's master wants, she can have a safe word. If not then the session will continue until I stop it."

I held my breath.

"No," Ben said quietly, and I breathed out in relief. I wanted this to go all the way. It was how it had to be.

"Gentlemen," Guy said. "I suggest that all these sluts are tied and blindfolded. That way their imaginations will amplify this one's screams and they will provide you with better sport later on."

Again I had to wait, but when it was all done the dungeon looked fabulous, the walls and various trestles and benches were festooned with naked female bodies. I could see their mouths were open and their chests heaved as they panted with apprehension and excitement. The air seemed to crackle with sexual tension. And at last Guy started. But not as I had thought he would.

At one end of the room was a shower area and a single toilet. He had me walk to it, my heels clacking on the stone floor — stockings and heels were always retained until we were ordered to discard them — once there I was ordered to kneel and place my forearms on the tiled floor. I could see the big syringe lying by the bucket of soapy water — the 'shit shooter', we girls called it. Guy gave me two full loads before letting me waddle to the toilet and expel them. That made it clear to me that I was to be spared nothing.

The treatment table was Guy's first choice of apparatus. It was a leather-covered table looking almost like a surgical item, with steel legs and shelving beneath it. It stood at right angles to a wall and I was laid out on it on my back while Guy stretched out my arms to left and right and clipped my restraints to iron hoops. Then he lifted my legs and bent them up before clipping my ankles to the same hoops. I was squashed double on myself, my crotch raised and spread. Looking up I could see my own sex, with its lips already engorged and peeled open. Guy stood between the two tight peaks of my stretched buttocks and regarded the body in front of him with a calm disinterest. I tried to remain impassive myself — determined to use my submissiveness to endure and accept his revenge with detachment.

But Guy knew what he was doing. From under the table he produced a big, ribbed vibrator and pushed it straight down hard into my vagina. He knew I was lubricated but even so I gasped as the thickness of the shaft spread and tested me. Just a quick couple of thrusts and it was out again, making me moan in shock. Then he slowly pressed it down into my anus, screwing it round until it shouldered aside the tightness of the sphincter and slid up into my innards. He reached down and took up another one just as big, but this time he plunged his hand into me as I stared up at him. He caught my eye and smiled just a little. He knew what he was doing all right. He was making me watch while his hand, the hand of a man I didn't like and who I had injured, screwed down into me, the fingers twisting and clenching until I was squelching with excitement; forcing me to enjoy this intimate invasion. Once he knew I had succumbed he pushed in the vibrator and then turned both of them on.

I fell at the first fence. Bent double and displayed for all the world to see, as the vibrators buzzed away inside me, shimmering against the septum dividing my passages as well as filling them to bursting point, I wriggled and strained at my bonds as I fought a losing battle against a humiliating orgasm. And then another one; and then a third one. Dimly I realised that my cries were echoing around the room, but just as I began the climb to a fourth peak, Guy stepped up and turned them off. He reached down between my legs and grabbed my face.

"You're just whip meat, Emma. I can hurt you till you come so much that everyone'll hear you beg me for a good long taste of the lash," he whispered through clenched teeth. The worst of it was that now I was sure I would, however much I didn't want to.

I was released and given a few moments to get my shaky legs to support me before I was hauled over to a padded whipping trestle and pushed down onto my back again, lying along the crossbar. Some of the other masters must have joined in then because my arms were wrenched down and shackled to the legs of the trestle while my legs were raised and spread. I realised at once that this position pulled my shoulders back and offered up my breasts. My head was lolling back off the end of the beam and I craned it up to see that my nipples stood up as two proud, dark red peaks at the summits of my breast mounds. Needles, whips, wax? I wondered as I let my head fall back. But before I even got that far, Guy put to good use the sight of me setting out on this long night of torment with all three entrances displayed. There were fourteen men in that room, not counting Guy and Mr Dixon. I don't know if they all took me, but it felt as if they did. My head jerked up as I felt someone pressing into my back passage, but my hair was grabbed before I could see who it was and I was pulled back down to gaze upside down at the underside of another shaft, hard and erect, which wanted my mouth. I opened wide, relaxed my throat as best I could while I felt my rectal tunnel invaded and spread again, and let this anonymous penis fuck my mouth.

They came inside me and they came over me. Sometimes, if my mouth was empty I yelled in frustration as someone pulled out to spurt himself over my stomach just as I was about to come, but then I was reduced to muffled grunts and moans as another shaft sank into my mouth and sought the depths of my throat. Some of the discharges were so big that I choked and spluttered on them, forcing the sperm painfully through my nose as I struggled for breath. Sometimes they pulled out too and I watched as the spurts of milky fluid jetted out onto my chest. Then that sex would be wiped on my throat or in my hair and another took its place. Sometimes the men enjoying my sex or anus were so energetic that the man who was using my mouth just had to hold still while I was jerked back and forth on his shaft, doing all the work for him. I have no idea of how many times I came under that onslaught, but when it stopped I felt almost as I had when Danny had finally finished with me. Sore, burning and almost delirious with the joy of being abandoned to the whims of others.

Mr Dixon lifted my head and I stared up at him groggily. He took my pulse at my throat, talked to me and I managed to croak some answers, then he stood back and pronounced me fit to continue.

I'm pretty sure it was the breast straps next. I felt the leather being looped round each breast and then buckled brutally tight so the blood pounded into the compressed, swollen lumps they made of my poor boobs. With one hand Guy held my head up so I could enjoy the sight of them, already going ruddy with trapped blood, the nipples engorging and the areolae swelling up fast behind them. Guy's other hand held a chain with a toothed clamp at either end. He helped me watch as he lowered one onto my right nipple and let it go, then did the same with the left. I let out a throat rasping scream both times as they bit into the swollen and tender nubs. Then Guy put his face close to mine.

"You've got spunk all over your face, your tits and your stomach. It's oozing out of your cunt like you're making it in there and your arse is so open I could get a kitchen sink up it. This is the real you, isn't it? Not the prick teasing bitch in London, who thinks it's fun to wreck men's lives," he said softly.

I could only signal my agreement by blinking. He was right and we both knew it.

The next day the other girls told me that they had all nearly come just by listening to me howl.

Guy took pinches of breastflesh and slowly passed needles through them. Someone stood behind me and held my head up so I could watch. I had had them before while we had been there but never while I was in the breast straps. It was still not as painful as it sounds, but the sight is one guaranteed to send any girl spiralling into the darkest reaches of pleasure pain. I knew my hips were drumming on the beam I lay on and all Guy had to do was touch one of the steel needles to my clitoris and I came in long spasms of agonised delirium.

Again I don't recall how many times I climaxed, but Mr Dixon appeared above me again and this time ordered me to be released. I lay on the floor, while the blood flowed back into my arms and legs. The breast straps remained on though and I ran my fingers wonderingly over the pierced skin, now purple and shinily distended. The nipples had almost disappeared into the swelling areolae. Mr Dixon ordered me to all fours and I made it, head hanging, drawing in gulps of breath and watching my tortured boobs sway under me, fascinated by the sight and drinking in the excitement of it. He helped me to my feet and looked at my eyes and talked to me again.

"I'm okay. Can go on. Want to," I managed.

"She's fine," he said curtly and I was put on the rack for hot waxing.

I was spread in the classic X configuration and put under enough tension to provide a suitable amount of discomfort while I twisted and bucked under molten cascades of blue, green and yellow wax. The pain of it landing on my constricted breasts was simply exquisite and I met Guy's calm stare as he watched me grimace, moan and then scream my way to yet another peak. The rack was a wonderfully designed piece of furniture; a body could be stretched on it with arms and legs straight up and down or the actual limbs of the table could be swung apart to form the X that the body was tied to. And so even while I was recovering from the waxing of my breasts, Guy shifted to stand between my open legs and started waxing my crotch. None of these treatments was new in itself but the steady, remorseless continuation without any respite was telling on me. My screams and wails choked off into hoarse croaks and my struggles became weaker as each scalding blob seared into the soft inner thigh and labial flesh. I came repeatedly, I know, but it was as if I was falling backwards down a long black tunnel. Then, with brutal suddenness I was jerked back as someone doused my face in ice-cold water. As I spluttered and gasped I felt the breast straps being released and gritted my teeth against the pain of the restored blood flow. It was agony, but it helped mask the squeamish feel of the needles being slowly taken out, one by one.

The rack was wound up another couple of notches and I felt real strain come onto my wrists and ankles, and the tendons in my arms and legs felt as if they were being stretched to the point of snapping. I craned my head up in a panic just as Guy stopped extending me. I glanced down my body and saw my breasts were now stretched almost flat, they were multi-coloured with streaks, runs and blobs of wax, and in places there were crimson spots where the needles had been. But at least they were still there! I could see, beyond my wide spread legs that some of the other girls had been taken down and were being used. The slap and crack of whips echoed through the dungeon and already some female groans accompanied them. Mr Dixon and most of the masters stood round the rack watching me, and as soon as Guy saw me looking around, he started in again.

The men were now stripped to the waist and they moved in while Guy held my head up so once again I could watch and enjoy what was done to me. The first of the men to arrive at my crotch held two straps, two clamps and two lengths of chain. I watched him reach down and encircle my upper thighs with the straps, which he buckled on tightly, then winced as I felt the clamps bite into my lips which were then wrenched apart and anchored by the chains to the straps. Now it seemed as though every part of my whole body was being stretched and utterly displayed. Even the pink flesh of my vulva would be splayed open now.

"Gentlemen," I heard Guy speak from above and behind me. "I believe this slut is in something of a hurry, so if you would care to make her wait a bit longer and enjoy her again before I move on, please do." He let my head fall back.

They took full advantage of the offer and once again I was used at both ends. But I was stretched so tight that I couldn't respond in any way to the penetrations of my vagina except by using my failing strength to clench my internal muscles around each shaft which filled me. Again I came but not enough to satisfy me. I was drowning in a sea of abuse, pain and the blackest pleasure and I knew what I wanted more than anything else.

So when they had finished with me that time, Guy heard what he wanted. I begged for the whip. I deserved it. I had earned it. I wanted it.

He let me up and Mr Dixon massaged my joints carefully while I leaned against him but once again he pronounced me fit to continue. I was ankle suspended with legs wide apart, still with my labia pulled hard open and in a gesture of such cruelty that it set my stomach burning and flooding all over again, he made me provide the light for my own flogging. He stuck candles in my sex and anus, lit them and dimmed the room's main lights. Ben said later that I made quite a sight, my swaying, limp body glistening with sweat and sperm in the soft candlelight.

I was too exhausted to writhe or twist much under that whipping but I came repeatedly nonetheless as Guy stalked round me, never letting me guess where the next stinging lash from the scourge he wielded would fall. Breasts then shoulders, buttocks then fronts of thighs, stomach then back. And in between, bolts of sharp scalding pain from between my legs where the wax was running down and falling on the tenderest of female flesh. On and on it went, Mr Dixon walking round with him, every now and then checking my pulse. I raced from orgasm to orgasm, peak to peak with scarcely time to breathe in between. And it was just reaching the point where I was terrified of the intensity of the next one when it stopped. I felt the candles pulled out and before I could react, the crotch whipping began. It was the icing on the cake and I found the last dregs of my strength. I twisted and yelled and cried and came to blinding peaks of tormented ecstasy as my sorely abused sex was laid waste by the whip. He didn't hurry even then. He took his time aiming and raising the whip before smacking it down along the pink gash of my splayed sex. It eclipsed the agony of my first crotch flogging in the same way sex with a master eclipses masturbation. Without doubt, this was real flogging. If a woman's innermost being is centred in her sex then he was whipping my very soul. Scouring it, scalding its helplessness with no pity, and I lost all traces of myself at last. I became pure pain, one white-hot flame of agony centred at my core. Each shuddering cry of orgasmic delight was the final measure of my defeat. I heard a voice urging Guy on to strike harder, to flay me, to take me to the blood.

It was my own voice.

And then there was Mr Dixon's voice at the last. "Session over!"

I came to with Mr Dixon holding smelling salts under my nose. I was laid out on my back on the dungeon floor and every bone, every sinew and every inch of my hide was hurting. Ben was propping my head up on one knee as he half knelt behind me. Guy stood over me. He said nothing until I had come round fully but once I had he clicked his fingers as an indication that I was to follow him, just as if I was his pet bitch. Without a second's hesitation I struggled to hands and knees — walking was out of the question — and painfully made my way after him. The rest of the dungeon was in full swing. And the next day I was to find that I was the toast of the girls. They all said they got the best canings, whippings and suspensions they had ever had thanks to the show Guy had put on with me.

At last we came to the shower area and he motioned me to go to the back of it. I did and then slumped down against it, panting, wrecked, exhausted, but looking up at him. He tore off his hood and stared back at me, then smiled fully for the first time that night. I watched his hands go to his flies and realised that he probably hadn't taken me once during the session. He pulled his sex out and it wasn't fully erect, but he held it pointing down at me and I understood. To tell the truth I was glad I didn't have to move, to kneel up and take him in my mouth. That wasn't what he wanted. All I had to do was stay slumped gratefully and accept the final token of Guy's victory. I closed my eyes and lifted my face as if for a kiss as I felt the stream of hot liquid hit me and drum against the skin of my face, my throat, my breasts, my stomach; and at the very last I shifted to open my legs and allow the acid, scented stream to beat against the throbbing flesh of my sex.

When I opened my eyes he was gone. I looked down at my beaten and bruised body and saw the gold drops hanging from my nipples where they had gathered after tracing paths through the wax. I could feel the urine in my eyelashes and running down my cheeks. Without even thinking I licked my lips and caught the hot acid taste of utter, utter defeat. And I welcomed it. Guy had made me come right at the start, without even hurting me and from then on he had played with me until I had begged him out loud to whip me. I had endured all right but I had not been able to retain any sense of myself, I had thrown myself into his hands begging for torment; just like the painslut I now knew myself to be.

Mrs Hepworth helped me shower and half carried me back to the stables. I never even felt the chains go onto my wrists, I was asleep instantly. And even then the night wasn't over.

I was woken by one of the night porters standing over me, shining his torch in my eyes. The stables were in darkness and I could hear the sounds of the other girls sleeping around me. My wrists were unclipped and only with the man's help was I able to sit, then stand and hobble after him on my lead. I was pretty certain where I was being taken and I was proved right.

The porter, a short muscular man we all called 'The Hulk' left me outside a room, having knocked on the door quietly. Guy opened it and I limped into his bedroom.

He was naked now and fully erect and when he stood beside his bed with an impressively long, though thin erection sticking urgently up from his crotch, I slowly and painfully knelt before him, and then bent further to kiss his feet. I had known that this scene had to be played out ever since I had staggered out of the dungeon, and I hoped he was enjoying the view I was giving him. I squatted back on my heels so that he could see the whip ravaged back, the slender waist and the swell of the buttocks with their dividing crease from which I had seen in the stable mirror, the scarlet flares of the final whipping emerged.

"I think you have something to say, Emma." His voice was soft but firm.

"Yes, sir," I whispered and gave one or two more slavish licks between his toes to aid my cause before I said what I had to. "Please take me as your slave," I stroked desperately at his ankles, his calves while I delved ever more desperately between his toes with my tongue.

"No," he said at last. Of course I had known that that would be his answer. But to make me beg had been his object all along. He knew that he had wrecked my life as certainly as I had damaged his.

But of course he took me. The long session had obviously inflamed him and he was in a hurry to spill his load into me. The pain of his penetration was the worst torment of the long night and the pleasure he took in prolonging it had me clinging to him like a drowning woman and tearfully urging him on to punish me all over again while I shook under each surging thrust; his fingernails digging hard into my welted bottom. And no sooner had he spent himself and withdrawn than I was squirming down the bed, heedless of my aches and pains. In a whimpering frenzy of abasement I licked him back into erection, burrowing between his thighs with my face, following the ridge behind his scrotum with my tongue, letting it take me to the place where the most abject of slaves lick their masters to express their devotion.

I wrenched my buttocks apart with eager hands, even using my own fingernails to score them yet again, when he ordered me onto my knees. And once he was inside me I begged him to show me no mercy in his use of that passage. He didn't, and like Ben wrenched himself out before he softened, making me yell in pain and leaving me with that gutted, wrenched open feeling before my entrance closed. For a moment we lay spent and panting, side-by-side and for a second I dared hope that my disgusting show of debasement had changed his mind. But he was made of sterner stuff and simply rolled off the bed to press the room service buzzer. When The Hulk came for me I was on my knees in front of him again, hopelessly, humbly licking him clean.

But just before I was led away in a state of dazed dismay at the depths of my betrayal of Ben and just as I was beginning to face the awful consequences of the night; Guy hit me with the final cruelty.

"You beg nicely Emma. Feel free to try again."

He didn't even let me go back to Ben with the whole thing behind me; he had left just a chink of light, so that I could never be wholly free of the memory of what I had hoped for and the depths to which he had driven me.

As he was permitted to, The Hulk took me before he chained me for the night. I knelt on my bed, bottom in the air and he had me doggy style while I muffled my sobs in the quilt until he had finished with me. It seemed a fitting end to the night.

For the next three days I wore the red disc that meant I was off limits for flogging. I hobbled around as best I could for two of those days until my muscles and joints eased sufficiently to allow me to move freely, and my breasts and vulva recovered from the lashing and piercing. From the other girls I got nothing but loving and amorous sympathy. I think all of them, except one, took advantage of the opportunity to explore such a severely whipped sex, and discussions in the leisure complex all seemed to centre around how many lashes I had taken there. The one exception to this game was Gina, Guy's slave. She must have sensed something had happened between me and Guy because she kept her distance and maintained a surly hostility towards me. Deep inside, her reaction gave me a hope I dared not even acknowledge.

Ben also kept his distance; there was nothing new in that. I was aware that he had brought me here to casually lend me out as a whore and whip fodder, but now there was an extra dimension to his reserve. I tried to catch his eye and smile at him but he never seemed to look my way.

Around the hotel I was fondled and groped almost continually and my cunt — as all the men referred to it — was much in demand which meant that by the time we left four days later, it was still stinging and the pain of the penetrations almost made up for the lack of whipping.

In the dungeon I had to make do with flat bladed pliers clamped onto labia and nipples, then twisted and pulled, or locked onto pinches of buttock flesh and left there. They were pretty effective when my breasts had been roped into tight, almost purple, swellings, with the areolae so blood engorged that the nipples struggled to stand out from them at all. Then, to have the gleaming steel clamped on and twisted was absolute hell; and I loved it.

As I was only lightly used, I had more opportunity to look around and continue my appreciation of my fellow slaves. Anna, my stall mate, after twenty years of slavery had the most amazing endurance. Her broad buttocks could soak up seemingly constant abuse. They were almost permanently welted, bruised and striped but it never bothered her; she obviously loved being beaten but never succumbed to the raucous orgasms I had. She was altogether more lady like. Her breasts were sensitive though, and a caning on those would have her screams echoing round the dungeon after only five or six cuts. There was a petite brunette called Angela who had very small breasts, but the nipples were the most up-tilted ones I had ever seen. She could support the most incredible weights pulling on those nipples though. I once saw her, hands tied behind her back, practically wrenched off her feet by chains run from nipple clamps up to and over pulleys and then wrapped around two bricks each. Her poor teats were stretched to the point where I was sure they would tear but she was calmly counting the strokes of a beating her master was administering to the fronts of her thighs.

On my last night I got quite a severe back and breast beating, but neither Guy nor Ben came near me. And I didn't see them talk to each other either. At one point, while Anna's master was making use of my back passage and I was bent over a leather-padded trestle, I looked up and surprised Ben looking at me. He had paused in the act of lashing a very slender girl whose wrist suspension made all her ribs stand out but gave her back a very graceful curve. It was that area which he was working on and when he saw me look up he turned back to it quickly and really began to leather the poor girl with his full force.

We left about midmorning on the following day. To add to my main concern about how much Ben knew or guessed about what had happened with me and Guy, my sun dress was badly designed for wearing to come away from there. It left shoulders, chest and upper back bare; exactly those areas which I had had worked over the previous night, so I was showing a network of weals to the world, and the anxiety that caused me made me very sad. I was going back to where I had to cover the marks I was so proud of, to where I had to hide who I really was. For the first time in my life I didn't want to be Emma.

However all my sadness was washed away the minute we pulled out of the gates. It was as though Ben had made up his mind to put aside everything which had gone on. He pulled over, wrenched off my blindfold and took me in his arms to kiss me. I melted. It was the slow passionate kiss of a lover rather than a master. And even as I felt myself swept away by the unexpectedness of it and the bliss of being in a man's arms again instead of merely on the end of his weapon or his whip, I resolved to belong to him and to no-one else. We are strange creatures, we women, because I can remember hoping, even as I sank into the pleasure of being embraced as a woman rather than a slave, that Ben would lash me until I bled to purge me of Guy.

I nearly got my wish. He stopped again fairly soon afterwards and I found we were back in the woods we had stopped in before. But this time he pulled something out of the boot before coming round to my door. And when he opened the door for me and helped me out, I saw he was carrying a cane and I laughed in sheer delight. What better way to show him I belonged to him again than to gladly take a caning.

This time we walked some way into the woods, and I was practically skipping ahead, trying to find a good spot for him to swing freely. At last I found a place where there was a clearing with some saplings growing round it. It was perfect. I wasn't bothered about being beaten out in the open, I just didn't want anything to interrupt us; and besides I didn't want a lift- the-skirt-and-bend-over quickie. I wanted this one on the full bare, and I was wobbling on my heels while I stepped out of the dress when Ben caught me up. He looked pleased and relaxed and he didn't have to tell me to bend over, spread my legs and hold my ankles, but once I had he put his hand between my legs and rubbed at my clit until I groaned with pleasure and then he slid his fingers into me.

"I've enjoyed passing you around, K," he said. "But I'm glad to have all of you back again."

"I'm your slave, sir," I told him. "Pass me around to whoever you like. But I'll always be glad to come home." And I gave my backside a flirtatious little wiggle around his questing fingers. He had barely touched me for a fortnight and I could feel the need in him, but there was business to attend to first.

It was a short but very whippy cane, one I hadn't had before and it gave me an awful beating. It was short enough so that he could work down one buttock and thigh without touching the other. Then he moved across behind me a little and did the same all down the other side. I counted and thanked him for twenty six blistering cuts. They brought tears of pain and relief flooding from my eyes and dropping onto the dead leaves and grass beneath me. Every biting stroke wrung a cry from me before I could speak, but equally every stroke carried me away from my moment of treachery with Guy. When he had finally finished he took me just as I was but had to pull back hard on my hips to stop me from falling. Some months later when I looked back on that scene of being naked and beaten in the woods, then impaled on Ben's cock, I realised that he actually made love to me then. He took his time inside me, thrusting then grinding against me, stopping at full penetration and letting me work myself on him; reaching under his shaft to finger my clit, driving me inexorably but gently to two beautiful, sensual orgasms, in stark contrast to the inferno raging in my hindquarters, before he let himself go. I can only think that I was too eager to get to my knees and take him into my mouth, and that was why I missed it. He had never made love to me; I had always been taken, used, fucked and thrown aside. From that I got my pleasure, especially after a good beating. If I had been a little more alert then I might have realised what was going on.

Somehow I never settled back into being Emma. The cut and thrust of political life never compensated for the real cut and thrust I craved nearly every minute now. But equally, although I threw myself at Ben at all opportunities and was a thoroughly 'sassy' little slave at times, the punishments, although terrible enough for the time it took him to inflict them, gradually left me aware of the fact that I wanted more.

Ben wielded the crop, cane, and whip as competently as ever, but it seemed that he used them simply as tools to make me howl and scream for a while; whereas I wanted to be terrified of them all the time. Insidiously, as the weeks went on I began to fantasise more and more. Almost without realising it I found myself, when alone in my bed, masturbating slowly while I played out a scene in my imagination. Ben would come storming in and find me with my legs wide apart and my fingers pushed deep inside myself, he would be furious and lash me and lash me without mercy until I felt the blood on my back. When I reached that part I would grind my fingers down on my clitoris and moan in delight at the mental picture I painted for myself.

But in reality, when I stayed at Ben's house overnight I would usually sleep in his bed after my session, and while it was everything a 'straight' girl could want; it wasn't what I wanted.

I began to get moody and irritable at work. My editor took me to task about lacklustre interviews and articles, but I couldn't shake myself out of it. And for reasons of his own, Ben wouldn't flog me out of it. Things came to a head when one night, in my own bed I slipped my hand down between my legs, into the warm moistness which was now virtually permanent there and played out my fantasy in my mind.

But I stopped dead in the deepest shock once I realised that in my mind it was Guy who had come storming in and who was whipping me to the all-consuming pain I needed.

I slept very little that night.

The honourable thing to do of course was to tell Ben how unhappy I was and hope that he could find it in himself to become the terrifying master I so wanted him to be. But I didn't do it. I thought about it all the next day and convinced myself that Ben simply couldn't do it; and that, in a way was a betrayal of my commitment to him, which freed me to seek another master without telling him. What specious reasoning we can use to justify ourselves when our sexes rule our heads! So the day after, I got a cab to Guy's house.

It was one of those half timbered, mock Tudor affairs you get in the affluent North London suburbs. A short gravel drive led to the front door and the crunching of my heels as I walked sounded very loud. What on earth was I doing? Suppose Gina answered the door. What could I possibly say to her?

It took me some moments to summon up the courage to ring the bell and my heart was hammering when I did. I breathed out a long sigh of relief when I heard a man's footsteps approach. The door opened and it was Guy. I was relieved, but that didn't stop my heart from pounding. He leaned nonchalantly against the doorframe and once again didn't miss a beat. "Yes?" he enquired.

"It's me Guy," I said stupidly. And then added, "Emma." How much more stupid could I make myself? I was supposed to be a professional wordsmith for God's sake and yet in front of this man I was reduced to a stammering, idiotic little girl.

He said nothing and let me stew.

"Can I come in please?" I whispered pathetically.

He thought about it for a moment.

"Yes, but if you've come to beg, you go back to the corner of the house and then crawl. Take it or leave it."

There didn't seem to be an end to the number of humiliations this man would inflict on me, but then what was I here for if not for that? I put my bag down on the doorstep and walked back to the corner of the house where I turned around and got down onto hands and knees. Thankfully the skirt of the suit I was wearing was short enough not to get tangled up under my knees, but as soon as I knelt I could feel the sharp little stones digging into them. And once I started to crawl I could feel them ripping my stockings to shreds. By the time I arrived at Guy's feet I was almost crying with the pain in my hands and knees, and when I stood up I knew I looked a total wreck; stockings in tatters, hair dishevelled and eyes red and puffy. But it seemed that that was exactly how he wanted me and wordlessly he led me inside. He stopped just inside the lounge door and turned to me.

"Beg then, Emma," he said.

I sighed and sank to my knees again.

"Please master..."

I got no further. In an instant he had stepped forward and landed a blinding slap on my left cheek. It was so unexpected that I was thrown out into the hall on my back. I lay there staring up at him in shock, while I sprawled inelegantly with my legs wide open, one hand held to my blazing cheek.

He was pale with fury and pointed a finger at me as he spoke. "Do not flatter yourself! Do not ever call me 'master', Mizz Stewart." He almost spat the words at me. "Not until I tell you to! Understand?"

I nodded and climbed shakily to my feet. His rage was truly frightening and without being told to I resumed my kneeling position.

"Please Guy," I began again. "I would like to serve you as your slave. If you'll have me."

"I've already had you, you slut," he said and then laughed harshly. "What on earth can you offer me that I haven't already got with Gina, or I haven't already taken from you?"

Good question. And I didn't really know the answer; all I could offer him was all I had.

"I can only offer you me," I whispered humbly. "Every part of my body to do with what you want. I can give you my fear of you, my pain, my obedience and my gratitude."

That stopped him. I don't think he was expecting something so abject, and when he spoke again his voice was a little less harsh.

"Well, you're a tough girl under punishment, I'll give you that. But I'm very attached to Gina... No. I don't think so Emma, although you're more determined than I gave you credit for. I never thought you'd have the bare-faced cheek to actually show up here."

I decided to push on; there was just a trace of doubt in his voice. "You know better than anybody how determined I can be, Guy," I said.

"I'll tell you what, Emma. I'll whip you here and now as a reward for trying but my answer's still 'No'."

"If I take it well, will you let me come back to beg again?"

He laughed. "The sight of the famous Emma Stewart on her knees and begging for pain is too good to miss. Yes, it's a deal. But I warn you, I have a special way of dealing with slaves in this room. Gina's terrified of it; and she can take a thrashing with the best of them."

I swallowed nervously. I had every reason to be fearful of anything Guy classed as 'special', but I got to my feet and tried to be brave.

"Strip to your waist, Emma," he said.

He watched me coolly as I shrugged off my jacket, unbuttoned my blouse with shaky hands and slipped out of my bra. So, it was going to be a breast whipping. Nothing I hadn't taken before, but Guy's use of the word 'special' echoed ominously in my mind as I faced him with my hands behind my back and my vulnerable breasts blatantly on show for him. I could feel the tightness in them and the tingling in the nipples as the prospect of imminent pain worked its usual magic on me.

Guy led me across the room to where an old card table with a green baize panel in the top and those X shaped collapsible legs stood against one wall. He pulled it out into the room a little way and then ordered me to kneel facing it. I did so and was then ordered to shuffle forwards until my breasts were actually resting on the table.

"Lift them up and make sure they're fully laid out for me," he said.

I cupped them and sure enough I found that if I pulled them from the crease beneath them there were a few more centimetres of tender flesh which could be displayed. I glanced down at them and allowed myself a little pride. They were good boobs — and I had seen enough recently to be able to judge — even laid out like this they retained their shape and roundness. The nipples were standing out hard and red, just a little bit off the tabletop.

I was encouraged to hear Guy's opinion. "They're not bad tits, Emma. In fact they're every bit as good as we always imagined them... do you know how many men in the House mentally undress you every time you go there?"

I had a pretty good idea and said so. Guy laughed as he reached behind a sideboard and took out a cane.

"Don't worry, I'll be as discreet as Ben. Though it'd be worth a few drinks if the others knew how I'd seen you."

I didn't thank him, I was too busy staring at the cane. It was the longest and thinnest one I had ever seen. My throat went suddenly dry.

Guy saw my expression. "You're right to be scared of this little beauty. Used lightly a girl can take literally hundreds of strokes on her back from it, until she's bright pink from shoulders to thighs. I've had Gina screaming under it for a whole afternoon before now. But used hard it can draw blood very quickly. Used for a tit whipping... well ..."

He let the sentence hang then ordered me to put my hands behind my head and pull my elbows back so that I pushed my breasts even farther out. Fear should have made my nipples shrivel, but it had the opposite effect this time. They were throbbingly erect and positively inviting the cane. He laid it across the wide upper slopes of flesh and left it there for a moment, just to let me suffer a little bit more.

"No restraints, Emma," he said softly. "Remember our deal. You've got to take this well or you're out of here forever."

I nodded and then looked down to tuck my chin in and keep it out of the way. He struck.

It was a deft flick, delivered so fast that I didn't have time to blink or look away so I saw the shaft of the cane blur and then crack down right across both nipples. A tidal wave of hot stinging pain engulfed my throat and brought tears to my eyes. I screwed them tight shut and bit my lip as the second cut fell — again right on the nipples. A scream tried to break through my clenched teeth but I held it. The third stroke mercifully fell on the main meat of the breasts. It was a hard, burning pain but nothing like as terrible as the first two. I blinked, gasped and sobbed my way through several more of those awful cuts before Guy stopped for a moment.

"You've had ten, Emma. Want to stop now?"

Oh God, did I! My whole chest throbbed and ached and burned. I took one hand from behind my head and wiped my eyes and nose, then looked down. I could almost see my nipples throbbing, and they were an angry, bruised crimson now. The upper curves of my breasts were striped with thin pink lines, just as Guy had described. And their thinness coupled with the fairly large expanse of flesh available meant there was plenty of room for more.

"No, give me as many as you want to," I managed, then put my hand back behind my head, gripped the other tightly and gritted my teeth.

He went back to work and continued slowly out from the roots of the breasts towards the nipples. I could tell because I began to sneak little looks downwards. The pain was throbbing through the whole of my mind and body by then but I couldn't help realising that this was what I had been missing all these weeks. This was what I needed, a slow masterful, savage beating. I even appreciated the way my breast flesh furrowed under each impact and then sprang back and rippled with the shock. It was as if I was back in the dungeon in the hotel, loving the way the female body reacts to the whip and the cane. And even as the pain mounted to the point where I had to start screaming, I knew I was boiling and flooding between my legs.

Guy stopped again but I went on screaming for a second or two. My arms were trembling with the strain of their position and the sheer force with which I was gripping my hands. My knees shook and my body was racked with shudders. I gazed down at my boobs again. The pink lines now stretched right out to the tips. All that was left was the nipples.

"Had enough?" Guy asked.

"Only if you have," I whispered, wiping my face again, which by now was soaked in tears and snot.

"It's time for the nipples again," Guy said unnecessarily. I knew damn well what was coming and steeled myself against it. It wouldn't have been so bad if I had known that he would take me when he had finished with the cane. But I knew he wouldn't. All I was doing was earning myself the chance to do this again, but if that was all I earned, it would have been worth it.

Three wicked cuts scythed across my nipples, my head snapped back and I nearly lost my balance but I held on… just. Guy stepped back to signal an end and I fell forwards across the table, my arms tucked under me, protecting my ravaged breasts. I hadn't even been able to scream during those last three cuts, not only because the pain had been so brain numbingly intense, but also because I had come. He held the cane out in front of me and I kissed it gratefully, then kissed his hand, making sure I looked up at him to signal my submission and consent to everything.

He left me to pick myself up in my own time and directed me to the bathroom so I could do some repair work. I slipped off my wrecked stockings and knickers and put them in my bag, the knickers were uncomfortably clammy after my orgasm. A cold flannel applied to the blazing flesh of my breasts reduced the agony to a supportable level and a face wash allowed me to re-apply eyeliner, blusher and lipstick. All the time I worked on my face in the mirror I couldn't help seeing and admiring how my breasts swung and shifted, and how the marks of the beating seemed to suit them. I was proud of them, both the breasts and the marks — it was how a slave's tits should look I decided as I smacked my lips to ensure the lipstick was on properly. .

It has never failed to amaze me how the application of makeup can affect a woman's mood. She can be beaten black and blue, but give her time to wash and put on a new face, and she'll be back for more. I don't think I could have gone back for more breast punishment just then, but as I winced while I put my bra back on I thought that I wouldn't mind a back or bottom flogging.

Dressed and refreshed but still smarting under my bra I went back downstairs. Guy was waiting in the hall.

"Well?" I asked. "How did I do?"

"You can try again if you want."

"When?"

He shrugged. "Whenever."

Just then the front door opened and Gina entered. She took one look at the two of us and flew at me, fingers outstretched, clawing and raking. I flung up an arm instinctively and stepped back, but one of her hands got over my guard and grabbed a fistful of hair. She yanked it forward hard and I had to stumble towards her. She kicked out and landed an agonising blow on my shin with the pointed toe of her shoe. I screamed and swung blindly at her, catching her under the ribs and making her lose her grip on my hair. I stood up just as she bent forward to gasp for breath and I swung my bag to catch her on the side of the head. It was all purely instinctive, just desperate self-defence. She staggered sideways and then lunged forwards to grab me round the waist and push me backwards, down onto the stairs. Then it was my turn to grab the hair. I took two handfuls of her thick black mane and pushed with all my strength so that she had to arch backwards, screaming in Spanish the whole time. I didn't have any time to wonder where Guy was; I just wanted this fury off me. And I had nearly accomplished that, her hands were clawing at mine but she was being forced further and further back, but then she managed to jerk one knee up and catch me right between my legs. Instantly I let go and curled up in shock around my crotch. Triumphantly she rained down blows on my back and head, and then suddenly she stopped; there was a split second's silence followed by an awful thump and a woman's sobbing. Slowly I sat up and looked around. Gina was lying in a heap on the lounge floor where Guy had thrown her bodily; a full six or seven feet. I got up, shaking with anger and shock.

"Okay?" Guy asked. There was a trace of real concern in his voice and if my heart had been capable of beating any faster it would have done.

"Yeah," I said immediately reaching into my bag for a comb to start repair work all over again.

Guy nodded. "Leave her to me," he said quietly and then walked towards the lounge where Gina had started picking herself up and was swearing in very fluent English. "Good fight though," he turned and gave me a slight smile which flipped my stomach over, then he shut the door behind him. While I tidied my hair I heard several fleshy smacks from inside the lounge, followed by the sounds of furniture moving and breaking porcelain. I felt like a voyeur and hurried out but I caught Gina's voice repeating Guy's name in the husky tones of an excited woman. Immediately there were more smacking sounds.

I hoped she was getting seven sorts of shit slapped out of her as I left. And maybe after that he got that breast cane out again, he was well warmed up after all, but I never did find out what he did to her. However my major concern, once I calmed down, was that while I had no intention of replacing her — I would have been quite happy to be just one of Guy's slaves — it was obvious that Gina would never, never share him. But then again maybe that possessiveness could work in my favour, it just depended on how much they loved each other.

On the whole I was well pleased with my visit to Guy. I wasn't his slave yet, but I felt it was more than a faint possibility that I might be one day. I was so pleased that I quite forgot to feel guilty about Ben. And even when it came to my, by now, nightly masturbation session, I stood naked in front of my mirror and admired my caned boobs all over again, cupping them, hefting them, stroking and tweaking at the bruised nipples until they hardened up and throbbed painfully. Then I selected the largest dildo Ben had left me and went to bed.

It wasn't until the next morning that I realised I had a serious problem. Yes, I had done well under Guy's cane, and, yes, my boobs looked great — but how was I going to explain the state they were in to Ben?

I took to deliberately leaving my mobile off and checked for messages in fear and trepidation, but I needn't have worried. For a whole week there was complete silence and I even began to feel put out that he hadn't rung! But as it turned out Ben was a great deal more shrewd than I had given him credit for.

It was nearly a fortnight after my caning before he rang.

"K, I need you to do something for me. Come to my house tomorrow evening," was all he said.

I turned up in a feverish state of excitement. A fortnight without any sex or punishment was the longest I had been without them since I had confided in Ben all those months previously. My marks had all faded and I was looking forward to getting a whole new set.

Ben wasn't in the hall when I entered, but that wasn't unusual, he frequently just opened the front door from the control unit by the lounge door and then waited for me, seated in his leather armchair. I stopped in the hall to retrieve my collar from its hiding place at the bottom of the umbrella stand and buckled it proudly round my neck, then entered the lounge and stopped in surprise.

He had company.

A tall but broad shouldered man was standing by the marble fireplace. He had a strong, handsome face with the hair brushed back from his temples. It was thick and black with just a few touches of grey.

Something about his bearing left me in no doubt at all that this was a man who was used to having women like me at his beck and call.

"K, this is Mr Hardcastle, an old friend of mine." Ben spoke without rising from his chair. The other man though stepped forward with a surprisingly warm smile, took my hand and raised it to his lips, exactly as Ben had been in the habit of doing, but hadn't done for some time now I realised suddenly. The man's touch was cool and I noticed that his fingers, like Ben's, were long and almost those of an artist or a musician, but there was nothing soft about his touch. He was strong, and as I felt his lips brush my own fingers I couldn't stop a little shiver of excitement from running through me. He must have noticed because his smile widened when he released my hand and stood back.

"I want you to strip for us, K," Ben said.

But of course. And it was fine by me; if I was right about this man the sight of my naked body would spur him on to take full advantage of my vulnerability.

"Yes, sir," I said quietly and went to stand by the sofa where I placed my bag and began to strip off. Under a dress which buttoned all the way down the front I wore my basque and stockings.

"She seems reasonably obedient," Ben's friend opined as I raised one foot to rest it on the sofa while I unhooked and rolled down a stocking. "Good legs too."

"I think you'll find the tits to your liking as well," Ben said. "And she is well endowed with inner muscles."

"A good tight fit in cunt and arse then?" his friend enquired.

Once again I listened to the coarse male commentary on my body with nothing but pride and that strange calm which always affects me whenever a master talks about me to another man. It's as if he is taking my body away from me so that it has nothing to do with me; it's his. I made as good a show as I could over rolling down the stockings and then undoing the hook and eye fasteners of the basque until I was naked apart from my high heels, which I knew I was to retain until told otherwise. I faced the men proudly, legs apart, hands behind back and eyes down.

"Yes, I see what you mean about the tits," the man called Hardcastle said. "Nicely in proportion but prominent and high. Some treatment to the nipples, I'd guess."

That was true, they were fully erect and standing out like little red bullets. Since my fortnight at the hotel and the repeated stretching and weighting they had undergone, they were definitely longer than they had been. Ben explained all this in graphic detail to his friend and then ordered me to turn around.

"Ah! An excellent back!" the man enthused. "Broad shoulders but a graceful line and a trim waist and hips. But the arse is wonderful!"

I heard him approach and then I started a little when I felt his cool hands explore my bottom. He dug his fingers hard into both cheeks, weighing the flesh and checking its firmness.

"It's just on the edge of being too big. But isn't quite, and the result is a truly inviting target. You were right Ben, she's a gem."

He let me go and Ben ordered me over to the wall in Position Five. I gazed patiently at the wallpaper with my hands on my head and my legs apart, counting the petals on the depicted flowers while the men discussed me.

Had I had the whip? Yes, and the crop and cane. Had I been crotch whipped, breast whipped? Yes, and although I sometimes had to be gagged, Ben said, I took it all very well and was exceptionally responsive to ill-treatment.

I listened proudly and could feel myself getting wetter and wetter between my legs as I looked forward to being put through my paces.

"Come over here, K," Ben said suddenly.

I turned and walked over to them, remembering to put one foot carefully in front of the other to get a good sway into the hips, just like Ben had taught me. Mr Hardcastle clicked his fingers imperiously and I altered course slightly to go and stand in front of him. He reached out and took hold of a breast with one hand and kneaded it as he had done with my buttocks. Then he pinched, twisted and pulled at the nipple while I bit my lip to retain the silence I knew Ben would want.

Then his hand went down to my pubic bush which I had carefully trimmed before coming out, and the fingers combed lightly through it before reaching under me and exploring my sex.

He laughed as soon as his fingers slipped between my already open lips and stirred the juices inside. "She's leaking nicely without having really been touched. She'll do, Ben."

"I'm sure she will. Now, K I want you to show Mr Hardcastle the respect he deserves from a slave."

I knew what he meant and was grateful for the command. I had appreciated the compliments he had paid me and was glad to get down onto my knees in front of him and reach for the zip on his beautifully tailored trousers. I could see a good sized bulge waiting for me and when I pulled his shaft free I found it was everything I could have wanted. As Guy hadn't touched me after my caning it felt like ages since a man had enjoyed me, and it was wonderful to feel that soft skin sheathing the ribbed hardness of an erect cock again. The polished smoothness of his helm beckoned to my tongue while with one hand I clenched the shaft itself and with the other cupped his scrotum, just letting my fingernails scratch lightly at the tightly wrinkled skin. I took a couple of long licks up and down the shaft before I opened up and took the whole of his helm into my mouth, exploring the slit with my tongue, then moving forward until it filled me and nudged at my throat. I felt his hands clench in my hair and knew that he had been looking forward to this as much as I had. Obediently I began the nodding motion, back and forth, inviting him to use my mouth for his pleasure and in only a few moments his urethra swelled against my lower lip and I felt the pulses of his ejaculation begin to race up him. His sperm was incredibly thick and heavy but less pungently salty than Ben's, and I had to swallow in big gulps to get it down and clear my mouth for the next spurt.

I was pleased with my efforts and their results, so I took plenty of time licking him clean before I tucked the detumescing and contented cock back into his trousers. Then I knelt back on my heels and awaited the next command. I reckoned, rather smugly, that my little display of servility should earn me a good thrashing at one of the men's hands. But it didn't.

"Dress and go, K," Ben told me curtly.

I couldn't help looking up in dismay but all I got was a steely stare from him. In that mood I knew that any disobedience would result in an even longer wait for the punishment I craved, all I could do was what I was told and hope that somewhere down the line I would reap the reward. The only consolation I could find as I dressed was the calm way in which Ben poured them both another drink and they ignored me. It was complete humiliation; I had stripped, been discussed like a slab of meat, knelt and sucked off a total stranger and was now being dismissed. Psychologically it was perfect domination, but physically it left me seething with frustration.

Only when I was dressed did Ben address me.

"Be ready at ten o'clock tomorrow morning. Mr Hardcastle will send a car for you. As long as he requires you, you will obey him absolutely and without question. Is that clear?"

"Yes, sir," I replied steadily. "Is there anything in particular I should or should not wear, sir?"

"Good question, K," Mr Hardcastle replied. "On the whole I think the dress you're wearing will do perfectly well. You will certainly be whipped, so the high neck will be an advantage. Oh and wear what you've got on underneath as well."

I began to flush with excitement. At least the evening hadn't been completely barren. Ben was passing me round again and a whipping, maybe more than one, was in prospect. I had proved that I was sluttish enough to be handed round like a pack of cigarettes and was happy that my master wanted to treat me with such contempt. All my devotion to Ben began to flood back and once again I felt terribly guilty about Guy. I determined to make Ben proud of me, whatever was required of me the following day.

The car was right on time and I had only just finished dressing and making up when the driver rang my doorbell. I had dressed exactly as instructed and was ushered into the back seat and driven in silence out past Heathrow and then well into the countryside before the car pulled off the motorway and travelled through the prosperous little towns of that area. After about an hour and a half we pulled up outside a building which declared itself to be a gym. The driver guided me out, took me up some stairs and then opened a door, gestured for me to enter and then closed the door behind me. Gerald Hardcastle lay on his back on a bench pushing up weights, but when I entered he rose to his feet and approached me. The room was a cross between a gym, a dance studio… and a dungeon. There were the usual exercise machines, but one wall was entirely given over to a floor to ceiling mirror and in front of that stood a whipping frame. My heart started pounding as I realised what I was looking at, and then noticed the coiled up whip lying next to it. It was the longest and most evil looking whip I had ever seen, its braided lash curling round and round on itself like a snake, its diameter narrowing as it neared its frayed end.

"I'm an expert with it," Gerald Hardcastle told me, seeing the direction of my gaze. "As you'll find out shortly. Get undressed, K. I'm going to thrash you first and then I have a job for you."

I swallowed nervously, looking from Mr Hardcastle's lean and muscular form to the wicked length of whiplash waiting to bite into me. And it looked perfectly capable of tearing me to shreds. All at once I wondered exactly what Ben had condemned me to.

Mr Hardcastle put a finger under my chin and tilted my head back to look into my eyes. "Fear makes your eyes very attractive. And I'm sure you look even better when you're in pain. Have you ever seen yourself under the lash?"

I shook my head but the prospect of seeing myself whipped had melted some of my fears and replaced them with the familiar pounding excitement. I reached up and began to undo the buttons on my dress. Mr Hardcastle smiled and went to stand by the frame, waiting for me.

"Shoes, sir?" I enquired when I was otherwise naked.

"No, take them off."

I padded over on the polished floor and raised my arms towards the chains which hung from the crosspiece, restraints already attached to them. By standing on tiptoe I could just reach them and while I was fastened into them I looked at myself in the mirror. The arms raised posture suited me, I felt; it made the sweep of my waist and hips extra smooth and raised my breasts very appealingly. Once my hands were fastened, Mr Hardcastle bent and took hold of my right ankle. Quite abruptly he wrenched it sideways, yanking it away from me and taking my left foot off the floor as well so I dangled helplessly, and then as I looked down in panic I saw he was fastening a restraint and very short chain to it, so that it was going to be held close to the side of the frame. Suddenly it became clear how I was going to be presented for the whip and it wasn't going to be a picnic.

I was right. My left ankle was similarly fastened and I was hung by my wrists directly over my head and then my legs were splayed almost into a splits position. Everything started to hurt straightaway. But through eyes screwed up in pain I could see myself helplessly mounted for a beating, breasts, stomach, back, buttocks, sex; all spread open and vulnerable to the whip. And what a whip it was. In the mirror I watched while Mr Hardcastle picked it up by the handle and approached me, trailing the immense lash out behind him. I whimpered in fear and he smiled.

"Just hold onto this, K," he said, and speared the handle of the whip up into me. I watched in the mirror as my labia were spread by the thing and how, with a twist or two he was able to screw it up into me. It was an intensely erotic spectacle which had me juicing helplessly and soon he was able to let go and my vagina gripped hungrily around every centimetre it could get hold of. Then he backed off and left me staring at a spreadeagled slavegirl with the lash she was about to be beaten with trailing out of her sex. I thought she looked pretty good, even though I knew exactly how much pain she was in.

Mr Hardcastle stripped off his shoes, tracksuit trousers and pants, then stood behind me again and eased the whip out of me. He examined the handle before drying it in my hair, which he then pushed forward over my shoulders to make sure every inch of my back was exposed.

"With one of these things, you really don't want my hand slipping," he assured me. And I believed him. In the mirror I watched in apprehension as he backed off and flicked out the full length of the lash. I saw his arm raise in an exaggerated sweep and screwed my eyes tight shut. There was a deafening Crack! and a blaze of agony erupted across my left shoulder blade, round my ribs and in the side of my breast. I opened my eyes in shock and saw the lash dropping back to the floor, and the path of its first strike already darkening on my body. Mr Hardcastle's arm raised again, the lash slithered back and I clenched my teeth and shut my eyes again. The second lash fell square across my back and carved a long line of pain from one shoulder to the other. The third mirrored the first and I opened my eyes and yelled as it struck. Then Mr Hardcastle changed tack entirely and began work on my stretched buttocks. He let the frayed tip of the whip crack home full on the main meat of my cheeks and even in my agonised suspension I saw myself jerk forwards under the savage impact. I counted seven, eight, nine lashes and then suddenly he moved slightly and the end of the whip slammed round one hip and bit across my pubic mound, the last few centimetres of the tassels just nipping at the junction of my labia. It was what I had most feared with my legs so wide open. I shrieked, more in terror than in pain. He cracked in another lash which curled around from my other hip and again I shrieked and tried to twist away. But then he went back to my shoulders and middle back, thudding in heavy blows which had me screaming almost continuously as my skin burned and blazed, the lashes came so constantly that I couldn't tell whether or not I was aroused. I was just on fire with a deep pain that was born of the suspension and the savagery of the beating.

Through a mist of tears I watched the tortured figure in the mirror writhe and scream as the lash snaked round and caught at my breasts, making them wobble despite how stretched they were. Again and again the whip was played over them until they too burned like my back. My cries began to fade as the relentless flogging went on and on, driving me much further than I had ever been taken before purely by the whip. The fires that consumed me were so intense that the orgasms I undoubtedly had were hardly noticeable. And just when my voice had almost gone, the lash curled round my hips and the ends of the leather snapped straight into my sex. I arched and went rigid before starting a demented wriggling and writhing as the next five lashes flew in on the same target. I couldn't scream any more, I just moaned hoarsely, resigned to passing out under the beating, the impacts of the lash were happening far away by then, the individual lances of pain were lost in the mist of agony I was drowning in and then suddenly there was silence. The swish and smack of the whip had ceased and the rasp of my agonised panting filled the room. My head fell forward and I realised that I had just taken the most ferocious beating of my life — including the ones Guy had delivered. And at last I could appreciate that it had been inflicted by a man who really knew what he was doing.

That whip could have torn me apart but instead it had given me one of the most intensely erotic experiences I had ever had. Mr Hardcastle had been in complete control the whole time, adjusting the flick and length of whiplash to terrify me, mark me, hurt me and thrill me in equal portions. He was a true whipmaster.

And when he came to stand close in front of me, I looked up at him with pure yearning in my eyes. He gazed back quite calmly and watched me arch as he pushed his fingers up into me between my splayed legs and began to stir me up. I moaned and closed my eyes.

"Open your eyes and look at me, Emma!" he ordered immediately.

I did so and he observed me with that icy calm as I heaved and cried my way to orgasm while his fingers made me squelch shamelessly. But once I had climaxed and was fully expecting him to take me properly, now that I was flooding and so wide open I could have taken three men in there, he withdrew his fingers and stood back. I cried out in shock and frustration but he smiled a tight little smile.

"There will be plenty of men to screw you where you're going now, Emma. Don't worry."

And with that he took me down, giving me some minutes to work the stiffness out of my arms and legs before ordering me to dress. The basque now looked like a refined instrument of torture as I was laced all over my torso with the snaking weals left by the whip and blotches of livid red where the tassels had struck. And it certainly did hurt when I struggled with the tight hook and eye fastenings behind me; the boning inside it digging in cruelly. But of course that pain, coupled with the frustration of not having been screwed after such a dreadful beating kept me very moist indeed as we made our way back to the car; Mr Hardcastle now dressed in a sober lounge suit and me walking stiffly and carefully beside him.

The car took us to a modern high-tech sort of office building on a development — one of many such that Mr Hardcastle owned as I later found out. I was ushered by him into a boardroom where four men were waiting for us. They had just eaten a meal and the waiters from the catering company were clearing away.

While they finished, Mr Hardcastle took a seat at the head of the table and had me stand beside him in Position One. And once the room was empty, apart from the guests, he addressed them. Apparently while he had been whipping me, his staff had negotiated a deal with these men and it was time to seal the arrangement with 'a gesture of good faith' as he called it. He meant me.

"This whore is here to do whatever you want with," he told them. Then he turned to me, "Take off your dress," he said quietly.

To add to the seething pains and excitement I had already been experiencing I got that stomach lurching jolt of arousal that I had felt at the hotel when I realised I was to be passed around. But this time it wasn't among members of the SM community, I was to serve ordinary men, just as any street prostitute would. Once again I was being lowered to new depths and for a moment I hesitated, but Ben must have known what he was sentencing me to and after that terrific beating I wasn't going to fail him.

My fingers trembled as I undid the buttons on my dress and shrugged it off my shoulders to stand proud and unafraid before the men. The livid traces of the whip brought whistles of appreciation and astonishment. But obviously the meal and the drinks had had their effect and almost at once a fat man on my right beckoned to me. I went to him and knelt when he told me to, opened his flies when told to and took him in my mouth. While I sucked at his thick stubby cock, I felt hands tracing the paths of the weals on my back and shoulders and once he had erupted in my mouth and I had swallowed his sperm, the floodgates were down.

They spent about an hour or so using me. And I tried hard to comply with all their demands, lying back on the hard table to take them between my legs, kneeling to suck them, bending over to be buggered and sometimes sucking at the same time. They didn't have whips but their nails dug into my weals and drew some specks of blood. But all the time I kept an eye, as best I could, on Mr Hardcastle. He was watching everything, calmly and impassively, as if he were assessing my performance and obedience. And it was only when all of them had finished with me and had gone, leaving me lying on the table with sperm oozing from every orifice and some already crusting on my breasts, did he approach me. Then he simply dragged me to him by my legs, lifted them so they lay on his shoulders and took me. I could hardly feel him inside me, I was so full of sperm and my own juices, and my vagina was both burning and strangely numb. But the thrill of at last having this strange, commanding whipmaster penetrating the body he had so thoroughly flogged and passed round sent me careering up to the heights of orgasm nonetheless, just as I heard him cry out as he spurted himself deep into me.

He used the bathroom to clean himself up while I had to lie there and wait, savouring the feel of five men's pleasure seeping out of me, but at last I was allowed to repair my ravaged makeup, comb my hair and wipe myself. I looked at my reflection in the bathroom mirror. I was a slut in all respects now. I was happy to be treated with contempt by all men, just so long as my master valued me.

But I still wasn't prepared for the wad of money I found waiting for me on the table when I returned to the room. I stared at Mr Hardcastle aghast. It was no wonder I had been called a whore during the whole afternoon. It was what I had been; I truly had been used by paying customers. Gerald Hardcastle smiled as he saw realisation dawning.

"Ben negotiated a good price for you, but you were worth it," he said, taking the money and thrusting it down my cleavage.

Angrily I reached down into my dress to retrieve the notes, meaning to fling them back at him. Yes, I knew I had been passed round like the commonest streetwalker, but I had done it out of my love of obedience, not for money. Mr Hardcastle grasped my wrist before I could do any such thing though, and his grip was frighteningly strong. I cried out in pain and sank to my knees as he squeezed remorselessly.

"Don't be stupid, Emma," he said calmly. "If Ben wants you to be a real whore, then be one. It is entirely up to him what you are and how you serve. Besides you enjoyed every minute and you know it."

He hauled me up, still holding my wrist in his paralysing grasp. And even as I had to submit to the truth in his words, I knew my body was once again thrilling to the strength of a man who had the courage to use me as contemptuously and as hard as he had. He gave me no chance to reply, just pushed me out of the door and slammed it, leaving me nursing my wrist and facing the knowing smirk of the driver who was waiting for me.

As I thought things through in the back of the car, I calmed down a bit. At the hotel I had played at being passed around and enjoyed the sluttish feel it gave me. Almost as if somewhere there had always been a part of me that wanted to be exploited sexually without any kind of relationship being involved. But now Ben had taken that to its logical conclusion and opened me up to a form of real prostitution by selling me temporarily to another master.

It was no one's fault but my own. I had flung myself at the feet of men and could only expect that they would take the fullest advantage of me; in fact wasn't that what I had been silently begging Ben to do these last weeks. I stopped feeling sorry for myself and instead concentrated on the feeling of my throbbing cheeks and back against the car seat and then retrieved the notes from my cleavage. I counted them and realised that Ben had certainly not sold me cheap. I looked up from my counting with a little smile and saw that the driver was watching me in the mirror.

I sighed. "Are you included or do I charge extra?" I asked, trying to be as matter of fact as I could.

He returned his gaze to the road but reached into his jacket and produced a further wad of notes which he passed back. I have still, despite everything which has happened to me, some shreds of ladylike pride and so I will keep private the amount I was sold for. But I will say that it was a generous amount as far as he was concerned because all he did was take me behind a hedge for a quick skirt lift, shaft and then blow job.

He took me back to my flat and I rang Ben from there. He told me to keep the money because as he put it, he enjoyed my being prostituted but took no pleasure in pimping.

I suppose I could have been forgiven for thinking that having sunk to the level of a whore, having been only a year before a high-flying journalist, that this time I really had hit rock bottom. But Ben told me to turn up at a fabulously exclusive restaurant for a late Sunday lunch on the following afternoon and when I did I found out that once again the world of slavery hid more challenges than I could ever have imagined.

I was ushered upstairs by an obsequious maitre'd and found myself in a small private dining room where Ben and Gerald Hardcastle were waiting for me. The meal was keeping warm on a hostess trolley and the two men sat on stools in front of a small bar in the corner on the counter lay my collar and lead.

"Lock the door, then you can strip and serve us, Emma," Ben told me.

So deeply was the habit of obedience ingrained in me by then that I was stepping out of my skirt before I realised that Ben had used my real name instead of addressing me as K.

"Please, sir," I enquired timidly. "Am I in session now... or what? I... I mean..."

"Just strip to your shoes, serve us drinks and all will be made clear," Ben reassured me.

I did as I was told, taking my usual pleasure in the way the men's eyes devoured my body as I worked behind the bar. I even took some extra time mixing Ben's cocktail with my back towards them so that Gerald could comment on the darkened stripes of my whipping. When I had done I was told to come and sit on a stool beside them and once I had eased my bottom onto the cool leather seat, Gerald took an envelope from his jacket and handed it to me.

"You may look at what it contains since it concerns you, and then pass it on to your master," he told me.

I opened the envelope and took out a cheque which was made out to Ben for a very large sum and signed by Gerald. I looked at both men blankly and then Ben took the cheque from me and pocketed it.

"Emma, it was obvious to me from the way you reacted to that session at the hotel that you needed a much sterner master than myself. So I have looked around and decided that Mr Hardcastle here will be ideal for you. We have settled on a price and as from now you serve him."

I must have looked truly ridiculous sitting there stark naked between the men, while I tried to speak but was overwhelmed by anger, humiliation, outrage and sadness. When it came to it I didn't want to lose Ben and in the end I couldn't speak and just burst into tears. Being naked, all I could do was bury my face in my hands and sob. The men left me to it until eventually Gerald took charge. I felt his strong grasp again on my wrists and he pulled my hands apart, forcing me to face him. As I was to get very used to in the coming months, his face betrayed no emotion at all.

"Dedicated slaves like you are frequently traded, Emma. I shall probably only keep you for a year or so before selling you on again. But in the meantime I think you will enjoy the suffering I have planned for you. Of course you can leave now and try to find your own master but if you'll take my advice you'll trust Ben's and my judgement," he told me.

He released my wrists and I slipped off the stool to stand shakily between the men who had bartered my body between them. As ever, my anger had wilted in the face of the stark truth; I was a slave and could be bought and sold, in fact I had been only the day before and it had excited me then just as it was undeniably exciting me now. Yes, there was sadness at leaving Ben, but I myself had begged Guy to take me on, so there was no point in crying crocodile tears.

"Do you really want to sell me, sir?" I finally asked Ben.

"It's for the best, Emma. Gerald is a far sterner master than I am; he's what you need now."

"Then I belong to you now, sir." I turned to face my new master. "I will submit myself entirely to your wishes, and try to be worthy of the price you have paid for me." I picked up my lead from where it hung on my stomach and handed it to him. He took it and nodded gravely.

"Good. But you will always call me 'Master' unless I tell you otherwise. I will call you Emma, as I do not believe a slave should have a slavename to hide behind."

"Yes, master," I murmured, and felt the tingle run from my nipples to my clitoris at the thought of all that that word implied. Yes, I was ready to move on.

At my master's command I knelt and kissed his shoes before serving the lunch. Of course I dined naked and kept my eyes fixed on my food unless I was pouring wine or waitressing, and the men ignored me while they talked about business and politics. Politics! It seemed a remote subject suddenly, one which had no relevance to the naked girl who was busily clearing the table and awaiting further instructions. I stood between the men with my hands behind my back and my legs apart, just as a slave should, silent and obedient.

Ben rose, tilted my chin with his hand and kissed me softly, then he left without another word. My master told me to bend over the table and felt between my legs to ascertain how much my submission had excited me. Almost at his first penetration I was squelching hungrily. I heard his zip unfasten and braced myself just before I felt him push my lips apart and thrust up into me. I sighed in pleasure as he filled me, drowning in the special joy a slavegirl takes from penetration by her master. And as if to underline his new status, I felt his fingers trace the lines of my weals across my shoulders and back.

"You will move into my house tomorrow, Emma," he said quietly. I jerked in surprise, but he pressed me down again. "I will explain everything to you once I have finished."

He reached under me and took my breasts in his hands while he built up a steady rhythm of thrust and withdraw between my legs. Relentlessly he built up speed until he was slamming me painfully against the edge of the table with each thrust and I groaned in gathering delight at the strength of his onslaught and finally yelled aloud as I exploded into orgasm while he still pounded away. I was so lost in my own world of pleasure that I didn't realise that he hadn't come until he suddenly wrenched himself out while I was still spasming and I felt his hot, sticky fluid splash out onto my back and bottom, then I felt him wipe himself on one buttock and heard him zip himself up. Again I made to rise but he pushed me down.

"Wait as you are. The bill still has to be paid. Tomorrow at eleven my car will come for you, and you will be packed and ready to leave. You will be taken to your workplace where you will tender your resignation. From now on you will work for me as my PR adviser and press secretary, at a considerably higher salary than you currently receive, your flat will be let and the rent paid to your account. Now don't move until you are told to."

He left without giving me a chance to protest or query anything at all. It seemed that when Gerald Hardcastle bought a slave he didn't do it by halves. I could have moved of course but post orgasm lethargy coupled with a perverse curiosity as to how the restaurant bill was to be paid kept me where I was, feeling the cool linen under my squashed boobs.

At last the door opened and the maitre'd entered. He closed and locked the door and immediately undid his flies. It was suddenly quite plain how the bill was being paid. Once again I had been prostituted; this time for the price of a meal. The thought of that humiliation suddenly had me tingling and moist all over again. The man came to stand in front of my face, his rigid erection rearing up before my eyes. Without having to be told I stuck out my tongue and began exploring the veins and ridges of his shaft, working upwards slowly until I could lap at the gleaming helm. Either he had had a hard day or he wasn't as hot on personal hygiene as he could have been. He tasted and smelled acrid, and this, added to the thought that I was giving myself up to this shameful treatment made the heat inside me increase still further. He bent his shaft down a bit so that I could get it into my mouth and then reached over me to stroke my back while I took in all I could with my throat so stretched. I felt again a man's hands caress my whip marks, this time overlaid with a generous smearing of sperm.

"You really are a complete whore, aren't you?" he said.

"Yes, sir," I mumbled through a full mouth, taking it as a compliment, although I knew he meant it as quite the reverse.

He withdrew from my mouth, moved behind me and slid himself into the vagina which my new master had prepared for him, and I now realised had avoided filling with his own spend. So, I reflected as I jerked again under a second barrage of thrusts, my master was cold, authoritative but scrupulous.

Once he was finished with me, the maitre'd couldn't wait to get rid of me. I was barely given time to dress, let alone clean myself up before he had hustled me into a cab and I was squirming with discomfort as two loads of semen, cooled, dried and crusted around my crotch, thighs, bottom and back. Not a bad afternoon's work, I felt. The issue of a new master had been sorted out and the adventurous part of my nature thrilled at the thought of what lay in store for me both professionally and sexually. The slave side of me was taking its usual moist pleasure in the casual way my body had been passed around and traded twice in the space of a couple of hours. In fact it really wasn't my body at all now. It was just a body. Just a collection of nerves and tissue, flesh and blood which could be made to scream and writhe in pain or pleasure for the amusement of anyone who controlled it.

PART THREE: GERALD

By early afternoon of the next day I was standing in the hall of my new master's house, still dazed by the speed of events. Everything had happened exactly as he had said it would. The driver had come for me precisely at eleven and I had had everything packed and ready to go. I kept three cases for clothes I thought I might need and the rest were scheduled for storage in this, my new home. All Ben's whips and dildos I had packed separately, with a note thanking him for everything he had taught me, and the driver assured me he would get them. Once he had carried everything down to the car he came back for me and took me in the kitchen while I bent forwards on the work surface. I was quite certain that he had the authority to do it and bunched my skirt up for him, stuck my bottom out and bent over as soon as he ordered me to. And as soon as his fingers found their way past my lips and into my vagina I was lost in the tidal race of pleasure that I was now becoming used to experiencing whenever I was so casually screwed.

From there we had gone straight to my office where I tendered my resignation to a surprised and furious editor. He assumed that I had been head hunted by a rival and paid me off immediately in lieu of notice, so after a quick visit to my bank we had driven down to the house, stopping only once for Mr Lee, as I found the driver's name to be, to pull off and enjoy me again. And so now I waited, legs pressed together once again, a cold dampness at the back of my skirt and my heart hammering. Mr Lee had disappeared with my cases and simply told me to stay where I was. I looked around at the wide expanse of parquet flooring and the airy, modern and light hall with its huge abstract originals by artists whose names I was unfamiliar with. The modernity of the house surprised me when I first saw it. It was low and rambling under a tiled roof which was steeply pitched and which rose to high gables at certain places. The windows were large and looked out over spacious, secluded gardens and, on two sides, woodlands — all of which I later learned my master owned — and which lent themselves to some pretty spectacular outdoor pursuits, as I also later learned.

I heard soft footsteps on the deeply carpeted stairs and looked up. A woman was descending them; she was in her mid forties, trim and slender but with a hard face and the darkest eyes I had ever seen. Her mouth was quite full and her lips could have been sensual if they had not been pursed in an expression of disapproval which I was to find was habitual. She walked slowly towards me, her heels clicking on the wood floor until she stood directly in front of me. She was almost exactly my height and we stared at each other, eye to eye for an uncomfortable moment.

I smiled nervously and held out my hand. "I'm Emma," I said.

"You're the new slut," she retorted, ignoring both gestures. "I'm Miss Dexter. You will always call me that, and now you will follow me."

So from the very first Miss Dexter put me in my place, and there I stayed.

But on that first nerve-racking day I meekly followed her on a tour of my new home. The house was very big and every room was furnished in cool, tasteful luxury. I detected a male hand in all the decorations and furnishings which were unfussy and just sparse enough to suggest a man who had very definite ideas about exactly what he wanted. I felt very flattered to think that one of the things he wanted was me, and he had been prepared to pay handsomely for me. But the rooms which really struck me were the library where I was to spend many happy evenings with Master Gerald, the swimming pool complete with gym, Jacuzzi and sauna, and my own room. I am writing this in that very room. It has a dormer window which looks out over the gardens and the woods beyond and beneath that is the desk I am working at. My left ankle is chained to one of the desk legs with an adequate length of chain for me to walk around quite freely, it slithers and rattles musically whenever I move. Apart from those rooms there were three others which had a profound effect on me when I first saw them. Above the swimming pool was the playroom, it was every bit as big as the room beneath it and was lined with sliding patio doors along one side with a veranda outside them, and on the other with frames, stocks, whipping benches and a rack. In amongst those hung every conceivable whip, flogger, cane, paddle and tawse plus all the restraints one could want. The floor was of polished wood and our footsteps echoed as soon as we entered it.

"You will note that there is no ceiling," Miss Dexter said.

I looked up and saw that the room stretched up to bare, polished rafters supporting the roof itself.

"Mr Hardcastle likes to savour every noise a slave makes in this room. You will also note that everything is recorded on camera and can be played back in the office."

On many sunny afternoons subsequently my master had his tea served on the veranda with the big windows open while I was whipped for him. That way he was able to look over the view and savour my cries and the sounds of my punishment coming from inside.

But on that day I duly noted the small lenses set about the room with a lurch in the pit of my stomach. This was where I would earn my money, I thought.

This was where I fitted into the household, strung up and beaten, screaming till the room echoed nicely... I instinctively clenched my thighs together at the tingle which started in my sex. Miss Dexter must have noticed a flush come to my cheeks because she gave me a rare and wintry smile.

"You will come to appreciate the acoustics, I promise you. In fact you will have a chance to try them out this evening. Mr Hardcastle wants you whipped in here."

I couldn't help feeling that losing myself under a hard whipping was what I needed to help me settle in — a familiar experience in amidst so much strangeness.

Next came the office itself where Master Gerald was working. He was sitting behind a very oddly shaped desk when we entered but politely he rose and kissed my hand.

"Emma," he said, with every sign of genuine pleasure at seeing me there. "What do you think of my house?"

"It's wonderful, Master. I... I'm looking forward to living here and serving you," I stammered.

He gave me a smile which warmed my heart after Miss Dexter's coldly threatening demeanour. He showed me what would be my desk and I was reminded that I was here not only to serve as slave to Master Gerald but also to work professionally and I ran a professional eye over the facilities. There was nothing lacking, everything was state of the art and I felt another thrill run through me. This time it was not sexual, but was instead the thrill of taking on the challenge of a new job. However I had been standing with my back to my master and he noticed the damp patch on my skirt, which I had forgotten in all the excitement of looking around.

"Ah, I see Lee has availed himself of you," he said.

"Yes, Master. I hope that was… I mean I thought he could…" All at once the sexual nature of my situation was re-established.

"Of course it was. He will not beat you, but he has the right to take you whenever it pleases him. Miss Dexter will beat you whenever I am too busy to do it myself, or if I just want someone else to do it."

I looked across at Miss Dexter and saw the expression of naked hunger on her face. I shivered a little at the thought of having this strange and cold woman let loose on me with a whip. But the idea of being beaten for my master's pleasure, without him having to be bothered with it himself, sent quite a different shiver through me. I was brought up short by the feel of Master Gerald's hand on my bottom.

"Now I think we should christen your desk Emma, as this is where your two roles will come together. Lift your skirt and bend over."

Ah! At last some comforting humiliation. I was back under a master's hand and without any hesitation, under two other people's gazes, I rucked my skirt up and bent over my new desk, being careful not to disturb anything. Not knowing whether I was going to be beaten, taken, or both, I stretched out my hands and gripped the edges of the desk, sighing in pleasure as I felt the master's hands pulling my buttocks apart and his fingers begin an intimate exploration of his property.

"Come here Miss Dexter," he said. "Take a look at this. Hasn't she got a splendid arse?" I felt that helpless thrill of delight at the casual coarseness of his compliment. "Plenty of good firm flesh for the whip. And look at her cunt! Deep flesh on the outer lips and beautifully developed inner ones."

"Her back hole looks like it could use some stretching," Miss Dexter opined. "And Lee has obviously had her more than once to judge by the state of the slut."

"I'm sure he has! And once I've had her as well you can clean her up, feed her then bring her to the library, after that whip her and bring her to my room."

Suddenly he thrust his fingers into me and he laughed as I jerked instinctively. "Try her, Miss Dexter. I tell you she's well worth her money. Just a mention of sex and whipping and she's creaming herself!"

It was true — as always. I felt his fingers withdraw and they were replaced with smaller female ones which twisted and clenched inside me until I could feel myself churning around them. Then they were withdrawn in their turn and wiped on my bottom. I groaned in pleasure at the degradation and then yelped as Master Gerald's sex rammed into me. I was driven hard against the edge of the desk and felt it cut into the tops of my thighs. But quite rightly that was no concern of his and he carried on relentlessly pulling me back and pushing me forward as he established his right to my body by using it for his pleasure. Despite the discomfort and the fact that Miss Dexter came around to stand in front of me and I could feel her eyes staring down contemptuously at me as I thrashed about on the end of the master's shaft, I came quickly and was on my way to another climax when I felt the final deeper thrusts as he spent himself inside me and immediately pulled out. I groaned in frustration and heard him laugh softly as I levered myself up. He knew exactly how far he had taken me and where he had left me. But I was well enough trained to dismiss that as irrelevant and dropped to my knees to finish paying homage to the manhood which would now control my every waking moment. In front of Miss Dexter, and without having to be ordered, I knelt and took the still tumescent shaft into my mouth. As men always do at such times he tasted richly of my own acrid excitement and his, thick, salty issue. I licked and explored him thoroughly, enjoying the thought that this was what I was enslaved to; this thick tube of muscle and tissue which mysteriously gave its owner the right to do anything he wanted with me.

The third room which made a huge impression on me was the dungeon.

But the rest of that first afternoon and evening passed in a blur of new experiences, new humiliations. I followed Miss Dexter to my room and she watched while I unpacked and hung up my clothes, she also went through every item of underwear and confiscated anything which might incur the master's displeasure. Most of it passed muster, but any knickers which covered even the smallest part of my bottom went, as did any bras which had much more than half cups. However, she nodded approval at the basques which I had collected up to date but we hit trouble when we got to the diaries which I had always kept hidden at the bottom of my knicker drawer. I had never thought that they would be controversial but Miss Dexter said they would have to be shown to the master and he would decide what to do about them. I wasn't happy about that but before I could even begin a protest I got a stinging slap which knocked me against the wardrobes.

"Into the shower with you, slut!" Miss Dexter ordered and suddenly my head cleared. What had I been thinking? That a slave should have some privacy, or some thoughts of her own? Of course not! The man who could prostitute me, beat me — do what he liked with me because he had bought me — he owned all of me. Not even my thoughts were my own now.

Later that evening Master Gerald began to read the diaries while I knelt at his feet in the library, and that was when he showed me his collection of SM literature. He was intrigued by the journal and allowed me to continue it, so long as I showed it to him every night. So you may imagine that he has read and enjoyed my descriptions of all the beatings and torments I have been through and sometimes I have been allowed to gently masturbate him while he has read my reactions to a beating which he had administered earlier. When he ejaculated though, I was not allowed to take him into my mouth, instead I had to hold a glass and collect it. I was then allowed to sip it as my equivalent of his evening whisky.

I have to say that cold sperm is an acquired taste, but by dint of much practice I grew to enjoy it.

But on that first evening I went from the library up to the playroom and duly got my first whipping under master Gerald's roof. Once I was naked I was put in a simple rectangular frame which stretched me out in an X shape and Miss Dexter took a long thin buggy whip to me. As I had suspected she had a formidable whip arm which had me in difficulties immediately, on top of my marks from only two days previously, it hurt appallingly. She had told me that as I was going straight from there to my master's bed I was not to come under the whip. But the soundness with which I was beaten and the way my gasps and cries echoed after the snap and crack of each lash had me melting very quickly. Added to that, Miss Dexter was well able to judge her strokes so that they wrapped from the sides of my back, round under my arms and the whip bit and cut at my breasts. I gritted my teeth and tried to concentrate on the pain but the thought of how well marked I was going to be when I went to the master was too much for me; particularly when my tormentor came round in front and laid a few lashes across my lower stomach and thighs. I spiralled helplessly up into orgasm as the pain burst into its strange flowering of pure erotic ecstasy and my groans of delight filled the room even while the whip continued to crack across my body.

When I was taken down Miss Dexter put a collar and lead on me then led me, still burning and quaking, to the master's bedroom where I met an item of torture I was to become intimately acquainted with; the bar. At the bottom of his huge four poster bed and slung horizontally between the bottom posts was a thick wooden beam which slid up and down in slots cut in them, the height being fixed by thick pegs pushed onto holes in the slots. Master Gerald was lounging on the bed when I was led in, his robe was open and both Miss Dexter and I could see his flaccid sex lying between his legs. Despite my soreness I was flattered to see how it twitched and began to pulse at the sight of my whipped nudity. He gestured curtly at the bar and I was pushed towards it and made to lean forwards under it. Then my arms were wrenched back and up over the bar, which had me whimpering immediately but then my wrists were joined together by a chain which ran in front of my stomach and dug into it. My hair cascaded onto the duvet below my face and I realised that with admirable simplicity I had been restrained in a painfully ideal position for the cane which was lying directly beneath me. I heard Miss Dexter leave and my master come to stand behind me.

"You disobeyed me Emma. I left instructions that you were not to come," he said.

"I'm sorry master. But it hurt so much I couldn't help myself."

"Ben said you were a painslut. Well I intend to make pain so much a part of your everyday life that you will come to regard it as nothing special and that will help you restrain your pleasure until it is required."

And then he gave me the first of the literally hundreds of canings I have subsequently endured at his hands. He worked slowly and methodically, one buttock at a time, using the extreme end of the cane to get every last bit of whip and bite out of it, sometimes striking over both buttocks when I least expected it. And he made sure to really lace the lower parts, just above the thighs, so that I would be able to feel it for days afterwards whenever I sat down. I yelped, screamed and gasped my way through the stages of dazzling fiery agony to the region where I was subsumed by the pain and floated in a blazing cloud — where the crack of the cane landing was happening to someone else and from where I usually went spiralling into orgasm, but I hung on grimly this time, willing myself to feel every increment of agony, counting the lashes to keep me anchored. Twenty-one … twenty-two … twenty-three. And it stopped. At least that time I had done it!

Master Gerald untied me and dragged me up onto the bed by my hair. My bottom was an inferno which sent its blaze right through my whole body but it faded into insignificance when I heard my master say that my screams of genuine anguish had been very enjoyable — and had been all the more so as they hadn't become screams of pleasure. Those followed very shortly afterwards though as he bored into me from behind and pushed his weight down onto my backside. I gave him a good ride, bucking and shrieking in my ecstasy as he filled me and pushed right up to my cervix while reaching under me to grind his fingers hard on my clitoris. Then, when he had spent himself inside me and rolled off, I didn't wait to catch my breath but almost dived down to bury my face in his crotch. I lost myself in the smells and tastes of man; sweat, sperm and woman juice. I was in that frenzy which I had come to know after my night with Guy in the dungeon. I wanted to display my slavishness, my love of utter degradation so I delved deep between my master's legs and licked and kissed my way up to his anus before coming back and toying with his scrotum, encouraging it to tighten as the sex above it reared into life again. And all the time I was whispering my thanks and saying how much I wanted him to give me all the pain he wanted to. When he pushed me off and positioned me on hands and knees I continued my babble of thanks which rose to a pained cry as he penetrated me and which then continued even more loudly as I savoured the discomfort and humiliation every second he was inside my rectum. And it was the thought of his pleasure which triggered my orgasm as he exploded in my guts and then pulled himself free. Immediately I went back to work with my tongue and I was still hard at it when Miss Dexter arrived to take me away, having been rung for. I knew better than to stop what I was doing and continued to cram as much of him into my mouth as I could so that he could see how eagerly I debased myself for him.

"A complete slut, Miss Dexter," I heard him say while I moaned in pleasure at the rich taste of him. "Take her away and chain her."

I smiled proudly to myself when Miss Dexter chained my wrists to the headboard of the bed all the while muttering about what a shameless whore I was.

Yes, that was what I was all right — and that was what my master wanted me to be.

There was an awful lot to get used to in those first few weeks. Firstly there were the rules; I was woken at eight by an already immaculately dressed Miss Dexter, and made to repeat the rules by which I was to live. I had to bend over the table under the window and recite them. I got one stroke of the cane or crop if I got each rule word perfect; three if I didn't. By the end of my first week I was word perfect.

The rules were:

1) The slave will always obey instantly and without question any order given her by her master or anyone he puts in authority over her. She will not speak until spoken to; unless she asks permission first.

2) Every morning when she first sees her master the slave will kneel and say the following; "Master, I am unworthy of the time you take to discipline me. So I will always seek to repay you for the honour you do me in flogging me or in any other way bothering yourself with me. I live only to suffer for you or to be fucked by you, or to be buggered by you or to suck your cock."

3) When the slave is required for discipline or her master's pleasure, she will always ensure that she looks her best. If the slave is unsure how to dress for her master's pleasure she must request permission to speak and then enquire.

4) The slave's body is always to be available for her master's pleasure at any hour of the day or night.

5) The slave must understand that any punishment she suffers is in her own best interests and she will

thank her master for that punishment even if he is too busy to, or does not choose to, administer it himself.

6) The worst punishment the slave can be condemned to is freedom. She must show that she understands that by her subservience every minute of every day.

I started my first day of full time slavery with eighteen strokes of the cane on my already badly bruised buttocks and had to shower off some trickles of blood.

But after the first fortnight I was so thoroughly indoctrinated that we dispensed with the rules ritual and went straight to the gym where I worked out under Miss Dexter's eagle eye and hair trigger whip hand.

On my first full day I was taken to see the dungeon. I was still tearful and smarting from the hammering my bottom had taken but even so it took my breath away. It was reached by going down a flight of stairs beside the swimming pool. In the tiled corridor at the bottom were the door to the pump room and the one to the dungeon itself.

I remember so clearly standing there naked, rubbing my backside and looking about me with stomach-churning fear and excitement. The myriads of chains fell like steel waterfalls from their racks while beside them were nipple and labial clamps of varying severity. There were literally hundreds of needles of varying lengths — going right up to skewers which made me involuntarily clasp one arm across my boobs. There were dully gleaming weights and hooks and breast presses, all pristine and neat and utterly terrifying but so, so erotic. The whipping equipment was not so extensive as in the playroom; but then it didn't need to be. There was a chair which looked for all the world like a dentist's but which I knew very well wasn't — it was equipped with stirrups and shackles. There were padded benches, adjustable frames and fixed frames; all designed so that a girl could be suspended, stretched, racked or pinned down for her master to work on in just about any position that took his fancy. And whichever part of her anatomy he wanted to work on could easily be made available to him. The walls, where they weren't covered by racks or frames, were quilted leather and the floor was carpeted. All of which made noises muffled and I surmised that that was to stop screams becoming too audible, and Miss Dexter gleefully confirmed that for me. My master enjoyed noise in the playroom, but down here he liked to work in relative peace.

However my abiding memory of that room is not one of noise, but one of almost library-like quiet. There were the occasional groans and shrieks right enough but mostly there was just the hiss of breath between gritted teeth or low moans of pain and pleasure. But they were separated by long periods when perhaps just the click of chains could be heard or the tinkle of metal in steel kidney dishes. The master worked slowly and deliberately, building levels of pain that I was to find the most blindingly ecstatic of experiences.

I was shaking and ashen with terror and anticipation that first day as I was led up to the dining room where the master was taking breakfast, but I remembered the rule and dropped to my knees beside him to repeat my promise and kiss his hand.

By ten o'clock that day and all subsequent weekdays we were in the office and hard at work. I had returned to my room to dress as if I was going out to an office and then adopted my persona of efficient PA and PR adviser. I kept my skirts short however as I quickly learned that my master was in the habit of absentmindedly putting his hand up between my legs and fingering me while he was thinking about other things. I learned to classify his moods by 'fingers'. If he put three or more up me there was a serious problem. Two was nothing he couldn't handle and one was purely for pleasure and just because he liked the feel of me.

I quickly came to understand that whether Miss Dexter watched him taking me or not was a matter of complete indifference to Master Gerald. She usually just stood quietly by when he took me or beat me and quite often he continued discussing business with her while he was doing so. And I have to say that hanging in chains while a master whips your back and bottom while he calmly discusses business with another woman is devastatingly humiliating and many's the time I groaned and heaved my way to orgasm while being completely ignored, except insofar as I provided a target for the whip or a receptacle for his sperm.

But I soon became aware that she would watch me while I was being put to use with a peculiarly intense expression. It wasn't hatred or contempt, but just what it was I couldn't make out.

In the office I came to understand the function of the strangely shaped desk the master used. At about half past three each day I would be expected to finish my work and resume my role as slave. And inevitably that began with my being strapped down over the desk. The centre of it rose in a curve rather like a barrel which has been cut in half lengthways. Master Gerald's monitor and keyboard swung out over this on steel stands and when he required me he would swing them aside, push his chair back and beckon. Immediately I would strip to stockings and heels, come around to stand where his chair had been and spread my legs. Miss Dexter would then buckle ankle restraints on and clip these to hoops in the desk legs, then I would bend backwards until my spine was arched over the curved section of desk. At that point Miss Dexter would do with my wrists what she had just done with my ankles and there I was, spread out like a starfish. And that was where the fun really began. Neat little clips with sharp teeth were clamped over my nipples and onto my labia, the wires from these ran to a small box on the back of the master's keyboard, which he then swung back so that it was over my stomach; the monitor being swung back over my chest.

The first time he did that to me he asked as he resumed his seat, "Have you ever been scared of a keyboard, Emma?"

"No, Master,"

"Then start being now," he advised me, then he began typing.

Immediately I leapt and twisted in my shackles like a gaffed fish. As he later explained he had had a sort of amplifier rigged onto the keyboard so that needle-like shocks of electricity were transmitted through me whenever he depressed the keys. It was impossible to ready myself for them because they varied constantly. If he was thinking carefully in the preparation of an e-mail, there would be sporadic bursts of shocks in between prolonged pauses. However, if he was well into his stride there would be long blizzards of shocks which would leave me limp and gasping in their wake, but aware that between my open legs I was seeping irrefutable evidence of my arousal. This was complicated by the fact that he used my wide-open quim as a pen and pencil store. And after two hours of this treatment, I made a pretty messy one and each day would get a couple of strokes with a plastic ruler from Miss Dexter right across my lips when she extracted them and found them wet and sticky. As if it was not enough that I was jerked about by the myriads of shocks to my nipples and labia, they used my breasts as pin-boards and deliberately wrote each other memos which they pinned onto me.

By half past five, when I was freed and we all went to supper — myself usually dressed again because the housekeeper served us — I was well set up for the evening. Quite often that would entail a flogging or a bout of breast beating in the playroom stocks if we weren't going out, and then my master would retire to the library to read or watch television and I would attend him; serving drinks or, as I have already mentioned offering more intimate service. Sometimes he would dismiss me directly from the playroom and Miss Dexter would chain me to my bed. On those nights he would come for me later on and I loved being woken by him and being taken in the dark with my hands still chained to the headboard. More normally though we would go from the library up to his room and he would use me there before sending me off to my own room, where the inevitable Miss Dexter was waiting. Her devotion to him was so obvious that I couldn't understand why he never seemed to take her or mistreat her at all, although I knew perfectly well that she would willingly give herself utterly to him. Every time she freed me after a beating or chained me for the night, she would examine me all over with her cool hard fingers. She would plunge them deep inside me, even if I was still full of my master's sperm, and then wipe them over my breasts or bottom, and there was always a look of anguished longing on her face as she did so. She seemed so sad at those times that it almost embarrassed me to look at her. For a long time I just didn't understand what was going on and can only put it down to the fact that I was head over heels in love with my master.

He was the calm, cruel master I had always wanted. He was always in complete control of himself and those around him and most especially of me. He took his time with me, sometimes making me wait for what seemed like hours, naked and fearful before telling me in minute detail what he was going to do with me in the dungeon or the playroom. And he always did exactly what he said he would; if he told me he was going to give me thirty lashes with that exquisite whip with which he was such an artist, then thirty it would be regardless of whether I was begging for mercy or for more. If he told me how many needles he was going to use on me in the dungeon; then I knew that it would be precisely that number. And his voice would be so calm and implacable that when he had finished telling me what my fate was to be and he reached for my arm to lead me away; the merest touch of his fingers would sometimes induce a knee-buckling orgasm.

At the end of my first week with him he strapped me into the chair in the dungeon, my legs raised and spread in the stirrups and he shaved and ringed me. One ring in each nipple; one ring in each of my outer labia. Of course he didn't bother with anaesthetic and when he had finished he clipped a lead to one of the labial rings and took me out into the garden to show me off to Miss Dexter before telling her to take me to the playroom and flog me. I was so proud of those rings and the nakedness of my sex! And sometimes, when we had company he would attach discs to the rings on my 'flaps' as he called them which had his name on them. I often used to beg to be allowed to wear them when we went out to dinner or to the theatre or cinema and sometimes he let me — at the price of doubling any discipline I was due when we returned home.

Perhaps it sounds odd but there was, despite all I have said some degree of normality in our lives. After all, even the most dedicated slavegirl can't take a full whipping each and every day, so although I normally carried some bruises around, it was business as usual nevertheless. I issued press releases, organised stands at various shows, liased with advertising agencies and planning authorities when a new factory was to be built; in short acted as Master Gerald's right hand on all matters relating to the image of his companies. And as always I took a secret and tingling delight in carrying the marks of my master's hands just under the thin material of skirt and blouse or sweater. I had my own car and frequently undertook journeys to conduct meetings which kept me away from home overnight. I hated those times, but my master had a way of keeping me occupied even so. He used me as a piece of 'corporate hospitality' or as a reward for services rendered, so even while I was away from him I was frequently being beaten and mistreated or just casually screwed in an office or hotel somewhere. So even though I hated being away from him, I could take some pleasure in the way he debased me with such utter authority.

For nearly two years I existed in a dazzling world of blinding pleasure and pain. There were parties at the house where masters, mistresses and slaves mingled in erotic celebrations of SM.

I can recall the 'My favourite torture' party where each master or mistress brought along something they particularly liked using on their slave and one by one in the playroom all the slaves were subjected to the chosen implements. Fortunately I was allowed to play with myself while I watched the girls take their beatings or piercings or suspensions — or all three — otherwise I think I would have gone mad with frustration. There were some beautiful sights. I remember one girl had clamps put on her labia with short chains attached to them which were then wrapped around a huge stone. While she sat back on her heels with her legs apart there was no problem, but when her master stood up and took out his cock for her to suck, then she had to kneel up and take the stone with her. Of course her hands were cuffed behind her back and so she got a rousing cheer from everyone as she dutifully took the pain of her outrageously stretched 'flaps' and sucked him to ejaculation while moaning quietly all the time.

When my turn came I was suspended face up by wrists and ankles from a four cuff spreader bar which of course left my bum and everything in between wide open and spread taut for cropping. And I got a good dose of that across my buttocks before my master turned his attention to using the crop up between my legs, slapping the keeper down onto my clitoris while the shaft cracked home right between my lips. He took me to the point of orgasm before he stopped and inserted a speculum into my vagina and then opened it up to its maximum, making me feel as though he was splitting me in two and displaying the inside of my tunnel to everyone, quite plainly. I had to fight hard to restrain my orgasm as the masters crowded round to have a good look, but then my right wrist was released and I was handed a thick, lighted candle. I ignored the increased pain in my left arm — we had practised this several times in the preceding weeks and I hot waxed myself all round my sex and even inside it; howling and yelling as I did so. I made so much noise and the pain was so intense that even I couldn't rightly tell when, or how many times I came.

But that show was stolen by a girl who was placed on knees and elbows while her master first widened and then fisted her anal opening. When he had got it fully stretched and she was groaning loudly he screwed a bottle into her. But not by the neck. He actually managed to get the bottom of the bottle up her, leaving the neck projecting. Her face was a picture of distress by that time, but better was to come. It was a bottle of champagne and he pulled the cork before attaching a chain to her clitoral ring, running it up through a ring on her collar and leaving it on her back. Then all anyone had to do was pull on it and she would kneel up, dispensing champagne from her arse as the bottle tipped. The dominants got through a lot of bottles that night and it must have taken weeks for the poor thing's anus to close again!

Then there was the master's fiftieth birthday party where Miss Dexter inserted fifty needles in my stomach, thighs and breasts, in the end of each plastic handle on each needle was a lighted candle. I was strung up by my wrists in the playroom and all around me the guests' slaves were displayed — with me as the centrepiece in the darkened room. Then my master was shown in and I could see the pride in his eyes as he surveyed me. Of course he didn't blow out the candles, he whipped them out with his beloved whip, and even as the light declined with the candles progressively extinguished, he never missed, and never touched my body. Not until the very last one had been put out and the room lights had come up did he turn his attention to me. And then he thanked all his guests and returned their kindness by inviting them all to beat me in turn, however they liked. Even my diary does not record the exact events which followed, and it's hardly surprising really. For what must have been about two hours I continued as the centre of attention; I vaguely recall being suspended in a hog tie, then taken down and hauled up again by my ankles. I was bent over trestles and tables on my back and on my front and all the time there was a steady rain of blows from whips, crops, canes and paddles until I was barely conscious. But one thing remained clear in my memory; whenever I was able to see through my tears, I saw my master laughing and talking with his guests but always keeping an eye on me. And his expression was one of pure delight in me and the pleasure his guests were extracting from me. Agony and orgasm blended and blurred to perfection and I dared hope that in some small way my master returned my feelings for him.

I was right. But by the time I found that out for certain it was far too late for me.

He had originally said he would probably only keep me for a year or so. Consequently as the second year wore on and I bathed in his complete mastery of me I began to relax and think that at last I had found my true home. Ben sometimes came round with his new slave; a girl called Lisa and on occasions we shared exquisite sessions in the dungeon. But I never felt a trace of longing for the old days. They were gone. And I loved Master Gerald.

It was when we were putting the finishing touches to a plan for a plant along the M4 corridor that disaster struck. Both of us were scheduled to attend a meeting with the director of a firm which had tendered for the work. My master had been dealing with him and had been very impressed with the tender and this was really just to tie up a few loose ends. Before we set off he told me that he had reserved a room at the hotel, and if all went as he hoped then I would be offered to this man for an hour or two. I was always told in advance when I was going to be lent out so there was nothing unusual in that.

We eventually arrived at one of those roadhouse hotels you get by motorway junctions and entered the big open-plan lobby. My master looked around and hailed a solidly built man with fair hair who was rising to his feet in welcome. It was Guy.

Of course I had read somewhere that he had resigned his seat in the House and taken up a directorship but he was so firmly part of my past and I was so bound up in my present that I hadn't paid any attention to what his company was. I felt the blood drain from my face and my knees go weak as the full danger of my position began to be borne in on me. This was the man to whom I had offered myself behind Ben's back — twice. And Ben was one of my master's closest friends. One word from Guy... I just couldn't bear to think of the fury and disappointment on my master's face if he ever found out that I had put my own pleasure before my allegiance to Ben. And apart from that he would feel that he himself couldn't trust me ever again.

I tottered over behind my master and before I knew it he was introducing us and Guy was shaking my hand. His flesh felt cold and hard against mine, and I wondered how I could ever have wanted him as a master. The answer was simple; I hadn't met Gerald Hardcastle then.

Through the pounding of my heart I heard Guy explaining that he and I knew each other, and I waited for the axe to fall.

"Oh, yes," he was saying, "we're old sparring partners. We used to see a lot of each other round the House in the old days, didn't we Emma?"

I stammered out some reply and then to my amazement the two men turned straight to business. I sat mutely as coffee was served and drunk and the deal was done bar the paperwork which would be sorted out on our return and sent to Guy.

Then obviously well pleased both men sat back. I continued to stare at the table top, convinced that now it would surely happen but instead I heard my master offer me to Guy to play with for an hour or so and Guy accept with no reference to anything other than his previous life as an MP.

"That would be an honour indeed, Gerald," he said. "You have no idea how many of us lusted after her! And she really is your property? Well, well, I never would have guessed she was that way inclined! And may I er…?"

"Of course you can beat her if you want to," my master replied with obvious pleasure. "That big shoulder bag she's got has a coiled up whip in it. Feel free…"

And with that he sauntered over to the bar while Guy grinned at me then took my arm to lead me over to reception and get our key.

"How did I do?" he whispered. "I don't think he suspected anything."

I didn't answer, just checked in, took the key and followed him into the lift. He was up to something, it was obvious from his wide grin, but what?

Once we were inside the room I found out. He thrust me straight up against a wall and his hands began to roam all over me but I was far too tense to respond.

"Come on Emma," he said, still smiling, but suddenly with a real hint of menace in his voice. "I saved your bacon down there and I expect some gratitude. In fact I expect a lot of gratitude."

He let me go and I stayed propped up against the wall, breathless and now really terrified; I suddenly began to see how fast his mind must have worked once he had seen me walk into the hotel. I began to shake my head.

"Oh but yes, Emma. One word from me and your master finds out how selfish and deceitful you can be. Poor old Ben. Gerald really isn't going to like finding out how you were prepared to walk out on him — maybe even two-time him. But don't worry, just tell me everything that Gerald is thinking and doing and I promise I won't breathe a word."

"No, no I can't," I managed.

"Yes you can. You'll find that deceit gets easier the more you try it."

I threw myself at him, screaming insults but he sidestepped and I crashed onto the bed with his weight on top of me and his hand over my mouth.

"Calm down, you stupid bitch! You know you have no choice if you want to keep your precious master, and it's your own fault. I don't care if you hate me; in fact I'll enjoy that," he whispered and held me until he felt me calm down. Then he let me up.

He was right about everything of course and all I could do was nod brokenly.

"Good. You'll sort out a time to ring from your mobile each week and keep me up to date on everything you know; and I'll bet that's plenty."

I nodded again and tried to wipe the tears of despair from my eyes. Guy said I looked even more desirable in my dishevelled state and then added that he would have to beat me just to keep Gerald happy. "You'll hate every second of it of course, so it'll be a whole new experience for you. Now strip and bend over."

With more reluctance than I had felt since I became a slave I did as I was told, feeling his eyes crawling over me. I spread my legs, bent and gripped my ankles while Guy turned on the TV and upped the volume to mask the sounds of the beating. I comforted myself with the thought that at least I would feel nothing but pain this time, so I could experience it as pure punishment — I needed that.

And I got it. Guy had lost none of his vigour with a whip and slashed it across my spread buttocks with enthusiasm. I blinked back my tears and fought the desire to scream as the stinging mounted but no pleasure developed. He kept it up until I was biting my lip and rocking forwards at each lash. Then he stepped forward and tried to ram his fingers into me. Even through the burning and stinging in my bottom I knew I was as dry as a bone and I cried out in pain as my lips were roughly parted with no lubrication.

Guy tutted and came to stand in front of my head, I felt the leather of the lashes tickle my spine as he laid them lengthways down my back.

"I can make you open up, Emma. You know it. And we both know how much you'll hate yourself when I do."

I gritted my teeth and felt the lashes lift then crack down along the length of my bottom crease and bite along the length of my slit. I could even see the ends of the lashes bite into my bent stomach. Immediately I felt that treacherous tingle start in my nipples and spread downwards as the second lash smacked in. Once again it was no contest; my mind just couldn't override my body. Three, four, five, six. I had my eyes screwed shut on my tears but when Guy tried me again, through the bitter pain at my crotch I felt his fingers intrude easily and wetly.

He had me from behind on the bed and even as I hated him I moaned under his thrusts as the inescapable pleasure of his penetration mingled with the pain of the beating. My cries of orgasm were the final signals of my complete surrender once again.

I was not allowed to clean myself and climbed stiffly into the car afterwards. Master Gerald was well pleased with the state he found me in when he pulled into an empty lay-by, had me get out and lift my skirt.

"Good," he said. "That's a man who knows how to treat a woman like you."

I kept it up for six long months. Betraying the secrets of my master's business empire every week, yet somehow still managing to stay cheerful and obedient even while my conscience gnawed at me, day after day. I told myself that I was only doing it for his sake, and that somehow I would find a way out of the mess I was in.

To make matters worse, Guy demanded the use of me regularly. I managed to disguise the marks he left by arranging it so that I saw him after I had been given to someone on an overnight stay. So I would dress hurriedly after I had been finished with, check out and drive to Northamptonshire where he had a cottage — sometimes not arriving until well after midnight. But that didn't stop him. The main room had exposed beams and from one of them he had hung chains. As soon as I was through the door I was put to stripping and buckling on restraints for wrist or ankle suspension. I always managed to take the floggings which followed as the punishment I so richly deserved, but Guy always managed to add a little extra something; nipple or labia clamps or needles; something I was helpless to resist, and he always made me come despite myself. Knowing in advance that I was going to be flogged and that I was not going to enjoy it at all was a wholly new torment; and it was one Guy played on, beating me hard and long and enjoying every agonised sound I made.

Fortunately my master was particularly busy at that time and we worked a lot at his office in the factory near the house, and he returned home tired and preoccupied, so somehow I managed to get away with just saying that I was going through a period of pretty hard use.

But I wasn't just passively putting up with all this. I racked my brains for a way out. Gina was obviously Guy's weak spot — that had to be why he always had me report to that cottage rather than his house in North London. He obviously didn't want to lose her despite her absurd possessiveness. But that was no help; if I blew the whistle on him, he would simply do the same to me and I had more to lose. But at last a desperate plan formed; I just had to silence Guy. I began to make some trips up to London and contact some old journalist friends and slowly I made progress. I was returning from one of these expeditions in high good humour, having made some arrangements and feeling better than I had done for months when I walked into the office in the house and found Gina there along with my master and Miss Dexter.

I stood rooted to the spot. I was too late.

My master looked ashen and suddenly older, Miss Dexter looked stunned and Gina was triumphant.

"Tell us again," my master told her in a dead tone.

Gina was a weird mix of slave and jealous mistress; she must have kept closer tabs on Guy than even he suspected. She had 'overheard' a phone conversation when I had rung Guy, she had heard him call me by name, she had also heard a lot of other names, including that of one of my master's businesses and once Guy was out of the way she had rung it and by sheer persistence had got through to the master himself. It was clear that she only saw it as infidelity and had no idea of what she had really overheard. Still, it was enough.

By the time she had finished I was leaning against the doorjamb for support. My master made out a cheque for Gina and thanked her for having come to him. She took it and pushed roughly past me and Miss Dexter hurried after to see her out.

My master stood up from behind the desk. "Well?" he asked

Gina had only touched on some aspects of the story, she hadn't been there when I begged Guy to take me as a slave, she only suspected something between us after that session at the hotel but I felt an overwhelming need to unburden myself of everything and just let things take their course. I couldn't fight any more and so I told him everything, going right back to my exclusive on Guy, the session, how I had begged him to take me, and how he had blackmailed me.

A powerful man like Gerald Hardcastle is no joke to be around when he literally shakes with pent up fury, as he did then. Apart from any sexual treachery, for six months his every move had been known to his rivals and competitors. And all I had to protect myself was my desire to take my punishment once and for all and to give him what pleasure I could while he did what he had to.

"If it'll give you any fun, I'll fight you," I told him as he advanced on me.

It came out all wrong, I meant it with heart-felt sincerity but he must have interpreted it as 'fuck you' sullen defiance because the dam of his fury broke instantly.

I was dragged by my hair, kicking and screaming in genuine fear from the office, down the main stairs, along past the pool and then down to the dungeon. We rolled and fought there for a while as he ripped my clothes off with a strength I had never encountered in him before, and to which I responded even through my fear. At last though, I lay in a tangled heap on the carpet, naked apart from laddered stockings. I looked up at him through a curtain of tangled hair, "Go on! Do it!" I urged him and then shrieked as he dragged me up and pushed me towards an upright rectangular frame; one that had a studded beam across it at breast height.

I managed another fight to make him exert himself before he could cuff and restrain my wrists and ankles to the corners. By then we were both panting for breath, but at least my master looked back in control of himself and had lost that drawn look I had hated to see. He was flushed and furious still, but at least he was where he liked to be. Sure he was going to take everything out on me — and why not — but at least he would enjoy himself now instead of just doing it as a duty.

Miss Dexter came in with a pile of folders.

"Right, you lying treacherous little bitch!" my master spat at me, "you're going to tell me everything you told that bastard! Everything! Miss Dexter, find me the Grosvenor file!"

I just clenched my teeth and prepared to hold out as best I could, so he would enjoy torturing me.

He went behind me and I heard him go to the whip rack. I glanced at Miss Dexter and saw she was spreading out the folders and getting ready to take notes. It was going to be a long and very painful session. There were a lot of files I was to be interrogated about.

I was distracted from that line of thought though as my first flogging got underway. Usually in our dungeon sessions the whips were used to warm up and sensitise the area of the body the master wanted to work on later. But this time he set off at full punishment strength. He used one of the thin bladed floggers and worked it hard across my back and buttocks, making me jerk forward as each lash slapped into me. I welcomed the burn and bite of the leathers and had no trouble in experiencing it all as pure pain, especially when he finished off with three scything upper cuts between my legs. I was still recovering from the shock of that scalding pain when he came to stand just the other side of the studded bar across my chest, reached out, hooked my nipple rings with his fingers and dragged my breasts out across the studs, then pulled them down. I shrieked again as I felt the studs begin to dig into their undersides.

He left one nipple and held the other while he reached to one side of the frame and took down a length of chain with a hook at each end and attached it to the ring. Then he did the same with the other. I braced myself for what I was sure would follow, and sure enough he went to one wall and took down several of the long steel weights I had always loved to hate. He placed them on the beam in a pile and then picked just one up and hung it on the end of one chain. I sucked in my breath as one nipple was elongated and its breast was pulled down onto the studs even harder.

"Now, you slut! The Grosvenor project. What did you tell him and when?"

Before I could even frame an answer another weight was hung off the other nipple and he was reaching for more. Desperately I racked my brains, even as a third and fourth weight were added. I glanced down and saw my nipples extended into grotesquely long pink tubes with the holes the rings passed through clearly visible. They hurt with a sharpness I hadn't experienced before and my stomach clenched in fear, but at least that freed my tongue. I began to babble out everything I could remember while remorselessly more weights were added until my breasts were stretched into almost flat wedges of flesh across the beam and the nipples themselves had all but disappeared over the far edge.

"Please! I don't remember any more!" I screamed.

"Did you get all that down, Miss Dexter? Good. Then we'll move on to the Pro-Con launch, in just a minute."

Oh God! The launch of some industrial software which had been 'mysteriously' forestalled by another company. How much Guy made on that I never did find out but I tried to marshal my thoughts against the intensity of pain from my tortured breasts, then sobbed in despair when I saw him approaching me with a riding crop. I opened my mouth to beg but could only scream instead as he flicked the keeper down across each breast in turn, stinging the stretched flesh and driving the studs in even harder. He did it twice more before I was sagging in my chains and he was removing the weights and unhooking the chains. But then he turned his attention below stairs.

He ducked down and I felt the chains being hooked onto my labial rings. I didn't wait. I began to mumble everything I knew about Pro-Con regardless of whether it was any part of what I had told Guy. But even as I gabbled the weights went on... and on. There was a searing pain from where the rings went through the flesh and panic was rising in my throat but I kept babbling faster and faster until I reached the end in a shrill scream.

"I got the bitch's every word, sir," I heard Miss Dexter's voice call.

Slowly the pressure was released as the weights came off and I breathed out in relief as my ankles and wrists were freed. My master walked off then to prepare my next torment and left me to peel my own throbbing breasts off that wretched bar and marvel at the fact that I still had any. A quick exploration between my legs reassured me that I still had my vulva intact. But then my master was coming for me again.

He pushed me over to a bench, whirled me round and made me sit down on its cold leather top.

"The plant in Aylesbury next," he announced as he lifted and spread my legs, strapping them into stirrups mounted on the end of the bench. I made no move to struggle and propped myself up on my arms while he worked, trying just to get my breath back. I didn't think for one second that my crotch or breasts had had their full ration for the day and was not surprised to see him go for the whip again and come to stand between my open legs. I shifted my arms behind me to get comfortable. I knew he wanted me to sit up so I could see the lashes landing on my already throbbing sex which was so naked and vulnerable. I gritted my teeth again and grimaced in defiance. I had always had a good tolerance of the whip, so he would enjoy giving me a good thrashing before I broke this time.

He raised his arm and brought the lashes down. I grunted as the scarlet blades of pain exploded inside me. But I kept my eyes open and defied him to do his worst. Again and again he lashed at me and at last I couldn't take any more.

My confession that time was punctuated by cries as he continued with the whip, "The Oxford meeting... Aah! I told him about the costings... Aah!" And so on until finally he stood back and I was allowed to collapse backwards, panting and sweating heavily while my hands cupped my abused and swollen lips. To the best of my dazed recall I had taken over thirty lashes. But almost immediately he was raising and cuffing my wrists and we were off again.

This time he went back to work on my breasts. He put them in the press and screwed it down till the bars squeezed my boobs into flattened travesties of their normal shape, immediately I could feel the blood pound in them and knew that within minutes they would start to darken and tighten even more against the brutal steel. But in the meantime I had the needles to contend with. He put three through each areola. With all his usual slow deliberation he took pinches of skin and threaded the sharp little points through. To my mind needle play is all about how it looks, not just the sensation of the sharp points pushing slowly at the flesh and then bursting through with their sharp jolts of pain. And even though I knew that my master's anger would rob me of any pleasure, I craned my head up to watch and gasp at each sharp prick of pain on entry and exit. He worked in silence and I knew the questioning would only start again when something worse was done. Indeed once my breasts were pounding and darkened to a deep pink shading into purple and the piercings were throbbing, he produced two large candles and lit them.

"Oh, no! Please!" I begged.

"Miss Dexter, get the Salford file!"

However hardened I have become to the whip, I have never got used to hot waxing. The sunburst of pain as each drop hits you and then intensifies before the heat dissipates, is to me a new agony each time I undergo it.

I began to babble everything I knew about the takeover of one of the master's subsidiary companies by a competitor. And all the time he tilted the candles each time the wax built up and let the scalding drops fall over nipples, areola and the breasts themselves.

"That's all, master!" I shrieked when I had come to the end of everything I could think of.

All he did was go and stand between my open legs.

"Who the fuck cares, Emma?" he said. "What I paid Ben for you isn't one tenth of what you've cost me! I'm going to get my money's worth."

I watched him hold up the candles and begin to tip them, then I put my head back and howled as the wax cascaded down over my clitoris, my already swollen labia, my inner thighs. My whole genital region was a blaze of pain under a stiff coating by the time he had finished and even my throat hurt from screaming. But at least that seemed to calm him down somewhat and the last part of my inquisition was carried out under a partial breast suspension, rings and chains attached to the needles and then hauled up tight to a beam overhead so that a good part of the weight of my torso hung from my suffused and pounding breasts. The questions went on and on, punctuated by slashes of the riding crop and my answering shrieks of pain which were followed by a whispered confession. At long last all the wax around my belly and my breasts had been sheared off, but the beating went on and I lay with my eyes closed and bucked my pelvis up to accept the next lash of pain. And at last I came. Behind my closed eyelids I bathed in the seething mass of aches and pains and eventually let myself drown in them as I heard my master's voice resume its normal quiet authority as he instructed Miss Dexter to come to him. I felt that I had paid my debt, ridden out the storm and now everything would be all right again.

But when I finally opened my eyes again, I could hardly believe them. Miss Dexter was kneeling in front the master and taking long, slow sucks of his stiffly jutting erection. As I watched in amazed horror, he put his head back and began to spend himself in her mouth. She made mewing noises of delight as he spurted into her and she ducked her head to cram as much of him into her as she could.

As he finished pumping, he smiled down at me while Miss Dexter dutifully licked him clean.

"Now, Emma. I'm going to punish you."

Terror and excitement immediately had my blood pounding. I knew what he meant; I had told him all my professional treachery, now there was the fact that I had betrayed a master.

He undid all my bonds and I cried out all over again as the breast press was loosened and then I had to remove the needles myself, a task which was as exciting as it was painful. Then I hobbled after him all the way up to the playroom, splaying my legs and waddling to allow some air to cool the tortured flesh between them. But once we were in the echoing space of the playroom, I forgot all my existing pains. My wrists were raised and clipped to a single chain which was then pulled up until I was on tiptoe. That meant only one thing; a full body whipping. With my wrists joined and with my toes just able to get enough purchase on the floor, I would be susceptible to every flinch and twist a girl is liable to perform under a hard flogging and that would in effect allow my own body to condemn itself to receive the next lash on whichever bit was presented. But at least my master was back with me, taking his pleasure with me and I knew how I would respond when I saw him take down his favourite whip.

"Master," I whispered hoarsely. "I'm afraid I'll come under this punishment."

He let the full length of the lash uncoil over the floor and watched my involuntary shudder. "You may. It makes no difference."

Then I knew I was in for a really hard punishment. He was quite well aware that repeated climaxes under a whip like that are every bit as exhausting as the punishment itself.

And sure enough he started on my back using every bit of his artistry to curl it around my ribs as well as crack it across my back itself and soon I was twisting on the end of my chain and the frayed tip was carving marks on my stomach. He shifted to my buttocks and made me jerk one leg up and then the other as he worked on them and my flanks. Sometimes he would flick in a quick lash before my leg was down and the tip would wrap round a thigh and bury itself gleefully directly in my sex and send me hysterically and helplessly spinning and hopping. Then he went back up to my shoulders, catching me by surprise and making twist almost right round in pain, so that I caught the next one across my stretched taut breasts. I could no longer scream so even when I came as a flurry of lashes cracked across my delta, I made no sound.

He gave me pauses to get my breath back every now and then. But as soon as my head was up again; he struck, and I went back into my agonised dance. At last even my well developed responses to whipping failed me. I could no longer tell what was pain or pleasure, I could no longer even hear the whip striking, I simply hung inert; absorbing the continuing flogging and enduring. I have subsequently seen the video of that monumental whipping and it is one of the most exciting things I have ever seen. By the time the slender figure dangling on the end of its chain is finally still, only the faintest twitches registering the impacts of the whip, it is striped from neck to knees, front, back and sides. Small rivulets of crimson trickle from cuts where some welts cross and the head hangs forwards between the straining shoulders.

But what made me come instantly when I watched it was the sound that filled the room when the master approached his whipped-raw slave, it was the hoarse sound of the girl rasping out her thanks.

The following day I was allowed to remain naked and in my room. I spent most of it under the shower or in the bath, easing off the soreness. Miss Dexter came and went, looking very much more relaxed and calmer than I had ever seen her before, and it didn't take a genius to work out why. Through her I got a message to my master to say that if he looked in my handbag in the office he would find proof of how devoted I was to him, all appearances to the contrary. I knew he would find a substantial amount of cash and a name and address. The journalist contacts I had renewed in London were all investigative and they had provided me with the name of a well known hit man, with whom I had agreed the price of working Guy over enough to silence him. Pretty desperate I know, but it had been all I could think of.

Master Gerald came to see me in the afternoon. I sat naked on my bed while he prowled round the room.

"What am I to do with you, Emma? I've checked on your story but it doesn't alter the fact that you, and no one else but you, got yourself into this, and the damage you've done..." He let the sentence hang in the air between us. "And of course you'll have to answer to Ben."

I nodded miserably; I had known I would sooner or later.

But any fear of that encounter was driven out of my mind by being told to undress him. He took me on the bed; his weight on me re-igniting the fires of my weals and I groaned and heaved under him in a long and luxurious series of orgasms until at last he spent himself deep inside me and I slept happily afterwards.

At the end of a week I was pretty well back to normal, apart from a spectacular display of bruises which were nevertheless fading. But the household had changed, I was no longer required to work with the master and sat, bored and frustrated in my room. At last I began to read over the diaries which recounted my downfall and began to make the notes which formed the basis of the story you are now reading. It also became obvious that Miss Dexter — Julia as I now had to learn to call her — had supplanted me. She was sent to me most nights when the master had finished with her and in the dark she climbed into bed beside me — no longer the master's servant in authority over me; now a sister slave. It was the master's way of comforting me while he thought about what to do, and each time she came to me I would seek out the traces of him, exploring her body in the dark, finding out which entrance he had used and licking his seed from her while my fingers traced the ridges of her floggings and canings. And as she progressed, I frequently found my fingers tracing the deep grooves that ropes had carved into her breastflesh during a suspension or bondage session.

From her I learned the nature of her particular slavery up to that point. The master had perceived how much she worshipped him and had played on that ruthlessly. He had held her at arm's length, allowing her only to reach him through the medium of his slaves. She could only taste and feel his spend at second hand, as it oozed out of our bodies, (I was the fourth slave to have passed through this house, I learned). And she was held perfectly between hating us, through envy, and loving us as the only point of contact she had with him; consequently she made an ideal punisher, wielding the whip with real venom and extracting all the pleasure she could from it. However neither of us could work out why the master had suddenly chosen to change her role so dramatically.

One damp and overcast day about two and a half weeks after my interrogation, Julia came to me with an order to dress and present myself in the main hall. It was the first time I had been dressed in all that time and went nervously and uncomfortably down to the hall. The master was waiting for me outside in the Range Rover and we drove in silence for a long time, heading south and east as far as I could tell.

"May I speak, master?" Eventually I had to know if my suspicions were correct.

Permission was granted and I asked whether we were going to Ben's house. We were and I relapsed into a tense silence.

It was raining when we reached the house, which had obviously been a family seat for generations, and it was just what I had expected, standing at the back of immaculate lawns and surrounded by horse paddocks.

My master stopped the car some distance down the drive and turned to me.

"Out you get, Emma. Walk down the side of the house and out to the stables. I'll be back in an hour or so when he's finished with you," he said. And then added in reply to my nervous swallow. "Go on. You know you've got to pay before you can move on."

I stepped out into the rain and watched the car turn and leave me. Then, feeling very small and alone I walked on. The rain was quite heavy by then and I quickened my step, skirting the porticoed front door and walking on a path which ran alongside the house, through an ornamental garden, through a walled rose garden and which finally brought me to the stable yard. It was obviously a working yard and was muddy and cobbled. Puddles were everywhere, in amongst bits of straw and the traces of horses. I picked my way across the morass, smelling the rich animal scent and trying to avoid the puddles and the droppings.

"Get a move on!" a voice called.

I looked up and saw Janet standing in the doorway of a stable. I smiled in instant recognition but received no encouragement; she just stood with hands on hips, dressed in sensible pullover and jeans and waited for me. I went as fast as I could and found myself in the deeply straw littered stable itself.

"You bloody fool, Emma," was all the greeting I got. "Get your kit off and get these restraints on."

I was pretty crushed by her hostility, but then she belonged to Ben's wife so the slur I had cast on Ben was obviously keenly felt even by her. I sighed and did as I was told, until I had the familiar feel of leather at ankles and wrists again, and was shivering slightly, my hair in rats tails from the rain.

"He won't be bothered with punishing you himself," a female voice boomed out. I turned to see Clair glowering at me from the door. "Says he wasted enough time on you. So I'm in charge, you slimy bitch — and by God you're going to know all about it!"

I stuttered out something about being sorry, but I might as well not have bothered. Janet grabbed my hands and clipped my wrists together behind my back. As bravely as I could I straightened my back and faced my final punishment.

"We'll start with a little walk, I think. The whip will bite better for her being cold and wet," Clair announced.

Janet pushed me towards the door to the yard but I hung back as I had discarded even my shoes, and the ooze outside did not appeal one bit. But Janet reached over to one wall and took down a crop which she swung hard at my backside, and yelping at the sudden sting I stumbled out naked into the rain and the muck. The mud squelched coldly between my toes and the rain immediately began to run in rivulets down my face and chest.

Clair was dressed for riding and as soon as I was outside I saw she had a horse already saddled up. My mouth went dry with fear as I saw a chain hanging from its saddle. But before I could do anything, Janet's strong hands grabbed my elbows and pushed me towards it. Clair mounted and stared down at me as I squinted up into the rain.

"Hitch her up Janet, and I'll take her for a spin before we get down to the real thing," she said with an evil grin.

Janet freed my wrists, brought them round in front and clipped them to the end of the chain. I stared at her in wide-eyed fright as she did so.

"You'll like this. I sometimes get taken for a spin before a beating, it makes it hurt like hell!" Then for the first time she smiled, but it wasn't friendly at all.

Clair put her heels to the horse and it set off. I tried to make some plea or other for mercy but the chain was paying out and I could see I had no choice but to follow it. And at first it was bearable, the horse walked slowly and I was able to hop and slither behind it, avoiding some of the worst of the slime, but very soon we were in an orchard and then it started. Without even glancing back, Clair set her heels to the horse again and it broke into a trot. With a wail of despair I tried to break into a run to keep up. But running with your hands in front of you is not easy. Clair guided the horse in a wide circuit which took us round the perimeter of the orchard, my feet were getting frozen from the wet grass even by the time we had made just one circuit. By the end of the second, I was gasping for breath, soaked and chilled to the bone.

At last Clair deigned to turn and look at me.

"Please! Stop!" I begged between gasps, but she simply turned away and once again urged the horse on. It broke into a canter and I was wrenched off my feet as my shoulders felt as though they had been dislocated. Suddenly I found the grass rushing by just below my face, big bits of earth flung by the hooves flew past me, while my whole front was now being banged and jolted by any unevenness in the ground, sometimes these threw me onto my back and I spun helplessly as I was dragged along with no hope of getting my feet under me, almost winded by the buffeting. But the real point of the exercise only came when we turned at the first corner to follow the edge of the orchard. My own impetus sent me spinning wide of the horse as it turned and I was into the long grass at the bottom of the boundary hedge. I screamed and yelled as I was pulled through nettles and trailing briars before the chain yanked me back onto the relative safety of the shorter grass. But at the next corner the same thing happened, and again a further two times before the horse stopped and I lay in a bedraggled heap, sore and burning from nettle stings and scratches to every part of my body; breasts, stomach, thighs, bottom crease and even the inner thighs and sex as well. But before I could get my breath back there was another agonising tug on my shoulders as the horse walked on, and this time took me back into the yard. It went slowly so I didn't get hurt by the cobbles, instead I just got a thorough dunking in every puddle and every pile of filth and mud until at last we stopped. All I could do was lie there wallowing in the dirt while I got my breath back, and as I was unclipped from the chain, ease my aching shoulders.

"Douse the filthy bitch down, then let's get on with it. Ben's got business later and he wants to see her once she's finished with."

I screamed again as a jet of icy water hit me, blasting off all the muck but hitting my skin like a shotgun blast of needles. I tried to roll away from it but Clair held my wrists and all I could do was twist and writhe until I was deemed clean enough to carry on receiving my punishment. I was dragged up by my hair and supported by both women as they half carried me into the stable again and blearily I saw what came next.

It was just as well they had weakened me so well. If I had seen that thing when I first arrived I would have run for it. At first glance it was just a wooden pony such as I had had to ride many times for my master's pleasure in the past. But even that had always been a particularly lingering torment; even when the crossbar between my legs had been smooth. This one's crossbar had been carved into serrated ridges like blunt saw teeth which ran along the top edge.

I whimpered and tried to pull away but had no chance against the two of them. They simply lifted me bodily and dumped me down hard, with one leg on either side of the bar. I shrieked immediately, the bar was narrow and immediately cut between my lips to dig at the inner flesh of my sex. Whoever had done the carving knew the female anatomy intimately. Even when my sex was in the valley between two ridges, the one in front pressed hard on the clitoris while the one behind was close against the anus. And apart from anything else I had been lacerated and stung even in those crevices and was shivering with cold.

Janet wrenched my arms up and fastened my wrists to a chain which hung from the rafters while Clair knelt and shackled my ankles to rings set in the lower beams which ran the length of the thing.

"Now then," Clair began, picking up a whip and running its lashes through her fingers. "I expect Gerald has thrashed you, but like any man would, I expect he took charge of your torment."

"Yes, mistress," I murmured.

"Well, you're in the hands of a woman today and I'm going to make you torture yourself. And right on that greedy cunt of yours so you'll know that the worst of what you're going to suffer is all because you just can't get enough. Janet, you flog from the left and if I even think you're holding back. I'll flay your udders off, understand?"

"Yes, mistress."

I was still too dazed to take in the full import of what had been said but it soon became clear. They flogged my back in turns, from left and right, the lashes overlapping in the centre and giving me a double dose of their deep stinging. The cold made it worse and the wet on my skin dampened and stiffened the lashes. I began writhing and crying out almost at once.

And then the second element came into play, as I wriggled and jerked under the heavy impacts I found I was grinding my clit harder and harder against the wood of the ridge in front of me. So despite my fear, my previous hurts and the whipping with wet lashes that I was now suffering I began the inevitable spiral upwards. Soon I was using the impacts on my back to try and hurl myself forwards onto the wood, but it wasn't enough, I needed to get my weight fully onto the clit itself. I couldn't use my feet so I grasped my chains and tried to haul myself up but of course the chains at my ankles pulled tight and hindered me. But as the whips smacked down relentlessly I hung and struggled, grinding myself and pulling up until at last, stretched as though on a rack, my whole weight teetered on the sharp summit of the ridge. The lashes came down even harder and I twisted and ground my poor nubbin on the point until starbursts exploded in my brain and I came and came again, and then slumped down into the next valley, jarring myself agonisingly as I thumped down onto the wood. They let me gather myself and started in again. This time yelling encouragements as I grimaced in pain and agonised pleasure, but grimly began to rub against the next ridge.

"Come on, you cunt! Get up there and grind that clit!"

"Come on Emma, you slut! Let me see you really hurt yourself this time!"

Once again I hauled at my wrists while the whips hissed and smacked, stretching myself and hungering for the climactic pain as I balanced my whole weight on my clitoris and crushed it against the crest of the wooden ridge. I made it and again exploded into orgasm before thumping down into the next valley. By now my whole vulva was one blaze of hot pain and as my wrists and ankles were fixed, by moving my pelvis two ridges along, my legs and arms were pulling back and my spine was arched.

The whips stopped for a second.

"Want to go for another, you slut?" Clair asked.

My head hung back between my shoulders and she pushed my hair forward to clear my back for more punishment.

"Yes, mistress," I moaned, well aware that I was condemning my crotch to more abuse but helpless to deny myself the pleasure.

"You're a greedy little painslut, aren't you Emma?" she asked again.

"Yes, mistress."

They drove me over another peak and I roared and shouted in hysteria as I bucked my pelvis on the summit once more, scarlet shards of agony mingling with the bright bursts of ecstasy as my stomach clenched, my cunt spasmed and I tortured myself into a merciful blackness. They left me for some time then, but came back and drove me over two more devastating ridges, until the pounding from my crotch was an all consuming physical shout. But I was so far gone I didn't care. I just wanted all I could take.

By then I was bent back like a bow, my pelvis thrust well ahead of the rest of me.

Janet gave me a drink of cold water and again I was allowed a rest; which was just as well because when they started again, they drove me back along the saw teeth.

This time they breast whipped me to make me draw back, and again I had to haul myself up to the point of almost dislocating my hips before I could mount the summit behind me and then make my raw clit and stinging vulva suffer some more as I bucked and howled under the whips. But from then on they hardly needed the whips. I was in some kind of trance; I just couldn't wait to torture myself again and hauled up on my wrists as soon as I could find the strength; just the occasional lash across my nipples or a hard twist on them was enough to spur me on.

Dimly I realised that I shouldn't be doing this to myself but still I couldn't stop. It was as though every ounce of masochism in me had been suddenly liberated and was out of control. I think I might have babbled some pleas for mercy, but it was me who was my torturer now and my next words were probably ones encouraging myself to find the strength for another pull and another agonising grind on a ridge.

Eventually I just couldn't go on and stayed slumped in a valley, though I was still making little thrusting movements with my pelvis. But I was lifted off and laid on the floor

Janet and Clair just left me sprawled there and stood over me for a minute or two before Clair dug the toe of her riding boot into my ribs and flipped me onto my back, still clutching my swollen and raw crotch.

"See?" she said. "With a slut like you, one only needs to give you the opportunity to torture yourself."

I understood that perfectly well by then. I knew I wasn't going to be able to walk for days, I hurt far more than I could ever remember having done before — and mostly it was all my own work.

"Haul her up, Ben's waiting," she added and they dragged my groaning carcass back out to the yard. There they let me fall into the muck and Janet pulled my arms down by my sides before cruelly kicking my thighs and ordering me to get my knees under me. I managed that and she clipped my wrist restraints to those at my ankles. This left me no option but to turn my face to the side as it was squashed down into the mud. She yanked on my matted hair and pulled me up a little.

"See where Ben is? Crawl to him!" she hissed.

I could see where he was alright. He was standing just inside the orchard — on the far side of the gateway where cars or tractors had churned the mud into deep, water-filled ruts, he carried an umbrella to keep the rain off him, I noticed.

Two things immediately became clear even to my pain-dulled mind. Ben might have humiliated me by not bothering to punish me himself, but he had saved the ultimate humiliation all for himself. The only way I could crawl was by shuffling one knee forward at a time, using my face as a kind of plough as I inched my way through the mire and muck. And to think that I had betrayed him because I wanted a harder master! This was exquisite submission and I began to shuffle my way out into the soiled straw, the puddles of water and the rest of the filthy mess. My cheek rubbed along the slick cobbles and pushed a brown and green bow-wave ahead of me. I pressed my lips tight together as I inched my way across the yard with Clair walking beside me. She whacked me hard across the buttocks if I dared stop for a rest or tried to raise my face to get a breath of clean air.

But when I finally reached the gateway I could go no further, they couldn't seriously expect me to nose my way through the depths of water that now lay in front of me. I clearly remembered that I had sunk in well over my ankles when I had had to walk through it behind the horse. I would drown at the pace I was going; it just couldn't be done.

I tried to protest but Clair raised the crop high and brought it scything down so hard that I saw a spray of moisture and mud fly up before I shut my eyes and screamed. Twice more she lashed me with all her strength and it was enough. I just couldn't take any more pain and I longed to abase myself before Ben and finally finish what I had started.

Grimly I drew a series of deep breaths and pushed into the first rut, burying my face in the inches of freezing, scum-covered water and the ooze which lay beneath. I lost my hearing as the water closed over my left ear. Desperately I spread my knees as far apart as I could and pushed frantically. My nose was blocked and I was close to panic when at last I broke clear and lay gasping, spitting and choking on the small bank in the middle of the track. But of course the last bit was the worst, and I moaned as I twisted my head to look forward. The far part of the rut had broken down and the water had mixed with the small lake which surrounded a nearby horse trough. There was about four feet of water and thick, glutinous mud ahead of me. It may not sound much but from ground level and when you are going to have to plough through it face first...

I was still getting an energetic thrashing as I squirmed forward and if I had had enough breath I would have screamed at Clair that I had had enough, but as it was I gathered what little strength I had left and wriggled forwards again. Once again the muck closed over me and my face shovelled slowly on until I thought my lungs would burst, but finally I felt grass under my cheek and realised that I had done it. Ben's boots were beside my face and Clair was releasing my wrists.

Thankfully I got up onto my forearms and looked back down my body. Every inch of my front was covered in slime and mud, and worse. My hanging boobs were chocolate coloured mounds and I had spread my knees so far apart to squirm forwards that even my crotch was dark brown. But at least the cold goo had soothed some of the pain in that region.

"Whip her while she licks my boots," I heard Ben say dispassionately.

Immediately Clair set to work, once again wielding her crop across my buttocks and back, the cord and leather smacking wetly onto my body and carving brilliant lines of agony into my dazed mind. But at least I was near the end now and I stuck out my tongue and licked every trace of mud from his boots, even finding the first stirrings of arousal under the lashing as I abased myself utterly at Ben's feet.

"Forgive me, sir," I said at last when the boots were immaculately clean. "I'm sorry." I dropped my forehead to the ground before him and waited. I was pretty sure what was coming and sure enough after a few seconds I felt the warm liquid splashing on my back and watched the gold droplets carve their way through the mud which caked me.

"It's no longer of any importance to me," Ben said when he had finished. "But if it helps you, then, yes. I have finished with you now."

Then he turned and left me.

My master arrived shortly afterwards and Janet helped the bedraggled, filth-streaked slave into the plastic sheeted boot, and in the dark I smiled amidst my pains. All my debts were paid.

POSTSCRIPT.

It took nearly a fortnight for the swellings and abrasions between my legs and all over me to fully heal and subside. And it was Julia who nursed me — as it had been she who had sluiced down the wreckage which had arrived back from Ben's, and which had rolled out onto the drive, completely limp and exhausted when the boot had been opened.

In the month which has followed from then, I have had nothing to do except to prepare this journal and that task is nearly done now so I can face up to my future. What that holds was explained to me when I was summoned to the library one evening. My heart was thumping as I followed Julia in; I dared to hope that I might be receiving my master's attentions once again. He had not touched me since my return and although I slept with Julia nearly every night, kissing another girl's welts is no substitute for the savage joy of taking the kiss of the leathers oneself.

But it was not to be. Julia and I knelt before him and he explained his plans. He had decided to reorganise his household; he would keep Julia as a slave for the time being and maybe purchase another in due course, but he would never again mix slave owning and business. I had got in behind his defences, he admitted ruefully — both emotionally and commercially — and he would not allow that to happen again, it was one reason why he had finally taken Julia — to demolish everything which had gone before. My heart sank as I realised how close I had come to obtaining everything I wanted, and had lost it.

I was going to be auctioned, he told me. He considered that kinder than setting me free and I have come to appreciate that fact. But on that evening I was devastated and even being allowed to watch Julia Dexter being soundly flogged in the playroom was small comfort. But when the whip was finally put aside and he buggered her while she was still bound on the trestle, I was allowed to lick him clean afterwards before licking his emission out of her. I knew it would be the last time I would taste him. And so it has proved.

The auction is now only two days away and tomorrow we travel up to London. In front of me as I write is the card which prospective purchasers will be given. The reserve price is flatteringly high! And the picture; a vidcap of me hung by the wrists in the playroom, is also very complimentary. All my vital statistics are listed, including my ankle and wrist cuff sizes, and then in a section labelled 'General' it reads.

'The slave currently goes under the name of Emma, but should be given a slave name. She is obedient and very tough under the whip, as well as responsive to all forms of mistreatment. However she is intelligent and can be headstrong, she really requires continual discipline — of the harshest nature."

And then under 'Reason for Sale'

"Master has become over-fond."

Several men have been to have a preview and I have been paraded in the library, naked and on a lead from my labial rings. I found it intensely exciting and am now really looking forward to a new life — how well my master judged me! Above everything else it seems — even him — I love slavery itself. I felt so wonderfully alive and feminine as male eyes devoured me, assessing me for the pleasure I could give them; speculating aloud with my master as to how many lashes I could endure on my back, buttocks, breasts etc. I loved the way their strong hands opened my sex and their fingers casually rummaged inside me and comments were passed about the speed and quantity of my lubrication, before it was wiped off on my stomach. All of them had me bend over while they explored my back entrance and my breasts and buttocks were closely examined and discussed for their contours, skin tone and ability to soak up everything from beatings to piercings. Best of all, once the examinations were over and drinks were being served, I was allowed to masturbate to orgasm in front of them; just to prove what a complete slut I have become.

And so the story of Emma comes to an end. I don't know what name I will live under in the future, or where I will live or what adventures in slavery lie before me.

But I am very happy to be leaving Emma behind; once and for all.

JANUARY 23RD. 2008. LEEDS.

I can't help but smile at those final words! Mr O'Kane did a splendid job of putting together all my notes and jottings and I'm very grateful both to him and the editor of Silver Moon for having given Emma a life in print. But those final words are perhaps best attributed to exuberant artistic licence! I am still stubbornly proud of being Emma!

The editor has informed me that some readers have been kind enough as to enquire what happened to me after the period covered by my original journals and so I am delighted and thrilled to contribute these extra pages to a brand new edition of 'Emma'.

The auction was held at a semi-derelict hotel, I was taken there hooded and trussed in the boot of the car so can't really tell where it was, and I was only allowed out when it was time to be bid for. I regained daylight in a room that had about ten other naked slaves waiting with their current owners, they were mostly, like myself once I had undressed down to high heeled court shoes, on leashes attached to their collars. One or two had their hands fastened behind them and were clearly not at all happy at being sold. The rest of them though were either sullen, frightened or excited, as far as I could see. As for myself I was nervous but definitely excited – after all that I had been through I knew I had finally left behind everything that I had been, except my name and my nature. Master Gerald held my leash and chatted easily with the other owners until a man stuck his head round the door and asked us to follow him.

We emerged into a big room full of sofas and chairs covered in dust sheets and looking very eerie indeed. From there we walked down a corridor and through double doors into what must have been the bar area.

All the tables were fully occupied by prospective buyers, mostly men but with a sprinkling of women as well, I returned their interested stares while my Master clipped my wrists together behind my back.

The man we were with looked down at a card.

"Lot Eight, ladies and gentlemen," he called and Master Gerald pulled gently on my leash. It was the viewing and I was led past all the tables and fondled and groped at each one.

I know that any 'straight' women reading this will be horrified at the humiliation and degradation of being led naked around a room full of strangers who have complete freedom to intrude into the most private parts of womanhood – and of woman. However, I know that most submissive women who read this will understand the thrill of being so utterly cast upon a master's wishes that they can find the deepest pleasure in the most degrading experiences. I can only plead in my defence, against charges of betraying all right-thinking women, that my nature is to find my identity as a woman immeasurably heightened by the very degradation a master condemns me to.

The size and 'pertness' of my breasts were commented upon frequently – and not always in a positive way – but it didn't matter to me. As long as carelessly arrogant hands were sliding over my skin and casual voices were assessing my capacity to provide pleasure, I was perfectly happy. I had no compunction in parting my legs to allow fingers to explore my genitals, in fact the more coarse the comments about the tightness of my vagina and its state of arousal, the more that arousal grew.

And despite everything, Master Gerald found it in him to pat me on the bottom occasionally when I had calmly undergone the most intimate inspection. And it became clear to me that serious money was going to change hands that day, because some of the inspections were very intimate indeed. For some prospective buyers, having the goods spread its legs and feeling carefully around it was not good enough. For some I had to really straddle my legs and allow hands to grasp and spread my labia while they crouched in front of me and discussed what they were looking at. All comments were, of course, directed at Master Gerald. They wanted to know what exercise routine I had to keep me tight, the skin of the labia looked smooth and of course they wanted to know if I had been subjected to needle play. Sometimes I had to turn and face away from them while Master Gerald pulled my buttocks apart so that they could inspect my anus. It was perfectly clear from a cursory glance and a quick probe that it was experienced at penetration but Master Gerald was plied with queries about what I had taken up that entrance. Fortunately he had clear recollections and even I was slightly surprised at some of the items he mentioned……..but then I had probably been otherwise engaged whilst they had been introduced!

And so it went on, sometimes hands would stroke my back as questions were asked about things like the greatest number of lashes I had taken at one time and had I been beaten with a singletail? A woman with a marked French accent spent some time feeling between my legs and stroking my thighs. Her fingers were cold and it seemed to me that she had hard eyes. As a result I was not as easily opened as I had been up till then.

She said something to the man with her that I couldn't hear and then with no warning smacked my bottom. I jumped in shock and there was a ripple of amusement through the observers but then her fingers dived back between my legs and achieved entry with no trouble. She smiled up at me with a warmth that completely changed my perceptions of her.

"Ah! Cherie, I understand you now!" she said and removed her fingers, wiped them on the front of my thigh, then marked her card and ignored me. For another twenty minutes or so I was led around, poked and prodded and examined with such casualness that by the end I was quite breathless with arousal.

Late in the afternoon the auction got properly under way and eventually I was led back into the same room and the same man who had taken us there earlier read out the details off my card and the bidding began. To this day I have only the haziest recollection of what figures were bandied about.

And here I suspect that any 'straight' women reading this may consider that I got my comeuppance. All excitement and perverse arousal fled from me as the crushing reality of what was actually happening left me horrified; and suddenly terrified. Certainly I had been bartered before but this was so formal and remote somehow that it was really threatening, it really was true slavery.

I was not *giving* myself to a dominant. My consent was irrelevant. I was going to be owned; bought and paid for, purely for the pleasure my suffering would bring to others. Normally that thought would have seen me through pretty well anything, but not then. Not at the auction.

I stood trembling at the end of the chain that Master held while my fate was decided, I couldn't look around me – I didn't dare - and I stared at the patterns in the carpet instead while the auctioneer's voice, calm and dispassionate, sorted through the bids until finally the impetus slowed and I allowed my ears to function. The bids had scaled heights which left me aghast. I suppose to some it might have been exciting to think that they were worth so much, and back at Master Gerald's house I had, but now all I could think of was that anyone who paid that much for a slave was going to want to get their money's worth out of her body.

At last the auctioneer banged his gavel and declared I had 'Gone!' With my heart thundering in my chest I looked over at Master Gerald who smiled at me and handed the leash to the French woman who had smacked me, shook hands with her husband, turned on his heel and walked out of my life. I was left shaking on jelly-like legs with these complete strangers who had God-alone-knew-what powers over me.

I returned to the changing room with my new owners who stroked me as they chatted in French and didn't seem too terrible. I was allowed to dress in the simple sweater and skirt I had worn on the journey down. We then adjourned to an office and I realised that the terms of the auction were much more limited than Master Gerald had allowed me to believe. A farewell punishment and one of his most severe in my humble opinion. It turned out that I – and the other slaves – had been sold for a two year period and I was required to sign a contract. At the end of the term my owners and I could extend it, or I could be sold on, if I so chose. Or I could be set free. A portion of my purchase price was transferred into my bank account there and then.

Once this was explained to me, I felt a little less terrified and sank gratefully into the back seat of their car as we headed for the Eurostar.

Monsieur and Madame Laferge divided their time between a large farmhouse in Normandy and a flat in Paris. When we were resident in Normandy I was quartered in the barn. It was quite comfortable and warm, the wooden posts that held up what had been the hayloft made pretty decent whipping posts for those occasions when the Laferges had guests. Those were terrific days and nights! Sometimes there would be as many as fifteen slaves in residence and with thirty or so dominants all working on them simultaneously, the place echoed to the thud and smack of the lash and the groans of we poor souls.

Groans which I have to say were regularly punctuated by moans of pleasure. Our dominants were never prone to denying themselves the delights our bodies could provide and I attained a high degree of competence as a slave to a

Mistress by dint of many exhausting sessions at the hands of Madame and her friends. Sometimes at these evenings the floor would be given over to one dominant who would provide a masterclass in one or other of the arts of sadomasochism. Thus I saw breathtaking displays of needle craft with slave girls' entire backs intricately laced with ribbon stretched between the piercing points, breasts turned into exquisite pin cushions and labia pierced time and again while the slave moaned her way to the threshold of orgasm and was then held back by a single command from the dominant. Usually the procedure would conclude with nipple piercing and the whole gathering would watch avidly to see if the slave could hold out against her excitement. Inevitably, failure led to delicious punishments and I have to say that I frequently fell at that last hurdle when Madame showed me off under the lash or the needles. She never seemed to mind very much, but then she did sometimes make the punishments last for a couple of days.

I was privileged to serve alongside some very talented submissives and I learned a great deal. There was a standing joke between me and the Laferges that I could scream fluently in four languages after only a few months with them!

The apartment in Paris was superb, all wrought iron and mahogany, it could have come straight out of 'O'! Indeed Monsieur did used to work from there and while Madame was out shopping, I spent hours standing under the chandelier in his office, naked and with my arms raised and tied waiting for him either to beat me or take me – or both. During those times I would gaze out over the Seine and watch the world go by, quite calm and patient, knowing that soon enough the whip and the Master's cock would be my lot. At other times Madame would take me shopping or out for lunch, but usually that involved us meeting other dominants of her acquaintance and I would often end up being lent out while Madame took another slave home for the evening. That was something I always enjoyed as I felt so utterly used and objectified.

And there were the parties! Monsieur and Madame had a cosmopolitan circle of friends and we would be invited to secluded chalets by Swiss lakes, where we slaves could be whipped and taken in the open and yet be unobserved. There were idyllic days on superb yachts in the Med when I would lie between Madame's legs on the sun baked decks and pleasure her until my tongue ached and then she would have me serviced by one of her domme friends' slave boys.

I recall one week-long outing on a three masted yacht. The doms played out pirate fantasies using their slaves to act as helpless captives from one of their raids. For the week they all drew lots to own different slaves and I was drawn by a bull-necked Swedish master. Every evening he would tie me down to his bunk and ravish me when he eventually came to bed, smelling of schnapps. He was enormously endowed and I was the envy of most of the other girls, but he played the part of rampant pirate, starved of female company, a little too well and my poor vagina was greatly relieved at the week's end! Two or three times every night with a monster like his was too much of a good thing. The daytimes however were heavenly. We were tied to the masts and whipped every day for any imagined infraction of whatever rules they dreamed up. I vividly remember being pulled up in ankle suspension, right up to the crow's nest almost and screaming as the deck spun and lurched dizzyingly far below me. The Swede held me there until I was begging for the lash – anything other than be left hanging there! He brought me down as everyone applauded and left me just above the deck – so my fingers just couldn't quite reach it! Then I got the lash I had abjectly begged for, and it was a beating to be proud of as four or five of the onlooking men asked for, and received, permission to take me where I lay when I was eventually let down in a sorry heap.

I lost track of time and became docile and wholly subservient in a way I could not have been before, so I thought nothing of it when, one night in the barn, Monsieur and Madame entered unexpectedly with a retinue of about thirty doms and dommes with accompanying slaves. The session that then ensued started with me being put face down on an X cross which was then tipped horizontal. And while the other slaves were put to use, in the middle of the floor I was beaten by what felt like everyone in the place. In the intervals between beatings, I was presented with cock after erect cock until I really didn't think I could swallow any more sperm. Fortunately those who hadn't enjoyed my mouth by that time seemed happy enough with one or other of my nether orifices.

Madame eventually unfastened me and made a great fuss of me, giving me a glass of wine and letting me kneel and lick her pussy while she talked to her friends. Then I was put back on the cross, face up this time and it was the dommes' turn. As women they gave my female parts the sort of patient, excruciating treatment that only women can. And all the while I was given pussy after pussy to lick out. It was a night of delicious surfeit, my face was running in the juices of the women who were whipping me, clamping my nipples, hot waxing me and doing so with such casual ease while they also tormented their own slaves, that eventually I almost passed out from the orgasms.

Only in the small hours of the morning did the reason for such an overwhelming session become evident. Madame announced to the whole assembly while I hung by my ankles beside her that I had served out my contract and that in the next few days we would decide on the future. I slept very little for what was left of that night and was very confused and out of sorts. Quite suddenly no one gave me any orders, I wasn't shackled in the barn and I was allowed clothes. I moved into the first floor flat in the barn and I had to decide what I was going to do. It was very unsettling after the years I had spent as a slave; a mere plaything with no will or mind of its own.

The whole subject of slavery had such confusing emotional baggage for me now that I was given the option of not serving. It had been the best and the worst of my life to that date and I just couldn't decide if I wanted it to go on or if I wanted to get off the roller coaster for a while. In the end one idea came to dominate my thinking. If I wanted to come back to SM, I had plenty of friends. But what I really needed to do first was re-establish myself as myself. And that meant going back to journalism; and that meant England. With the decision made, I fell out of love with SM entirely and I'm afraid I was a bit surly and ungrateful towards the Laferges for the last few weeks of my stay.

So here I am again, back in England! The Laferges were wonderful, now I have been able to stand back, I can see that. I appreciate them properly now and I write to them regularly. In fact I fully intend to serve them again for a year or so when I can. In the meantime, I am beginning to experiment with writing longer pieces and am hopeful that I will soon have the courage to embark on a full length novel in which I shall draw on my wonderful experiences as a slave.

Emma Stewart.